LET
THE
GOOD
PREVAIL

LET
THE
GOOD
PREVAIL

A
NOVEL
BY

LOGAN
AND
NOAH
MILLER

A Barnacle Book • Rare Bird Books

This is a Genuine Barnacle Book

A Barnacle Book | Rare Bird Books
453 South Spring Street, Suite 302
Los Angeles, CA 90013
rarebirdbooks.com

The authors would like to thank their tireless agent Shannon Hassan and Editorro

Set in Dante
Printed in the United States.

10 9 8 7 6 5 4 3 2 1

Publisher's Cataloging-in-Publication data

Names: Miller, Logan, author. | Miller, Noah, author.
Title: Let the good prevail : a novel / by Logan and Noah Miller.
Description: First Trade Paperback Original Edition | A Barnacle Book | Los Angeles, CA; New York, NY: Rare Bird Books, 2016.
Identifiers: ISBN 978-1-942600-46-6
Subjects: LCSH New Mexico—Fiction. | Veterans—Fiction. | Marijuana—Fiction. | Cartels—Fiction. | Brothers—Fiction. | Suspense fiction. | BISAC FICTION / General.

Classification: LCC PS3613.I528 L48 2016 | DDC 813.6—dc23

And no smooth tongue of fire,
Or liquid poured on the ground,
Or tears will now dispel,
The quick edge of sharpened rage,
Sing, sorrow, sorrow, but let the good prevail.

—AESCHYLUS, *The Oresteia*

1.

L IFELESS PRAIRIE BENEATH A ghost-blue sky without clouds and beyond that the lonely mesa land of bleached bones and pueblo ruins. A spiral of dust gathered and whispered into oblivion. Then a flash of chrome winked in the sunlight as a car grew out of the distance on the old ranch road. In the opposite direction another vehicle traveled at about the same speed, in no hurry. The two would soon intersect, but for now they rolled along at a casual pace, methodically drifting over the barren land, a timed rendezvous on the outskirts of hell.

The cars slowed and parked. The trailing dust swirled around them and then settled upon the ground. One was a rented Chevy Impala, gunmetal grey. The other was a sheriff's cruiser painted in the American flag, a blue hood spangled with silver stars, red and white stripes undulating along the doors and side panels and down the trunk.

Sheriff Darius Gates stepped out, opened the rear door, and removed a young man restrained in handcuffs with a strip of blue duct tape across his mouth.

Marlo emerged barefoot from the Impala. He had given up shoes years ago and preferred to connect directly to the energy of the planet with his callused flesh. He carried a clear plastic cooking bag and a long yellow zip tie as he strode noiselessly across the fine layer of silt that covered the old road.

"How's my nephew working out?"

"He drinks too much," Gates said.

"He's got the gene, that's for sure. I'll have a talk with him."

The young man in handcuffs stood as a terrified witness, mute behind the duct tape. His ordeal had been one of long suffering and his frame sagged under the weight of terminal despair.

"Where'd you find this all-star?" Marlo asked.

"Where they always go when they're scared—his mother's house."

"And where is she?"

"The poor lady had an accident with a handgun. Thought it was a popsicle."

Gates produced a bindle of cocaine from his breast pocket and tapped a bump of the Peruvian flake on the back of his hand. He contemplated the pearly alkaline crystals, a dull, mindless, organic compound. *When am I going to be able to put this shit behind me? Tomorrow. Always fucking tomorrow. At least it's the pure stuff, not some synthetic horror show cut fifty different ways with baby laxative and Rolaids.*

He raised the back of his hand and hoovered the coke up his nose. It stung with brilliant intensity, a little discomfort for a half hour of mind-blowing heroism.

"That shit will take you down the rabbit hole," Marlo said. "Superman one minute. Commander fuckup the next."

"I want the handcuffs back," Gates said over his shoulder, sniffing and wiping the remnants from his nostrils and the groove of his upper lip. He climbed into the patriotic cruiser and drove back down the ranch road the way he came. The shocks and chassis creaked over the ruts fainter and fainter until the vacuum of desolation took hold again.

Marlo stared at the young prisoner. Only the sibilant hush of the void would bear witness. The sun-scorched wind blew faint and thin over the last trails of summer grass that were clumped like ancient broom heads inverted toward the sky, brittle and decayed, uprooted and dissolving back into the earth when the monsoon downpour raged each afternoon. The smell of rain approached in the gathering towers of clouds. The flood was coming. He began:

"You can't control your fate. That is certain. It's happening right now. There is no cosmic puppeteer. No one to weigh and balance your soul at the end of the line. Those are invisible ideas invented by frightened and primitive creatures. So don't beat yourself up about the situation you're in—about the stupid decision you made that brought you here. That is behind you. In less than five minutes you won't even know you're dead—you won't even know you were ever alive. You won't know anything. There will be no more you. No more thought. Not even darkness. Only your corpse will remain—but that's my problem. You shouldn't worry about that."

Marlo circled the young man, not in a menacing way but in a perversely thoughtful manner, a deranged shaman imparting advice to the condemned.

"All you have left are these precious few minutes. And you have a choice—the last one you'll ever need to make. And it's this: You can choose the way in which you spend these final moments. You can choose to spend them peacefully—or you can spend them in a wild and terrified panic, pissing and shitting yourself all over the prairie. Either way, whether peaceful or panicked, you're dead. But you can decide, you can choose how you leave this place. How powerful is that? In this respect, you are more powerful than me."

But the young man, like anyone in his doomed position, could not heed the impossible advice, nor hear it. His face boiled with sweat and tears and his nostrils flared wildly for oxygen, heaving through the duct tape. His world was violent with his own noise.

"How much time do people waste fretting about their death? But you know. You know exactly how it's going to end. It's ending right now. So be kind to yourself. Love yourself. Follow your memories to the past and rest amid those youthful dreams. Your first love. The nurturing warmth of your parents. A Little League game where you were the hero. Dwell there. Don't be here."

Marlo pulled the plastic bag over the young man's head like a hangman with a hood. Then he wrapped the zip tie around the man's neck and ripped it tight.

"My conscience is clear. You were warned."

The young man staggered into the prairie land, suffocating inside the plastic bag, powerless in the handcuffs and shivering with convulsions from a defiant nervous system that did not want to die. And then he did it. His crotch bloomed with wetness as his bowels and bladder emptied into his jeans.

Marlo observed the death-struggle with pathological detachment. A malevolent cipher. A bipedal sphinx.

The young man faltered and then collapsed to the parched earth—his life ending in a spasm of twitches.

2.

A STIHL MAGNUM CHAINSAW ROARED through a felled pine tree and kicked up a spout of wood dust that fluttered through the sunlight of Carson National Forest. Caleb Boyd worked his way down the tree with the screaming blade, cutting the trunk into two-foot sections—bucking, in logging parlance. He had the rawboned frame and weathered skin of a man who worked outdoors and burned more calories than he ate. Sinewy muscles told of a functional strength and endurance, and he negotiated the uneven tinder with a severe limp. His shoulder-length hair was tied back with a coiled red bandana, salted with sweat stains.

He stepped through a tangle of branches, which gave way, and he sunk to his knee. He laughed to himself—he should've broken his ankle. But his new prosthetic leg was composed of carbon fiber and aluminum and some other industrial-powered materials that he'd forgotten the names of. It would take a lot more than a misstep in the woods to snap the motherfucker. He set down his chainsaw and yanked his boot free. The branches clawed at his jeans but there was no flesh to damage anymore.

The sudden movement caught the peripheral attention of his older brother. Jake eased on the throttle of his saw and brought the scream to a low belching idle. Caleb threw him a huge grin and fingered a can of Skoal Long Cut from his back pocket. He pinched out a gob of mint tobacco and tucked it into his chapped bottom lip and then winged the can over to his brother. The disc floated above the forest floor and slapped Jake in the chest and fell onto the dry pine needles. Jake packed a lipper and the forest began to howl again.

For another hour the brothers wielded the dangerous tools of their trade with the ease and dexterity born from long use. They ate tamales for lunch on the tailgate of their wood truck and packed another chew of tobacco and began splitting the logs from the morning harvest.

Into the afternoon the forest boomed with the driving maul of the log splitter and the brothers stacked the truck bed with several cords of firewood to the height of the plywood siding. They covered the hump with a blue tarpaulin and tied it down with ropes fastened into the truck spurs.

They drove down the mountain to the flat mesa land and pulled the truck onto the shoulder of the paved road, brushed their teeth, combed their hair, and threw on rumpled collared shirts with their names embroidered above the left breast pocket below their company name: BROTHER FIREWOOD. GET SOME.

"Let's go sell this shit," Jake said as they turned off the paved road and steered toward a scattered community of mobile homes.

♎

THE APACHE WOMAN WITH deep creases in her face stared at Jake from the doorway of her doublewide that rested at an angle on cinder blocks in the alluvial sand. The attempted sale was not going well.

Jake adjusted his belt and switched tactics.

"The Farmer's Almanac is predicting the worst winter in fifty years," he said. "Are you prepared for that reality?"

"Dunno."

"Can I ask you a personal question?"

The woman barely nodded. Maybe it was her age. Perhaps she didn't like Anglos, which was understandable considering the history of her people and his. But it was hard for Jake to tell for certain. He could only hazard a guess.

"What kind of heater do you have, ma'am?"

"A big one."

"I'll bet…electric?"

She nodded.

Jake shifted his weight from one leg to the other. He showed her his recently brushed teeth.

"What happens if your power goes out in a storm? How are you going to heat your home? Keep your family warm? This is a very serious consideration, considering how cold it gets around here— don't you think?"

She said nothing.

"Firewood never breaks down, ma'am. Ever-reliable. It's been heating homes for thousands of years. It warmed the castles of Europe, the kings and queens of my people, and the pueblos and the chiefs of your people. More importantly, it's twice as cheap as the average family's heating bill. Those are facts."

He waited for a response. *This woman could win a staring contest with a statue*, he thought.

"I'll tell you what," he continued. "I see you run a hard bargain— and I appreciate that in my customers. Money is hard to come by, and one shouldn't part easily with it. A customer should demand more than average service, and that's what people have come to expect from Brother Firewood. Ask around, they'll tell you."

Jake paused, the closer on the way. "And that's why me and my brother there will even stack the wood free of charge. No cost. Won't even accept a tip."

Jake glanced over his shoulder at Caleb sitting in the cab of the wood truck. Caleb smiled and waved at the woman as if on cue. The Apache woman shut the door.

"Have a nice evening, ma'am."

Jake walked back to the truck and jumped inside.

"That cocksucker tarantula fucked the sale for me—I knew it the moment I ran over him."

"Fucked the sale? The tarantula's dead."

"The fucker just jumped in front of the tire when I turned in here—fucking suicide mission. It's bad luck running over one of them, especially during mating season. You're supposed to be my co-pilot."

"I pointed it out a hundred feet down the road, bro. The thing was big as a turtle. I said, 'Watch out for the fucking tarantula.' Can't get any clearer than that."

"That hairy cocksucker." Jake backed the truck through the sandy lot and tumbleweeds and turned onto the pavement. "I hate this door-to-door bullshit. I'm thirty goddamn fucking years old. I was a Boy Scout a long time ago."

"I don't like it either. But it's effective sometimes." Caleb grinned at his older brother. "If you know what to say and how to say it."

"You got the next one asshole." Then Jake said under his breath, "That tarantula fucked me."

🦂

ABOUT A MILE DOWN the road Caleb stood on the front steps of another doublewide looking up at a shirtless man whose skin wore a circus of faded tattoos rendered by a poor artist. Across his stomach were the letters PIMP—and below that he wore a pair of fraying jorts and further down a pair of white socks with red stripes and no shoes. He had a considerable gap in the front of his mouth where several teeth used to be and the involuntary twitches and agitated movements brought about from the prolonged use of methamphetamines.

"I'll tell you what," Caleb said. "Me and my brother there will even stack the firewood free of charge."

Jake smiled and waved from the truck.

An orange tabby meowed and slinked through the doorway, ribs protruding through a mangy coat. It brushed against Caleb and made a figure eight through his legs, leaving a track of dust on his work jeans.

"What will you trade for the wood?" asked the shirtless man.

Caleb paused. Trades were uncommon but sometimes they worked out. "What do you got?"

"A bike."

He disappeared into the back of the trailer and wheeled out a banana-seater with pink and white streamers flowing from the handlebars.

"I got eighteen of these," he said.

"I don't need a bike."

"That's cool."

The shirtless man ghost-rode the bicycle back inside where it crashed into some other junk before clattering onto the floor.

"How about a phone charger? It works in the car and the house. It's got a convertor thing."

"Two-hundred and fifty dollars, sir," Caleb said. "That's a great deal for a cord of wood."

"Two-fifty? Bullshit. I know where I can get a cord for one-fifty."

"No you don't."

"Sure I do."

"Four feet by four feet, by eight feet?"

"What's that?"

"A cord of firewood," Caleb said. "We don't dump it loose like some of our competitors. We stack it and measure it. You get a true cord from the brothers."

Somewhere near the back of the trailer a toilet flushed something heavy and then an irritated woman growled from the dark interior.

"Who is it?" she said.

"Firewood, ma."

"Shut the goddamn door. We don't have a fireplace, you fucking idiot."

3.

CORDS OF STACKED PINYON and oak cured in the open air while others rose in great heaps waiting to be stacked. The brothers had sawed and split for seven hours and tried selling their hard work for two and a half and were now back at their wood yard, which served as both home and office for them. Independent contractors: if you don't make the money, nobody does. But they had cold beer and a fresh can of chew and a New Mexican sunset of purples and reds and colors of flame they could not name, and that was all right for now.

Caleb sat on the tailgate of the wood truck and rolled up his pant sleeve above his knee. He unhinged his prosthetic and tapped out the pine shavings and needles from the forest. Jake opened a bottle of Lagunitas IPA on the side of the truck with the pound of his fist and sipped the foam spilling out and handed it to his brother. He popped one for himself and the brothers chinked bottles and drank.

"You see," Jake said, "what we need is a big ass sign at the front of the driveway that says 'FIREWOOD FOR SALE.' That way people driving by will know that we're here and selling."

"But nobody ever drives by. We're the only ones on the road."

"You know what I mean. Down on the main road, pointing down our road. We gotta do something. The Internet thing that guy talked us into doing doesn't seem to work around here. I mean we've got a couple of calls from Albuquerque, but that is way too far to make a run and make any profit. Gas alone will cost us damn near fifty or sixty. And posting up at the market has not paid off like I thought it would."

"We'll figure it out," Caleb said. He sipped his beer and stared at the blazing skyline.

"And why don't we have a goddamn dog around here?" Jake said.

"The last two ran off."

"I know why."

"Then why'd you ask?"

"It wasn't a question searching for an answer." Jake paced the dirt, animating with his left hand, his beer in the other. "You're telling me you don't want a dog?"

"I'd love to have a dog, I just ain't thinking about getting one right now is all. It's just another responsibility we don't need."

"Responsibility? Hell, dogs take care of themselves."

"And that's why the last two you brought home run off."

"That wasn't my fault," Jake said. "They were the wrong breed."

"And what kind of breed wouldn't run off?"

"A pure breed."

"Pure breed what?"

"Any of them."

"That so?"

"Yep. Pure breeds make good dogs. That's why they cost more."

Caleb laughed and shook his head.

"Stop badgering me," Jake said. "I know what the fuck I'm talking about."

He unlaced his boots and sat on the tailgate beside his brother, the six-pack between them. "You meditating or something?" he asked.

"Just relaxing."

"Why are your eyes closed?"

"It feels good."

"Don't go getting weird on me now, Caleb."

The beer washed down their throats in calming waves and numbed the conversation for the time being. The land was quiet and they were quiet as they shared a deep appreciation for the light that was sinking behind the red-earth mesas and pine forests that shaped the horizon. The buzz from the beer was mixing with the buzz from the tobacco and they were flying westward into the dying embers of the day.

Jake hurled his empty bottle into the yard somewhere and opened another.

"Why don't you just give Lelah our mom's ring?" he asked.

"I thought about it."

"It's the only inheritance we got. You might as well put it to good use. Mom would want that."

"But half of it is yours," Caleb said.

"Well, when it's my turn to settle down we'll just have to saw the fucker in two."

"That'll work for now."

"What time are you guys heading out in the morning?"

"Five," Caleb said. "You're welcome to come."

"You think I wanna be there if he says no?"

"He ain't gonna say no."

"A man's only daughter? Shit, he's liable to shoot your dick off."

4.

H E WAS SOBER. TODAY.

Well, at least at the beginning of it. If you started at midnight and counted forward.

I can do this. One day at a time. One moment at a time, more like it. One fucking second at a time.

Gates the Sober Sheriff.

But it had started whispering to him, insistent, calling from the darkness or wherever it was it called from, that remote and nameless region, mounting with intensity until it was a full-blown feral scream. The urge, the gnawing, relentless and unremitting—but what was it? It wasn't merely a voice, no, that was too simple. It was a force of excruciating power that compelled the entire spirit, the soul, every molecule and atom, wouldn't let you rest, wouldn't let you sleep— wouldn't let you think—until it was gratified, satisfied, appeased.

And now it was.

The beast had stopped gnawing, bathing in the intoxicating broth of victory, a leisurely backstroke, spitting water out of its mouth like a gentle fountain and grinning with cunning satisfaction at its ability to prevail.

And it always fucking won didn't it?!

Vicodin. Micodin. My whole wide world's a Vicodin. He was doing the ditty thing again. *Gates the Sober Sheriff. Gates the Noble Sheriff. Riding a Vicodin. On the goddamn Mic-again.*

They said he lacked the tools, the means of expressing himself clearly and constructively, compassionately. They said he lacked *empathy. You don't understand me.* That's what his wife always said, his ex-wife, that is—*and she always let me know it.*

He'd tried going to therapy with her—actually his wife had insisted—in the death throes of their marriage, but it was bullshit. His wife, of course, hired the therapist, a woman, naturally. It was a total set-up.

A total goddamn set-up.

A fraud—like Obama and his birth certificate.

They always ganged up on me. Everything was always my fault. My fucking fault! How could it always be my fault! Those fucking cunts. If there's anything women are good for—it's men-bashing. They were fucking raised for it, bred for it, it drips from their hot fatty mother's milk. It's stuffed up their vaginas like evil. Maybe it was my wife's fault. Maybe it was my wife who didn't understand ME! But those two cunt bitches never thought about that, never even raised the question. Two college degrees, two sticks rubbing together, one in each pig head, and they never even suggested THAT.

THAT.

THAT.

THAT.

ALL FUCKIN' RATS.

HIT THE BITCH WITH A BAT!

She tried to turn Lelah against me. Turn her against Daddy. But it didn't work. No, no, no. Lelah had decided to stay and live with me. Not you. She'd decided to stay with her father. With Daddy. Haha. Who's smiling now, you cunt?

That was all the proof he needed to know he was right...

Where are you?

You're on an alien fucking landscape. There aren't even humans here anymore. They've all been killed off. Removed. This is one big fucking turdhole. And you're nothing but a turd floating around in it.

Darius Gates continued staring out the bug-splattered windshield into pure night and strolling the sordid corridors of his mind, kicking and knocking over things, his emotional circuitry on haywire and surging, the adrenal gland blowing high-octane inferno gas, bursting in a syrupy slather of neurotransmitters and infusing him with wild fantasies—a phantasmagoria of only the most inappropriate and lurid visions, visions of a fecal-sexual nature, an orgy of foul deeds, each one darker and more disturbing than the next—a novel of sadistic intrigue and blood-soaked retribution with dildos and sharp weapons, manacles and sweaty ropes, and two medieval bludgeoning instruments.

The radio could be heard again but he couldn't understand what it was trying to communicate. The lyrics and the song were a primitive mystery in a world without music.

And then he had the thought, the thought that had haunted him ever since he was a confused boy, ever since puberty when the first hairs sprouted on his balls like fuzz on a peach—*maybe I'm a space alien. A real-life Martian.*

They landed here once. Maybe they left me behind.

None of it made any sense right now. None of it. None of the voices whoring around his drug-addled mind.

Man make mudcake with man.

He maketh cake.

He baketh cake.

Pattycake. Pattycake.

I am the Baker Man.

Why doesn't my brain work right? Why-why-why? He begged. He pleaded. *Why-why-why?*

He screamed the final pronouncement between his lobes and then started crying into the steering wheel as hysterical tears and strings of snot unspooled from his nose.

Pull yourself together. You're going fucking hunting.

It was 4:00 a.m.

He pumped Visine into his eyes and the whites became clear again. He snorted a key-blaster of coke and his senses became terrifically alive. He pulled into the truck stop and filled his personal plastic coffee mug. It said DAD on the side.

The fresh coffee steamed in the cold before dawn as he stood against the patriotic cruiser and stared into the darkness that draped the desolate badlands. Not a house light anywhere on the western horizon. Only the unseen wilderness below a vault of stars.

🪱

Two hours later Caleb and Darius Gates cradled hunting rifles through the high country grassland. The bordering pine and aspen forest climbed the bowl of mountains around them and they searched where the grassland met the trees for a shadow or movement of any kind. Gates had slammed two 5 Hour Energy shots and a thirty-two ounce green Gatorade and he was starting to feel human again.

They wore bright orange vests and camouflage pants. It was an interesting contradiction in clothing, thought Caleb. The visible invisible.

"As you know, supporting a family ain't easy around here," Gates said. "I know I'm stating the obvious, but as Lelah's father, I feel the need to bring up certain issues."

"I've been giving that a lot of thought lately, Mr. Gates. Well, for one thing, me and my brother are looking to grow our business. We've got a bank loan pending, which would allow us to invest in larger equipment and hire a few employees."

"Look, I know you don't want to hear this, but I'm going to tell you anyway. Your brother is a fuckup. Always has been. Mark my words, he'll be making the same amount of money at fifty as he is now."

The candid assessment of his brother stung but Caleb limped alongside Gates and listened without making objection.

"Life doesn't get easier for guys like Jake," said Gates. "It only gets harder. It squeezes and squeezes them. And men like Jake get desperate. And they do desperate things. And when that happens, you don't want to be anywhere near him. My advice to you is get away from your brother and do your own thing."

Caleb bowed his head and watched his pant legs swish through the high grass.

"My brother has made some mistakes, that's for certain. All of us have. But he works damn hard."

"I'm not saying that he don't. It's just I know the type. I see it every day. Economic pressures will bury a man quicker than the undertaker."

"I respect your opinion, Mr. Gates, and I'll give it some thought."

"You would've made a hell of a lawman, Caleb. It's a shame I can't pull any strings for you. If you had lost your leg on the job as a sheriff, you'd be set for the rest of your life."

"Bad timing, I guess."

"No. Wrong fight."

"Yeah… I had it all figured out. Join the military after high school. See the world and then come back home and get a job in law enforcement. I had never heard of an IED."

"How much they give you for your leg?"

"A thousand a month."

"That's criminal."

"I try not to dwell on it too much. I don't regret my time in the Marine Corps."

"The poor fight the wars for the rich. It's always been that way."

They crested a slight rise in the meadow and Gates paused and turned to Caleb.

"Make sure you and my daughter tell your kids that." Gates extended his right hand to shake. "I'd be honored to call you my son. But you gotta make me one promise first."

Caleb nodded vaguely and shrugged.

"Shave your face and get a goddamned haircut before the wedding."

Caleb grinned. "I'll think about it."

There was a sudden crashing and snapping of branches and a bull elk charged out of the forest some two hundred yards in front of them and across the meadow as if he'd been flushed or spooked by another predator. Or perhaps he had heard their human voices and was deceived by the direction. Neither Gates nor Caleb questioned the nature of their good fortune. They merely raised their rifles and pressed them tight into the grooves of their shoulders.

Gates fired first—and missed. The shot sailed wide and buried itself into an outcropping a thousand yards distant.

Caleb tracked the bull in the crosshairs of his riflescope. Its powerful haunches ripped up tufts of sod with each muscular stride as instinct propelled it toward some unknown haven on the other side of the divide. Steam burst in brief clouds from its nostrils and clashed with the chill air. Its healthy coat of fur held a tawny-brown shimmer in the mountain sunlight and showcased the full-rutting force of its virility, the months of feeding off the nutrient-rich grass, a crown of endless points.

Caleb could take its life in the next moment. But as he was about to squeeze the trigger he deliberately pulled the rifle a bit, ever so subtle, not enough for Gates to perceive, but enough to miss his prey. The shot rang across the valley and by the time the echo came back to the hunters the forest had swallowed the elk on the other side.

He had hunted men before, and after that, he had never wanted to hunt anything again.

"I thought you were a crack shot," Gates said.

"Used to be."

"It's different when guys are shooting at you, isn't it?"

"Sure is."

5.

He THOUGHT THE SONIC trick was pretty clever. The tequila was taking its confident hold when Caleb stepped to the edge of the promontory and started arguing with his echo. The canyon plunged below him to the sandy arroyo and rose hundreds of feet vertically to monoliths of Jupiter-swirled stone on the other side. Tequila, badland cliffs, a hazardous combination on most nights, but the amphitheatre was bathed in surreal sunset hues and it emboldened him to the precipice for the prelude of the evening's show.

"I love her!"

His declaration flew across the canyon and then reverberated back to him from the wall on the other side.

I LOVE HER… LOVE Her… love her…

"No, I love her!" Caleb shouted in response.

The invisible responded: *NO, I LOVE HER… No, I love her…*

"I'm going to marry her!" he shouted again.

The canyon replied: *I'M GOING TO MARRY HER…*

Caleb turned around and smiled down at Lelah, sprawled on a Navajo blanket with a bottle of Cuervo and the picked bones of a rotisserie chicken.

"Who's it gonna be, babe?" he said. "Me or that asshole on the other side?"

"Whoever asks first."

"I think I can beat him to it."

Caleb limped across the sandstone and rummaged through the picnic basket.

Lelah gazed across the canyon and continued the charade.

"Better hurry," she said. "Here he comes. Boy, is he cute. And he's got a real nice car. And he's rich. And he wears a suit and tie to work and golfs all the time with his buddies at the country club. And he was in the best fraternity in college—the very, very best one, Phi Beta Phucko. Wow, he's a real asshole."

Caleb finally produced a black velvet ring box from the picnic basket and kneeled before her. He looked into her green eyes at the sunset reflected within them. He wanted to stay there, but everything inside him told him to look away. For some reason, the sheer acknowledgement that he was supposed to stare into her eyes, a physical act performed thousands of times over the years of their relationship, made him self-conscious and he started to blush.

She knew what was coming and she could not keep from smiling. It all felt terribly cheesy and at the same time terribly right. They were teenagers again on the first date seconds before the first kiss and she nearly started giggling.

"You don't mind parking in the handicap spot, do you?" he asked.

"Nope. It's always up front."

"For the rest of your life?"

"That sounds awfully long," she said.

"But the man always dies first. So you'll be able to get married again."

"I'll be a prune by then."

"Fine. We'll do a five-year trial phase."

"Five years, that's it? I'm only worth five years?"

"Goddamnit Lelah, will you be my wife?"

"Can we get married on a Friday? It usually takes me at least two days to get rid of a hangover."

"Is that a yes?"

"Yes—Yes—Yes. Till death do us part."

"I think I like the five year idea better."

Lelah whacked him on the shoulder.

"Till death do us part," he said.

She wrapped her arms around him and nuzzled into his neck and kissed his warm skin. The tang of his salt excited her tongue. Even after working all day in the forest he tasted sensual to her. On nights when they were apart she slept in her bed with shirts that he had worn.

Caleb removed the antique diamond ring from the box and slid it onto her finger.

"It was my mother's," he said.

"I remember."

"I'll get you a proper ring when we get married."

"As long as I got you, this is all the ring I need."

"How did I get so lucky?" he asked.

"Small town. I didn't really have a lot to choose from."

"That's what I figured."

Caleb poured them each a shot of Cuervo.

"To our lives together," he said.

"And the assholes on the other side."

They chinked shot glasses and downed the Mexican heat. He pulled her tight and hummed in her ear and they swayed in the dance of their song together and he smiled and kissed her on the forehead and then her lips. He caressed her back in slow circles and she caressed him and she rounded her hands over the muscular strips of his lower back running down his spine.

The sun had vanished in the west and taken with it the painted shadows that now ran away to a cold blue without fire and the darkness came with the first stars. The air was slack and warm around them in the pocket of the canyon. They were happy and their lives together stretched out before them and the memories to be made and cherished and they held each other in the grandeur of nature complete. Afterward they made love atop the sandstone cliff and needed a flashlight to hike down to his truck on the dirt road below.

6.

His venomous puppet.

His murderous Pinocchio.

Deputy Sparks.

Third-generation white-mongrel trash. A dash of Mexican sperm in there somewhere. Grade-A toilet fly. The cognac of forlorn hope. Cud served as salad. A stream of piss tapped and bottled as Vitamin Water. Pure zero multiplied to infinity. A cur beaten to a shrieking aggressive shiver. Acne pocks, small womanish hands, thinning hair combed to the side, a wispy mustache, an unhealthy sweat to his greasy skin, angry to the bone with frail yellow teeth like sucked-on Tic Tacs that leaned at angles like old fence posts. DNA, what a motherfucker.

He'd come a long way indeed, started a long way down, plucked out of the hot frothy muck of poverty and reckless breeding by a silver-starred god from the machine. He'd been harshly judged the first day of kindergarten and lived painfully with that judgment until he dropped out of school midway through seventh grade. After that it was a predictable route to crime and an unpredictable route to the badge.

It had now been over a decade since Sheriff Darius Gates rescued Lester Sparks from a murder rap and, once rescued, knew that he could play puppet master with him until the end of his days. He'd caught the kid cold, a once-in-a-career catch, the murder weapon still in his hand, miles from nowhere in the badlands. Gates was napping in the cruiser along an empty county road, feet kicked up on the dash, hat knocked over his eyes, when he heard the gunshots *bap-bap* out of a ravine. Yes, a once-in-a-career catch.

Lester Sparks had killed the hitchhiker just to see if he could do it.

He was still a juvenile at the time, sobbing in the jail cell, praying to God for salvation. Well, that night Sheriff Darius Gates was God and Lester Sparks was going to become his experiment. The murder weapon disappeared, the body of the transient never found, and Sparks walked free without so much as an incident report.

But he owed him. And he would happily repay the debt. Lester had found someone who cared.

Two years later Gates helped him get his GED, then a slot in the academy. Within five years he was deputized and patrolling alongside Sheriff Gates in the patriotic cruiser.

Gates had given him a new life, dignity and respect, standing within the community. A badge and a gun. A uniform. The emblems of power and authority. The son he never had. The father he'd never known.

To own someone's life. That was real power.

GATES PARKED THE CRUISER outside the squat building that sat on a square of concrete in the unincorporated prairie. A lone outpost for lawmen. His outpost. He pushed through the front door. Sparks was eating a bowl of cereal at his desk and reading something on his computer. It was only the two of them. And that's how they liked it. Thousands of square miles all to themselves. The only authority. The final authority.

"My daughter's getting married," Gates said.

"Congratulations."

Sparks slurped a spoonful and stuck out his fist to give him a bump. Gates slapped it away. A wounded look from Sparks.

"Stand up and shake my hand like a man," Gates said.

"Sorry."

Sparks set down his bowl and rose out of his chair and they shook hands.

"When's the wedding?"

"Don't worry, Lester, you're invited."

Lester nodded and then said, "I got that coin for you. It's on your desk."

"It's a chip."

"Well, it sure looks like a coin."

"Well, it ain't."

Gates lifted the bronze medallion from the surface of his desk and read the inscription. "To thine own self be true."

"Didn't Jesus say that?" Sparks asked.

"Sounds like it."

"He said just about everything else."

"Him and Shakespeare."

Gates turned over the medallion and read the other side.

"God grant me the serenity to accept the things I cannot change, courage to change the things I can, and wisdom to know the difference."

"That's definitely Jesus."

Gates did not answer and slid the medallion into his pocket.

7.

T HE SUN WAS CASTING low across the prairieland and there was only gold about its color when Gates rolled down the dirt driveway toward his home a half mile from the blacktop road. At night the house was only a faint globe in the darkness beyond and a traveler passing in a car could only squint and wonder who lived out there and why. He and Lelah had moved there after the divorce halved his savings and forced him to sell the family ranch he had hoped to grow old and die on.

He pulled to an easy stop in the withered grass behind the house and checked himself in the rearview mirror. He squirted Visine into his eyes and made sure his nostrils and face were clean. He put a stick of peppermint gum in his mouth and exited the cruiser.

When he stepped through the backdoor and into the kitchen he jumped from her loud greeting.

"Surprise!" Lelah said. Three sparkling candles fizzed from the chocolate cake in her outstretched hands. "Congratulations, Dad, three years clean and sober."

She set the cake on the kitchen table and kissed him on the cheek.

"Hurry, blow them out before they melt all over the frosting."

Gates leaned and blew on the candles. They went out for a moment in swirls of gray smoke and then flared and sparkled anew. He leaned and blew again. The candles sputtered out and then flickered and the flaming trick was rekindled. He smiled and conceded to the magical candles and she laughed. She plucked the candles from the cake and carried them sparkling to the sink and ran water over them. The small kitchen was suffused with the smell of burned paraffin and they fanned at the smoke with their hands.

"Did you get your chip?" she asked.

Gates fished the bronze medallion out of his front pocket. Lelah placed the medallion on the windowsill beside two other bronze medallions with edges aglow in the backlight from the falling sun. One medallion for each year of sobriety.

"How was the meeting this morning?" she asked. "Did you speak?"

"Not this time."

Lelah cut into the cake and looked up at her father before finishing the wedge.

"More?"

"That's perfect, honey," he said.

She gave them each a slice and they sat at the little round table. Gates took the gum out of his mouth and tore a strip from his paper napkin and balled the gum inside.

"If you ever want me to come to a meeting for moral support," she said, "or just to have me around, I'd love to be there for you."

"It's sort of a private thing for me, honey. Something I have to do on my own. But I appreciate the offer. Everyday it gets easier. I don't even crave that junk anymore."

"I'm so proud of you, Dad."

She looked at him and her eyes were wet with emotion. He nodded and dug his fork into his cake.

"You might want to have a sip of milk first, Dad. Or else it's gonna taste like gum."

She poured him a glass of milk from the half-gallon carton and he drank the gum taste from his mouth and then ate the first bite of cake.

"It's good, huh?" she said.

"It's delicious. Did you make it?"

"I just finished spreading the frosting when I saw you pulling down the drive."

She smiled at her father and he smiled back at her.

"I think you're really brave for making the changes you've made in your life." She looked down at the table and twisted her napkin. "I had some real doubts at first about you staying sober. And I'm sorry that I did. I never should've doubted you."

The intimacy was excruciating for Gates but he managed to hang on without changing the subject. "That's all right, honey," he said. "I was a real jerk."

"I've read a few books lately on addiction. I understand now that it's a disease. And I just want to tell you again that I'm here for you, whatever may come. I'm here with you every step of the way. One day at a time. I love you. And I'm done with my speech. That's it."

"I love you too, honey," he said.

They sat there in the waning daylight, lifting their heads and smiling at one another in between mouthfuls, the cake delicious and warm from the oven, the milk cold and silky, the rays of the setting sun through the country window amber upon their faces.

"I told Caleb that he's gotta cut his hair and shave before he marries you. He looks ridiculous."

"Dad, you just ruined a beautiful moment."

"It's my moment," he said as he brought his fork to his mouth. "If it's gonna be ruined, then I wanna be the one ruining it."

"I like the rugged look. I happen to think Caleb looks very handsome right now."

"Hey, if you wanna marry a hippie."

"Maybe I do."

"Glad I'm not."

"You can if you want to, Dad. It's legal now."

He rolled his eyes.

"You set yourself up for that one," she said.

"I did."

Lelah stood out of her chair and took her plate to the sink and washed it with a sponge and set it in the drying rack. She grabbed her purse off the back of her chair and kissed her dad on the cheek.

"I'm going to stay with my hippie tonight," she said.

"And leave me all alone on my birthday? After all that talk about support and being there for me?"

"Redtube, Dad. Check it out. You'll be just fine tonight."

"What's that? I thought it was YouTube."

"You'll like Redtube better."

"Is that one of those sex sites?"

She giggled and opened the backdoor.

"You're hurting my ears," he said. "Drive safe."

"Love you."

"Love you too."

She closed the door and he heard her truck start up and pull down the long dirt driveway into the dusk. He stared down at what remained of his cake slice. He thought that he would feel bad about spinning such lies to his daughter but he felt nothing at all. He waited for the sting of remorse but it was not in him right now and would be a long time coming if ever it came again.

There was only one thing on his mind. A singular bladed focus that cut out everything else. He took the bindle from his shirt pocket and tapped a line on the table beside the chocolate cake.

What the fuck is wrong with you?

If there's a hell, Darius, you're gonna burn in it.

Yeah, but I'm betting that there ain't. Not beyond this one.

He took the cocaine into his body and his eyes flamed and he saw fire dancing up through his ribcage and across the walnut folds of his brain and he exhaled mightily and sat there in the kitchen until his breathing calmed and he could think clearly again. It was dark outside now.

One of these days, Darius, your chameleon skin is gonna run out of colors.

8.

"WE HAVE REVIEWED YOUR application, and unfortunately, we are unable to provide you with a small business loan at this time."

The brothers sat across from the loan officer of Southwest Capital Bank.

"Why not?" Jake asked.

"As I said, we've reviewed your application and—"

"No shit. But why not? We're only asking for fifty thousand dollars to grow our business."

"As everyone knows, these are economically hard times."

"When have they not been hard? We didn't fuck them up. You did."

"Jake—relax. C'mon, bro."

The loan officer suffered the insult with a short inhale and sigh before continuing.

"According to your financial statements, your business took in just under twenty-eight thousand dollars last year. Frankly, without any collateral or capital to speak of, you are a high-risk applicant. Ten years ago, maybe. But not today."

Jake leaned forward, lowered his voice, and geared up for a proposal that would resolve the issue happily for both parties—a fair trade.

"Look, we'll give you and all the employees of this bank free firewood for the next two years. All you can burn."

"Sir, that's illegal."

"For who?"

"This bank does not traffic in bribes for loans."

"My brother is a goddamn veteran of this country. That's gotta count for something."

"Sir—"

"What the fuck have you done for it?"

"I'm gonna need you to leave."

"No, you need to leave." Jake raised his voice and looked around the bank, trying to rally support for his cause. "We want to speak to someone else. We want to speak with the manager of this piggy bank."

"That would be me."

Jake's voice dropped. "You're the manager?"

"And the President."

"Well, that's a real fucking stupid policy. You should hire someone else. No wonder you're a rinky-dink wannabe outfit. I bet you're not even on the stock exchange."

"And which stock exchange would that be?"

"You know the one."

"No. I don't. Please tell me."

"That's your fucking job to figure out. Not mine."

"Leave before I call the police."

Jake pondered his options. His face was burning. He could feel the sweat rising through his pores. It had always been this way with the white-collared men with college degrees. They had the power and he had none. He could kick the living shit out of these pasty donut pussies, but to what end? The world favored these assholes. All the laws too. They created the system. They owned it. Built it. He threw his chair back and strutted across the shiny floor and pushed through the glass doors. Caleb followed behind his older brother and then turned around and limped back to the loan officer.

"I apologize for that, sir," Caleb said. "My brother is just a bit frustrated, is all."

"My job isn't easy either."

"When can we re-apply?"

The question caught the loan officer off guard. But there wasn't a hint of irony in Caleb's tone or demeanor.

"I'd give it at least six months."

"Thank you, sir. Have a good one."

THEY WERE FIVE MILES down the road and Jake had lit his second cigarette before a word was spoken between them.

"Bro, can you do me a favor?" Caleb asked.

"What?"

"Next time, try and see it from his perspective."

"He's an asshole."

"He ain't the boss."

"He said he was."

"Even if he says he is, he ain't. He don't own the money in that bank. He's just following orders, doing his best not to get fired."

"What are you a fucking financial expert now?"

"There's just no use getting riled up is all I'm saying, and taking it personally. That won't do us no good."

"If it ain't personal, then what is it?"

"It's just a man trying to keep his job."

"Well, at least one of us is trying hard. Fuck. I'm giving it all I got."

"Then take it by the smooth handle, Jake."

"What the shit-fuck does that mean?"

"Don't grab the saw by the blade. How's that?"

"As long as you grab the saw when it ain't running and with gloves on, you'll be fine."

"You've got all the answers."

"I know an asshole when I see one."

"Remember, Jake," Caleb said, half-serious. "Smiles are contagious."

"So is the middle finger."

Jake threw him the bird. Caleb responded in kind.

"See," Jake said, smiling. "It's goddamn fucking contagious."

"And please don't bring up the military stuff anymore. Okay?"

"I'm proud of you. That asshole should know what you've done for this country before he decides to reject us. He should know who's sitting in front of him."

"Please?"

Jake nodded and took a long drag of his cigarette. He curved his mouth and blew the smoke out his window.

"You're moving out, aren't you?" he said.

"Me and Lelah are gonna look at some trailer homes this weekend. There's one for rent near the Chama."

"I'm happy for you two."

"I'll still cover my rent for a few months."

"How you gonna do that?"

"Get a night job. Lelah is asking her boss if there's anything available. I told her I'd clean toilets if I have to."

"I'm happy for you," he repeated. "Really happy. You got a good lady."

Caleb looked across the cab at his brother, his eyes fixed on thoughts beyond the road, cigarette pinched between work-swollen fingers, the lines on his face bending downward in slow defeat, engraved with growing shadows that would never brighten again, only become longer, larger, deeper—he'd aged ten years in the last three. Caleb could see now with clarity what had always been there. Underneath the hard exterior, the raw male energy, the sweat, the dirt, and the grime, there was a pervading sadness about Jake; he'd never be what he wanted to be, and deep inside, perhaps subconsciously, he knew it now. Jake's quick smile and rough charm had always concealed that sorrow, but it was there, ever-present, churning below the surface and growing with intensity in each passing day as the sands of time escaped him.

"I've always tried to look out for you the best I could," Jake said. He stole one more drag from his cigarette and then stubbed it out in the ashtray. "I can't say that I've done a very good job of it."

"You're my older brother, not my father."

"Thank God. Anybody would've been better than that asshole."

Caleb took the can of chew from the dashboard and packed a lipper and spit the first tobacco juice into an empty Sprite bottle.

"Hand me that will ya?" Jake injected more nicotine into his system. Then he said, "We're gonna lose the wood yard if we don't find us a loan soon. We got too much debt. Got nearly four thousand dollars in bills and operating costs each month. Our saws ain't even paid off yet."

"We should try some banks down in Santa Fe and Albuquerque."

"What makes you think it will be any different down there?"

The truck drove out of the pine trees and made a right onto the interstate where the land opened up again and flat-bottomed clouds rested on the doldrums of a skyward ocean.

"The money will work out, bro," Caleb said. "It always does."

"It's just never as much as you need."

9.

*J*ACK AND COKE. *JACK and Coke and real coke. Another Jack and Coke. More real coke, the powdery kind—the kind they used to put in Coke.*

He was making a ditty out of his night. He was sitting on the toilet. But he wasn't shitting. *Sitting and shitting*, he said. *Shitting and sitting.* The world was a song for Darius Gates right now, off-duty, on the toilet in Buffalo Thunder Indian casino, sitting but not shitting on shit land given back to the Redman after his near extinction by the Great White Man. He wrote the song and visualized the stanzas in his head:

Jack and Coke.

Jack and Coke and real coke.

Sitting without Shitting.

Shitting without sitting.

Buffalo Thunder.

My Buffalo Thunder is in the toilet, thank you very much. Don't flush it. Let some sap discover it. Blow his mind.

A Buffalo Thunder Pie.

My, my—my Buffalo Thunder Pie.

He snickered and bumped one last charge of white power up his nose.

Toot.

Toot.

He launched from the toilet seat and nearly kicked the stall door off its hinges with the heel of his lizard skin Lucchese's. He was looking at himself in the mirror that spanned the opposing wall above the line of porcelain sinks, legs bowed, hands poised, gunfighter-like. *Billy-the-goddamn-Kid.* He loved what he saw right now. He loved his image. He was enraptured. He could starve to death staring at himself. He was so powerful and handsome and doing everything right with his life.

Dashing, came to mind. He'd never used the word before. But he'd heard it spoken in movies with British actors.

Dashing. You're goddamned right.

He snapped to attention and saluted himself.

The war on drugs, sir? We're winning.

Darius, you're hilarious.

He strutted out of the bathroom and across the gaming floor and plunked himself back down in the stool beside Sparks at the blackjack table. The waitress minced along with a tray of drinks. He nearly pinched her ass to get her attention. She turned to face him. She was smiling. Of course she was. He was so goddamn powerful right now. It was like some sort of undeniable supercosmic force. *The Secret: Cocaine.* Why couldn't he always feel this good?

"Another Jack and Coke please." He tossed a twenty-dollar chip on her tray. He wanted to say, *I got a hard dick too, hard as the wood on this table,* but refrained, merely adding: "With a heavy hand, sweetheart."

The waitress winked and minced along with her freight of beverages. He watched the sway of her childbearing hips.

I can keep it hard all night for you… All fucking night… I've got special powers. I'll lift up that tight skirt of yours and bend you over in the parking lot and blow my balls all over your back.

The sudden impulse to commit acts of extraordinary violence rushed fiercely through Darius Gates as he took in the faces huddled around the card table, drawn and spiritless, ruddy from drink, ruddy from the soil of poverty, ruddy from the slur of history, ruddy from abuse and neglect. *A bunch of degenerates*, he shouted to himself. *You're all a bunch of degenerates.* He wanted to scream at them. *You fucking degenerate goats!*

He wanted to leap onto the card table and issue the diatribe publicly, hose them down with pepper spray and a couple of hard whacks to the ribs with the old club, throw them in handcuffs and let them ride out the night on the putrid cement of a jail cell—when a bucket of shit-water was dumped on his delicious reverie. His face creased with anger as he stared across the casino. Ruben. Ruben. Ruben. Ruben. What the fuck was he doing down here?

Gates elbowed Sparks and motioned with his chin.

Sparks followed the gaze of his superior through the tangles of cigarette smoke and card tables and across the burgundy carpeted floor to where Ruben staggered drunkenly over to a slot machine and braced himself against the gaudy electric payday.

A quarter slipped from Ruben's sweaty fingers and rolled under the machine. He got down on his knees and peered underneath, then moved into a push-up position for a better view. He spotted his quarter amid the fuzzy lint and candy wrappers and reached for it with his right hand. He touched the quarter with his fingertips and tried to scissor out the coin when a boot heel pressed his cheek into the carpet.

"What are you doing down here, Ruben?"

"I dropped my quarter—"

Gates grabbed onto Ruben's belt and jerked him off the carpet. Then he ran him through the glass doors and into the parking lot where his face met the side of a Chevy truck. The force of the collision buckled Ruben onto the asphalt.

"I got my girlfriend watching over it," Ruben said. "She's up there right now."

"Don't lie to me."

Gates pinned Ruben against the hood of a green Taurus and ground his forearm into his throat.

"I swear," Ruben said. "Everything is safe."

"You'd better hope so. You'd better pray that it is. Now get your ass back up there."

"I'm too drunk to drive."

"No you're not." Gates kicked Ruben in the tailbone. Ruben staggered over to a four-wheeler ATV parked under a street lamp.

"I'm gonna tell my uncle about this shit," Ruben said.

"I'll tell him myself."

Ruben climbed onto the ATV and hit the start button. "Fuck you, Gates. Fuck you too, Sparky—you fucking pussy."

He throttled the ATV and attempted to speed away.

But Gates vaulted the short distance that separated them and punched Ruben in the face. Ruben flopped onto the asphalt with a painful wet smack. Then a swift boot from a Lucchesi knocked the wind out of him.

"Apologize," Gates said.

Ruben rolled over and rested on all fours. Blood dribbled from his nose and freckled the asphalt between his hands.

"Apologize," Gates repeated.

Ruben raised his chin and the words frothed out his bloody lips. "I'm sorry."

"To Sparks as well."

"Fuck him," Ruben said. He was in terrific pain and disorientation and as soon as the words left his mouth he tried to suck them back in.

Gates plowed a short jab into his ribs.

"I'm sorry…" Ruben said, coughing. "Sorry… Sparks."

Gates lifted Ruben and threw him onto the ATV. Ruben wobbled in the saddle and grabbed hold of the handlebars. The ATV kicked out exhaust and he pulled down on the throttle and shot forward. He swiveled around and flipped off the cops before disappearing into the night.

10.

HE CAME INSIDE HER and rested in the warmth of her body, the two of them coiled together and panting with pleasurable fatigue until their breathing calmed and heartbeats slowed.

"That's the best lunch I ever had," Lelah whispered into his ear.

"Free delivery seven days a week."

Caleb traced the contours of her breasts, the sheen of sweat around her nipples, his fingers barely touching her skin. Her breasts were at their peak of life and the full ripeness of them in his mouth made him hunger again to be inside her. He bit her nipple. She shuddered and kissed the top of his lip and pulled on it with her teeth. Then she kissed his chest and down his abs. He had no chest or stomach hair above his bellybutton, not from the razor but from genetics, smooth and soft and tight with muscle.

"My boss said they have an opening for security guard at night," she said.

"How much they paying?"

"Seven fifty an hour."

"That much?"

They shared a laugh.

"I'll see if I can get him up to eight," she said.

"If you wear that pink push-up bra, you might even get him into the double-digits."

"You smell so good I could eat you."

"I'm gonna eat you first."

His mouth slid down the centerline of her torso and his lips kissed along the way. Her back arched and she moaned softly as his tongue massaged her and licked the wetness running down her inner thighs. She rocked her hips and moaned louder and grabbed his head with both hands and pushed it down harder, deeper, with greater pressure. Her head flopped back onto the bed and she turned her cheek to the side and her eyes wandered over to the digital bedside clock—

"Oh my god," she said, trying to push his head away.

That's right. Her words encouraged him. He was pleasing her, on the path to ecstasy, and he slid his hands around her hips and cupped her butt with the raw strength of his workingman hands and pulled her deeper into his mouth and probing tongue.

"Oh my god!" This time she managed to push him off and she sat up. "Oh my god! I gotta get back to work. We gotta go."

She jumped out of bed, slid on her panties, snapped her bra and stepped into a pair of slacks, and buttoned her blouse with her nametag fastened over her left breast.

"We were so close," he said, catching his breath.

"Wipe your face, baby. You have me all over you."

He licked around his mouth, slow and dramatic, his tongue curling and making a circuit of his lips.

"Gross." She giggled.

Caleb took his prosthetic from the floor and slid into the sleeve.

"I think my penis has grown since I lost my leg. All that extra blood that used to be in my calf now flows straight into my pecker."

"I didn't notice," she said with a smirk.

"It was just a theory."

"I was kidding, babe." She bent down and kissed him. "You've never had an issue there."

He threw on his jeans and shirt and laced his work boots.

"Help me make the bed, honey," she said. "Room service already came."

There was a distracted hitch to Lelah's movements as they tucked in the sheets, fluffed the pillows, and smoothed over the bedspread. She glanced nervously at Caleb several times and tried to make eye contact with him. There was something she needed to say but she was having trouble coming out with it. She had been having trouble coming out with it for the last two weeks.

When Caleb reached to open the door for her—

"I missed my period," she said.

He paused with his hand on the doorknob and said the first thing that came to his mind.

"Thought you were on the pill?"

"I am. It's probably nothing."

"I'm not afraid if it isn't."

His words were warm with feeling and they comforted her.

"Neither am I," she said. "I just always wanted to be married first. I don't want to look like a big white blimp in the wedding photos."

"We can go down to the courthouse and get married any time. Have a real wedding later on."

"I'm not getting married in a courthouse. But you're cute." She kissed him on the lips. "It's probably nothing."

They stepped out of Room 17 into the bright midday sun and strolled down the cement walkway in an attempt to conceal their clandestine sexual romp.

"Shit, I knew it," she whispered as they approached the office. There was a tourist couple waiting in front of the "BACK IN FIVE" sign that hung from the door. "Every time you talk me into this I get in trouble."

"Talk you into it? You texted me and said, 'Meet me in room seventeen.'"

"Yeah, but I didn't know you were going to attack me. I thought you were just going to bring me lunch."

"Then you shouldn't have been waiting for me with your clothes off."

"I was hot," she said.

Caleb stole a pinch of her butt before heading toward his truck in the gravel parking lot.

Lelah ran her fingers through her hair and gave it some body and life. She flattened the wrinkles on her blouse and plucked a piece of fuzz from her slacks.

"Hi," Lelah smiled. The couple turned around. "How are you doing today?"

"Oh hi," the man said. "Do you have any rooms available?"

"I believe room seventeen just opened up."

11.

A FEW MILES UP THE interstate, Sheriff Gates and Deputy Sparks followed an eighteen-wheeler down the empty stretch of asphalt. The eighteen-wheeler downshifted and its blinker lights flared and it made a wide right turn onto a dirt road. Out in the open, middle of the day, was the time they made their runs, most of them at least. Amateurs made runs at night—or those without a police escort.

They followed the eighteen-wheeler through a saddle of mesas and into the scattered shadows of a pinyon forest where the road opened to a clearing with an adobe ranch-style compound perched on a grassy bluff.

The eighteen-wheeler pulled inside a pre-fabricated metal warehouse and dragged the swirling dust with it.

Gates parked the American flag cruiser in the gravel.

Marlo nodded from the doorway. He was shirtless, shoeless, sweating from exertion of some kind. He walked across the gravel without a wince or hint of discomfort, his feet tough as moccasins. Gates shook his hand and hated it. Marlo had long spidery fingers and a strength in his grip that Gates despised and could not match. It was the kind of handshake that Gates had always wanted but could never produce with stubby fingers and a shallow palm.

"How come your partner never comes inside?" Marlo said. He smiled at Sparks through the windshield and waved at him flirtatiously with his long spidery fingers. Sparks turned away.

"Queers scare him," Gates said.

"Let him know it's not contagious."

"I've told him. He doesn't believe me."

They walked through the warehouse where several men had begun to unload bricks of what Gates assumed was cocaine or heroin from the eighteen-wheeler, the product concealed behind cellophane wrap and duct tape. The specific contents of the product didn't concern him. He was paid for the safe delivery of the truck, a thousand dollars per wheel.

Marlo and Gates strolled through the cholla cactus garden and along the adobe walls that were tiled with spirals of lapis and malachite and then through an arched oak door.

"Would you care to dance?" Marlo asked. He pirouetted across the laminated floor of his dance studio and the mirrored walls captured his reflection on all four sides. "I can teach you."

"I think I'll pass today."

They crossed the dance floor and through another arched doorway into an unusually large kitchen of stainless steel and chop-block cutting boards for the preparation of lavish meals and then down a long hallway decorated with a grim mélange of artwork from Cindy Sherman and Hieronymus Bosch and Durer and Goya that showcased death and the sexual macabre and then into a workshop where a sixteenth-century naval cannon was in the process of being restored. The heavy vapors of lacquer and paint thinner made the air taste flammable.

"Does that thing fire?" Gates asked.

"What good would it be if it didn't?"

"Did you build it?"

"It belonged to Coronado."

"Who was he?"

"A criminal."

Marlo lifted a manila envelope off the work shelf and handed it to Gates.

"Do you think about retirement?" Marlo asked.

Gates paused at the oddness of the question. But there was nothing in Marlo's expression that suggested it was anything but a normal piece of conversation.

"Sure," Gates said.

"What would it look like for you?"

"I don't think too deeply about it."

"But you must think something."

"I can't wait for the day when I don't have to clean up other people's shit."

"There is no such day," Marlo said.

"Maybe not."

"But you know you can't."

"Can't what?"

"Retire."

The conversation was becoming absurd and Gates had little patience for absurd conversations, especially deep ones, or more specifically, those of a philosophical nature. Such nonsense was a waste of time. But his business desires and personal finances compelled his patience to endure the claptrap for a bit longer.

"I'm going to retire some day," Gates said. "Soon. Very soon."

"No. You never will. You crossed a threshold years ago upon which there is no future, only evasion from the past, which, by the sheer force of it, permits no future. Only those without a past can retire."

"And who's that?"

"A forklift driver at Costco. Do you think he can look back on his employment career trundling from one section of the dusty warehouse to the next and remember one day from the other? He has created nothing more than a mathematical accumulation of time, calendars burned from the wall, until the day his employer tells him—thank you for your life, now go enjoy yours, what little you have left, that is: retirement. Suddenly he finds himself on alien ground, with no one telling him what he must do each day. He is lost in his own mind, a tenant he never cared much to know, and he is now forced to create his own world, unhindered and unpursued by a past that he never created. There are no years following him."

"If you say so."

"He is free to create his future."

"So are we."

"No. We already traded that away."

Gates opened the door to leave. He'd had enough of this street-poet-hippie-crystal-vagabond-woojie gibberish, he'd indulged the crackpot for a time because of the money in his hand and had now fulfilled his fiscal obligation.

"I would appreciate it if you allowed me to discipline Ruben."

Marlo's tone had changed and Gates turned around to meet the challenge. *I'm not afraid of you, faggot.*

"If he's going to be hurt," Marlo continued, "I'm going to be the one hurting him."

"He disrespected me."

"His mother is my sister. I love her very much. A father may beat his own child but he would never allow his neighbor to do so.

We accept this as part of our social contract. Would you allow me to discipline your daughter?"

"I'd kill you."

"Good. We understand each other."

"I'm the fucking law around here. Remember that."

Marlo took a pair of handcuffs from the work shelf and tossed them across the room. They had been sitting beside the manila envelope. Gates caught them.

"You are one form of law," Marlo said. "I am another."

12.

THE OLD WOOD TRUCK labored up the wilderness road that snaked through the mountainous forest, gears grinding, belching plumes of black diesel over the dried water ruts and gnarled depressions, its worn tires firing stones against the battered steel undercarriage and dust flaps.

"I had that dream again," Caleb said across the cab to Jake, who was behind the wheel.

"Did you tell her?"

"Yeah."

"Why'd you do that?" Jake said. "That's something I'd do. Why don't you just hang out with her and let her be? Keep your mouth shut and not hurt her feelings."

"I don't know. Can't figure it out."

"Well next time take it easy on her. She's dead for Christ's sake."

He first had the nightmare a few months after their mom had died. She was sitting in the passenger seat of his truck with her purse on her lap, eager to go somewhere with him, a much anticipated day trip. Her hair was pinned back in a bun and she was many years younger than the time of her death. Jake was at the wood splitter. He waved at them from across the yard. He was not coming with them for some reason.

"Where are we going?" she asked. "I love surprises."

She smiled at Caleb and rubbed his shoulder with the tender affection a mother always carries for her child, from infant to adulthood, the touch never adjusting for the years and ages gone by. He would always be her baby.

He turned off the truck and swiveled to face her.

"You're dead, Mom. We're not going anywhere."

She turned away and stared out her window and began to cry and then admitted through her tears what he had just told her. She said she was sorry. Sorry that she was dead. Sorry that she'd left him and his brother for this other place.

He had the dream often and loathed it for the pain it caused her, for the pain it caused him. And yet it was always the same and he did not know why he felt the need to tell her she was dead and make her cry. Always he awoke with crushing guilt and a dark anger toward himself. Why did he have to tell her? Why couldn't he just let his mother be? Why couldn't he just drive down the road and enjoy his time with her? He had no answer.

Jake lifted his steel-toed boot from the gas pedal and the diesel slowed and stopped where the road forked in the wilderness.

"Let's try the western slope today," he said. "I remember seeing a bunch of dead snags up there last spring."

Then suddenly it was upon them, shooting out of the forest. Loud. Screaming. Two-stroke engine. The ATV barreled around the corner from above and hurled a cloud of gritty dust into the truck cab as it thundered down the mountain, its driver some crazed blur of a lunatic negotiating the ruts with reckless agility. His red-mirrored goggles flashed in the sunlight and his long black hair kicked around without a helmet.

"Whatever happened to forest etiquette?" Jake said, waving at the dust.

"I bet he was never a Boy Scout."

The two-stroke engine noise was now far down the mountain and they didn't think of the ATV again until later in the day.

"Western slope?" Jake said.

"Let me text Lelah before we lose service."

"Tell her to put the beer on ice this time."

"Get your own lady."

"I'm working on it… Tell her to hook me up with one of her friends. She doesn't even have to be good-looking."

"You already fucked them all."

"Yes I did." Jake reflected, quite pleased with himself. He'd fucked them multiple ways, not only in the biblical sense. "But I've matured. I can honestly say I'm a one-woman man now."

Caleb glanced up from his phone. "No. You're a no-woman man right now."

"They weren't exactly church girls. Just saying."

"You're the one humping your hand."

"Yeah, and I'm tired of it. My dick's got fucking calluses on it."

"That's why they invented lotion."

"What about butter?"

"Shut the fuck up and drive."

The wood truck lurched forward and climbed the mountain toward the ridge several miles above them.

EARLY IN THE AFTERNOON Lelah set the case of Lagunitas IPA on the counter at Bode's General Store.

"And a bag of ice, please," she told the cashier.

Then a hand touched her shoulder from behind and she started.

"Is there a party I should know about?"

She turned around to face her father. Fresh coffee steamed out of his plastic mug that said DAD on the side. She'd bought it for him last Christmas. He must have come in through the back door. She hadn't seen the cruiser out front.

"Invite only," she said.

Gates leaned over and kissed his daughter on the cheek.

"I'm just bringing the guys some beer," she said.

"Where, the wood yard?"

"Jeez, Mr. Nosy, I'm not a suspect."

"It's the job. I can't help it."

"I've been an adult for a long time, Dad."

"But you'll always be my little girl."

They were the only customers inside. Gates strained to read the peculiar name on the case of beer.

"Lah-goo-KNEE-tuss. Is it any good?"

"The guys like it."

Lelah paid the cashier and grabbed the case from the counter.

"Love you, Dad."

"Love you, too. Say hello to the boys for me."

She pushed through the glass door and climbed into her Ford pickup. She turned over the engine and shifted into reverse when a knock on her window startled her again. Her father opened the passenger door.

"You forgot your ice." He laid the bag inside the cooler resting in the passenger foot space.

"Thanks, Dad."

"You gonna be home for dinner?"

"Probably not. Don't worry, we'll drink responsibly."

Lelah pulled onto the blacktop and headed toward the pine-forested mountains.

Gates planted his coffee mug in the dash holder and drove the cruiser out of the gravel parking lot in the opposite direction toward the lonely mesa land where the afternoon gusts had whipped the horizon a dusty orange.

⚥

CHAINSAWS WAILED THROUGH THE forest as Caleb and Jake harvested pinyon on the western slope four thousand feet above the arid valley that ran north to Colorado and south to Santa Fe.

Caleb could see the wind sweeping through the canyons below them and wished for a little breeze at least. They were on the lee of the mountain and the sun beat harshly on the back of his neck with brief mercy from a few passing clouds. But it was always good to be outdoors. Couldn't pay him enough for an office job. Sit in a starchy suit in a stuffy cubicle. Nope. The burned skin, the rough, grease-stained hands that looked twice his age, the splinters that swelled his knuckles and inflamed the meat of his palms, the swamp crotch that rashed and chafed like road burn from his balls to the top of his ass crack in days of fierce heat, it was all worth the freedom of the mountains and the open air. He could chew tobacco when he liked. Spit when he liked. Fart when he liked. Piss wherever he pleased. Not that he and his brother could ever qualify for an office job or anything other than labor outdoors. But he liked to entertain the thought that he was controlling his destiny, that he was doing the work he wanted to do, by choice. In war, you had very little choice.

They killed the saws and started hauling the cut sections of wood over to the log splitter.

⚥

LELAH NEARED THE TURNOFF for the wilderness road. In the approaching distance there was a man walking on the shoulder against traffic. He was carrying a jerrican and his red-mirrored goggles winked in the sunlight as she drove past him. She rounded a bend and noticed what she assumed was the man's ATV parked in a turnout. Bummer. Running out of gas. Oh well, Bode's isn't that far. If she had recognized the young man she would have stopped. But she didn't know him.

She continued down the asphalt a short ways and made a left turn onto the wilderness road that would take her to her man.

13.

CALEB SET A LOG on the holding plate and the maul drove down and halved the wood with a ferocious clack. He tossed the halves to Jake in the back of the truck for stacking and repeated the process. An assembly line of firewood making. Chop, toss, stack. Chop, toss, stack. Chop, toss, stack. Hours of it. Thoughts wandered but not too far. Always be cautious of the driving maul. One lop, chop off your hand.

Then Caleb saw her truck approaching through the dry tinder. He thought about kissing her and the cold beer that she was bringing and he turned off the log splitter and smiled.

Lelah parked at the edge of the clearing and craned her head out the window.

"Anybody thirsty?"

"Do my balls hang low?" Jake said.

Caleb threw a piece of split wood at him and it banged off the plywood siding and rattled around the truck bed.

"What, now it's all formal 'cause you guys are finally getting hitched?"

Caleb helped Lelah out of her truck and kissed her glossy lips. He walked around to the passenger door and removed the cooler from the foot space. He opened a bottle for Lelah and underhanded a bottle up to Jake in the bed of the wood truck. But Lelah handed the bottle back to Caleb and said in a whisper, "I probably shouldn't have one. I'll just have a sip of yours." She glanced down at her belly. "Just in case."

"Just in case of what?" Jake said.

"She's driving," said Caleb.

"That never stopped me from having a good time."

"Maybe it should have."

"Whatever," said Jake. "I've only lost my license one time."

Jake opened his bottle on the side of the tailgate with a bang of his fist. He took the cap between his fingers and snapped it into the forest where it caromed off the side of a pine tree.

"Hey Jack-Dick," Caleb said, "this isn't your bedroom."

"It's just a bottle cap."

"Give a hoot, don't pollute," said Lelah.

Caleb dropped his bottle cap into the cooler and then took a swig. Jake nearly downed his beer in one hungry thirst.

"Thank you, Lelah," Jake said. "Damn that is good."

"Anytime."

"You might want to marry her, brother," Jake said. "Before I do."

Caleb and Lelah sat on the tailgate together and stared through a break in the trees at the valley far below. A hundred miles south the Sangre de Cristo Mountains appeared to float above the haze. And then a light breeze finally carried through the trees and cooled the sweat below his eyes. *Yeah*, thought Caleb, *it doesn't get any better than this. A hard day's work. Cold beer. Your lady beside you.*

He nuzzled up to her neck and placed a kiss just behind her left ear.

"You smell so good," she whispered.

"I smell like ass."

"No, you smell like man."

He chuckled and kissed her again and threw his arm around her. He brought the beer to her lips and she took a self-consciously small sip.

"I gotta pee," she said.

"And we were just getting romantic."

"Sorry, babe. I'll be right back."

Caleb hopped down from the tailgate and limped around to the cab. He took a roll of toilet paper from the bench seat and handed it to her.

"Any tree you like, babe," he said. "Do you want me to come with you?"

"Enjoy your beer."

"Watch out for mountain lions."

Lelah turned around. "Seriously?"

"Bigfoot too," Jake said. "He's a horny fucker. Sneaks up from behind. Boom, bam, you're pregnant."

"Lovely image," she said.

Caleb threw another piece of wood at Jake and Lelah disappeared over a rise in the forested slope.

SHE STEPPED THROUGH THE undergrowth and looked behind her. She could no longer see them. She paused and admired the wind in the treetops and watched them sway as if in a chorus. There was an ageless harmony in the woods that awakened her senses in new ways. They became sharper, more acute. She remembered first experiencing the sensation on a camping trip with her father. The air seemed alive, humming, touching her skin. It felt good to her in a way that she could not explain. Since then she always had an affinity for nature, for the beauty that held a mystery and origin of its own, not wrought by man. The outdoors were a spiritual place to her and it was where she wanted to die if ever she had the choice.

She searched the pine needles with her eyes for snakes and bugs and dropped her jeans and started to pee. The stream of urine disrupted her thoughts until it felt as though the entire forest vibrated with the sound. Her face reddened and she reminded herself that she was alone. There was no one for miles.

She was nearly finished when her body shuddered and her eyes snapped wide. She pulled up her jeans, breathing heavily, her stare fixed on the—

What was it?

A man-made clump of camouflage.

A sleeping bag?

No, much too large.

A tent? Yes, that's what it was.

Looking over her shoulder the entire way she hurried back over the rise.

"What's wrong, babe?" Caleb asked, noticing the alarm on her face.

"Did you see Bigfoot?" said Jake.

"I think there's someone over there," she said.

"Were they watching you?" Caleb asked.

"I didn't see anybody. Only a tent... I think it was a tent. I'm not sure."

"Maybe they want a beer," Jake said, leaping down from the truck bed.

The brothers started up the rise and Lelah followed behind, catching up with Caleb to hold his hand.

It was indeed a tent, a camouflage green pup tent, crouching in the undergrowth.

"Hello," Caleb called out as they approached. He listened for an answer but there was none. He motioned for Lelah to stand behind them.

Caleb unzipped the door flap and looked inside. He saw a sleeping bag, an empty bottle of whiskey, cigarette butts, a stack of canned goods, and a large pile of trash. Jake peered over his shoulder.

"Been up here awhile," Caleb said.

"They need to call a cleaning lady. It stinks in there."

There was something unsettling about the scene for Caleb. It didn't feel right and he had come to trust his gut when it spoke to him.

But Jake snooped around the campsite, not sharing the concern, his curiosity driving him. He noticed something peculiar on the ground. He kneeled to investigate and pulled a thin plastic drip line out of the pine needles. It ran along the forest floor in both directions, up and down the slope.

"Check it out," Jake said.

"No, let's get out of here."

But Jake had already started following the drip line down the slope deeper into the forest, ducking under the branches and clawing undergrowth, like a dog on a scent.

Caleb called after him. "C'mon, Jake. Let's go."

Jake couldn't hear his brother right now or any voice other than the one in his head calling him further into the unknown. To what he hoped to find. He had his suspicions. He'd heard rumors. Heard tales about the gold growing in the hills and the men that grew it.

The powerful smell hit him first.

And then it was there.

He pushed through the evergreen curtain and beheld a clearing of ten-foot high marijuana plants, laden with ripe buds, days from harvest.

"Holy fucking money trees," Jake said out loud. "There you are."

Caleb and Lelah parted the branches and halted beside him. An elaborate network of drip lines fed water to the illicit garden from an aluminum water trough, which was partially concealed in the undergrowth at the base of a trickling spring.

"Jake, this is nothing but trouble. Let's get out of here while we still can."

Jake stepped further into the garden, indulging his lust and curiosity, the plants towering above him.

Caleb grabbed Jake by the arm and yanked him back.

"Let's go, Jake."

But Jake shouldered him off and admired a large bud drooping from a plant. The THC crystals glittered like iridescent fairy dust in the slanting light, rubies, diamonds, and amethyst floating in the mist of an ethereal water globe, a treasure growing in the silent intimacy of the forest, a treasure to be found and claimed by the worthy. He brought the pungent fruit to his nose. He could smell his dreams in the cannabis. He could smell the money. It was literally in his fingertips. Here, growing before him was the lucky break he needed. The lucky break this poor hardworking white boy had been waiting for his entire life. Right here. Right now. It's yours. Take it.

♃

To THE DOME. To the dome.

Ruben had slugged two Mickey's wide mouths to the dome on the walk back from Bode's and now didn't give a fuck about the gas mishap. He set the green case of Mickey's on the back of the ATV and rounded the bag of dripping ice over the top of the case and fastened the load with a bungee cord. He twisted off the gas cap and let the jerrican empty into the tank.

Galugga.

Galugga.

Galugga.

He spaced out and imitated the sound of the tank filling.

Galugga.

Galugga.

Galugga.

And then he decided, while waiting, to *galugga* another malty brew. He deserved it. He'd been working hard up there all by himself, for months, living in filth. He didn't get paid enough to live like a rat. He deserved more money. But that would come. He was paying his dues. Look at his uncle.

He *galugga*'d the beer and his dome expanded to an even higher consciousness. The ride up the mountain would be epic, a real screamer of wind and two-stroke howl—nothing better than speeding with a raging buzz and no helmet. Fear? He had none on the quad. Helmets were for pussies and punks who crashed.

The jerrican went silent. It was empty.

Ruben bungeed it next to the beers and straddled the seat. He searched for his red-mirrored goggles and realized at that moment that he had never taken them off.

He readjusted his .40 cal Beretta in the back of his waistband before ripping onto the asphalt and then pitching left across the yellow lines and up the wilderness road with the bag of ice leaking a trail of water droplets.

♪

"WE'RE OUTTA HERE," CALEB said. He took Lelah by the arm and headed back through the forest toward the trucks on the other side of the rise.

Jake crashed through the low branches and caught back up with them, charged with excitement, the prospect of it all.

"I know what you're thinking so stop thinking it," Caleb said without breaking stride.

"And what am I thinking?"

Caleb began packing up the wood truck.

"Hold on, brother." Jake stepped in front of him. "And hear me out."

Caleb lifted the chainsaws into the truck bed and hitched the log splitter onto the ball joint.

"Caleb," Lelah said, "what's wrong?" She hadn't opened her mouth yet.

"We're getting outta here before we get mixed up into something that don't concern us."

"Just hear me out, bro."

"I know what you're going to say, and it ain't good."

Then Lelah said, "Caleb, wait a second."

This stopped Caleb. Had he heard that?

"Are you serious, babe?"

Jake placed his hands on Caleb's chest in an attempt to calm him.

"Listen, brother," he started, "you're your own man, and so am I. A gift was just dropped in our laps and we're fools if we don't accept it."

"That ain't no gift."

"You don't go to prison for stealing pot. It's practically legal."

"No, you get killed."

"Nobody is going to catch us."

"What if they come back? They haven't been gone long."

"We could cut it down and have it stacked in the back of our truck in ten minutes."

"It ain't ours," Caleb said.

"They shouldn't be growing it up here in the first place."

"So that's how you rationalize stealing?"

"We steal wood from this forest all day long if you really want to get philosophical on my ass. What's the difference?"

"We pay for the permits."

"Those plants could turn our lives around," Jake said. "There's a bunch of money over there. A whole shitload of it. Lelah, what do you think?"

"She's not part of this—don't even think about dragging her into it."

"She's here. I'm sure she has an opinion. She's gonna be your wife, which now makes all of us business partners."

"Babe, you don't have to answer anything."

"It's between you two," she said.

"You're neutral?" Caleb shot back. "You're fucking neutral?"

"I don't know," she said. "I don't know. Like Jake said, there's a lot of money there, I guess. I know how hard you guys work. It hurts me to see you struggle for money, Caleb."

"I ain't struggling. I'm happy to get up and go to work each morning."

"You're gonna be working two jobs just to pay the bills," she said, raising her voice slightly. "When am I going to see you, babe? We've got a wedding to pay for."

"It ain't always gonna be this hard."

"It can get a hell of a lot easier right now," Jake said.

Then Lelah added, "They're not supposed to be growing it in the first place, right?"

"Have you two lost your minds? I can't believe what I'm hearing."

"I'm going in the truck," Lelah said.

"I think that's a good idea."

Lelah opened the driver's side door to her pickup and sat inside.

Caleb exhaled and stared at Jake, a few feet separating them. "How are you going to get rid of it once you got it? You thought about that?"

"I know a guy in Albuquerque who's in the business," Jake said. "He'd buy it from us."

"You don't know that."

"It's worth a shot."

"And since when do you know anyone down there?"

"We met while you were overseas."

"We got a good life, bro. We don't need to mess it up."

"A good life?" Jake snapped. The pressure. The dream. The life he imagined and the future he'd seen so clearly in the few minutes since he found his treasure was being threatened. "A good fucking life? We share a goddamn trailer. We ain't got no health care, no college degrees, no retirement fund, we're about to lose everything we got—and it ain't because we haven't worked hard for our slice of the American Dream. Our backs are gonna be broken by the time we're fifty. Knees shot. We can't even get a goddamn bank loan. We've done things by the book. We've done it the right way. You lost your leg for this goddamn country and what did they give you? Some cheap medals and a thousand dollars a month—they should've given you a room in the fucking White House."

"This ain't about that."

"This is like one of those fairy tales where the poor woodsman comes across the treasure in the forest."

"And it always ends badly."

"Not this time."

Jake climbed into the back of the wood truck and grabbed his chainsaw. He jumped down and stood as close to Caleb as he could without getting punched. "In or out?"

"Out."

"I'll still split it with you, bro. But I ain't leaving it behind."

Jake marched back up the slope toward his El Dorado and was soon lost behind the trees.

Caleb yanked open the driver's side door to Lelah's truck.

"Scoot over."

He nearly snapped the key when he turned over the ignition. He wheeled through the crackling tinder and turned onto the wilderness road.

THE VISTA WAS EPIC and he felt a sense of wild accomplishment as he gazed upon a hundred miles of desolation, a necessary pit stop on the ten-mile ride back up the mountain, the perfect time to *galugga* another brew.

Another wide mouth.

To the dome.

He felt like some videogame warlord marveling over his kingdom. From horizon to horizon, he couldn't make out a single structure, a note or vibration of mankind. The road was the only sign of human intervention. But the ghosts traveled below, he knew that much. You couldn't see them. They were invisible. But they were there. They never ventured into the high country though, into the pine forests where it was cool with shade. The lowlands were their precinct, the windswept pueblos, the lonely mesa land, and the ruins of bleached bones. He never would have taken the job if the spirits swam through the trees at night up here. Never. It would've scared the shit out of him. Ghosts didn't climb mountains. Thank God.

This could all be mine one day, thought Ruben. *All mine. Why not?*

He pulled the Beretta from his waistband and waved it over his domain, threatening his subjects to obey his rule. A pistol in one hand and a frosty green grenade in the other.

He'd have twenty G's cold cash when he was through. He'd slap some iced-out wheels on his Civic. Drive over to Tanya's and show her his wad of hundreds and his .40 cal. She'd say yes this time. She'd be his lady. A fine piece of ass. Finest piece of ass he ever seen.

Nineteen years old and living large. Deep in the game.

He tilted the green bottle and the wide mouth dropped malt liquor down his throat and he floated on the fumes. His vision had begun to blur and he could feel the oncoming escape when he would disappear into his thoughts. But first he had to get back up the mountain, back to his tent. It was safe there, safe to get zombie drunk, become temporarily blind, do as you please, jerk off to Tanya all night long. All night. In the four months that he'd been living up there he hadn't seen a soul near his campsite. Not within five miles. It was safe to be free up there. To be yourself. To howl at the moon. To be shit-housed—and alive. To bang Tanya. For when he was drunk he was most alive. He was almost there. He'd be there soon enough. They were a few days from harvest. The home stretch. He could celebrate a little. He could celebrate a lot.

♪

Under the blaze of Jake's chainsaw the ripe plants toppled onto the forest floor. There was no resistance, no pushback from the thin stalks, and they fell in great *whooshes* of stinky bud. The three-foot blade was made for chewing through the hardwood forests of the world, mighty trees that towered above every living thing. These weren't even saplings. They were weeds. He felled a half-dozen with each swoop of the blade, whirling in semi-circles, giddy with moneystrokes—for that's what each stroke of the blade generated—MONEY. CASH. DREAMS.

He killed the saw and dragged an armload of plants through the undergrowth toward the wood truck. He heaved the plants into the truck bed and headed back into the forest for more green gold.

♩

THE FORD PICKUP CREAKED and rocked along the ruts of the wilderness road.

They were not speaking.

They hadn't spoken.

Caleb wanted to punch the dashboard. His stupid fucking brother. That dumb motherfucker. And she nearly sided with him. His fiancé. The woman he was going to marry. Fools. He shook his head, his arms extended and flexed, hands clenched on the steering wheel, wringing the water out of it.

Lelah looked across the cab. She wanted to slide over and nudge up to him but she could feel his anger. She'd let him cool a bit. At least till the bottom of the mountain.

Caleb turned a sharp corner and stomped on the brake pedal. The truck slid in the loose earth as the ATV swerved around them and motored up the road without paying them any notice. A jerk of the handlebars, a shift of his weight. Throttle and rip. The rider was gone.

Caleb remembered the red-mirrored goggles. It was the speeding idiot they had seen on the way up the mountain. They had nearly hit him or he'd nearly hit them both times now and he didn't so much as slow down and wave or venture an apology. He just kept tearing up the road with a middle finger to the world.

Lelah looked at Caleb again, hoping that he would meet her eyes with his. But he did not return her gaze.

He could feel her watching him. But he was still too angry. Afraid of what he might say. Wait. Cool off.

He took his foot off the brake and they continued down the mountain.

♃

JAKE SURVEYED THE MARIJUANA garden. He'd nearly cut down the entire crop. He hauled another bushel through the forest and over to the truck now loaded high with plants.

He looked through the trees to the nearest ridgeline where fingers of sunlight shafted through. He thought about leaving. The afternoon breeze was barely a whisper through the pinyon and he searched far into the shadows of the wild with his ears and eyes. He searched the arroyos and canyons of the mountain and the recesses beyond them. There was only stillness.

Again, he thought about leaving. But the vault was open and the bank tellers and the guards were gone.

He looked up at the truck bed, the heap of marijuana higher than he could reach, the tantalizing and powerful scent of the sweet leaf. The strong fragrance spoke to him of one thing—money.

And there was more.

A little more and he would have it all, the entire garden. He listened again. Nothing stirred. No birds. No squirrels. And no more wind, not even a whisper this time.

He was alone in the wilderness and free to exercise his will.

He felt a rush, an audacious thrill, an energy and sense of adventure that hadn't been there in a very long time. He felt powerful, triumphant, the adrenaline and perverse satisfaction of a misdeed done well. An inner applause rose in a great swelling wave of endorphins—*continue,* it said—*keep going. Don't stop now.*

He nodded to the cheering arena, proud of his resolve, and strutted back into the trees for one more haul. To finish the job.

RUBEN HAD TURNED OFF the road a ways back and was cutting his own trail up the mountain, slaloming through the forest. Making a game of it. Speed was enhanced with a good buzz—it made everything seem twice as fast, like driving a spaceship at warp speed. The quad was made for this type of high-octane action.

He carved close to a knotty pine, inches away from scraping himself off the vehicle, and chuckled with alcohol-fueled recklessness.

He could win the X Games.

He was a light-speed warrior.

He was Han-muthafuckin'-Solo.

He came to a small clearing and whipped the quad into a donut. He straightened the vehicle and gunned it down into an arroyo and over a rise when his brow furrowed and he eased on the throttle. He squinted and then silenced the engine. Through the trees he saw what appeared to be a wood truck and heard the scream of a chainsaw suspiciously close to his camp.

He sat there in the saddle and deliberated.

No way, he told himself. There's just no way.

But it was harvest time and the thieves came out during the harvest.

Had somebody followed him one day on a run to the store? Or his slip that one night at the casino? He hadn't told anyone about his secret job up here in the mountains. He'd disappeared for the summer. It was the longest time he'd ever kept his mouth shut about anything. Only a few people knew he was up here—and he was growing it for them. He wasn't even from this part of the state. He was a hundred miles from home.

He tracked through the drunken haze of his memory and he cursed his luck. Adrenaline surged through him and he became sober in the moment. He drew his .40 cal from the back of his waistband and stalked into the trees.

♣

THE FORD PICKUP APPROACHED the cattle guard at the mouth of the wilderness road. They still hadn't spoken to each other and it had been a twenty-minute ride down the mountain.

A suspicion, at first remote and distorted with anger, had become an immediate concern for Caleb as he turned over the events of the day. Who was the guy on the ATV? What was he doing up there— riding down in the morning and back up in the afternoon? There were plenty of off-roaders and thrill seekers who drove around the hundreds of miles of wild roads in this part of the country. They'd done it with friends when they were younger. They still did it. But this guy, at this time, on the same seldom used fork of the road that led to nowhere and dead-ended a short ways from where they harvested wood today would not leave his thoughts.

Caleb was no longer angry. He was worried about his brother.

You dismiss coincidence in times like these and act. He stopped the truck.

"It's gotta be him," he said.

"Him?"

"The guy on the quad. It's gotta be him."

Caleb whipped the Ford into a 180 and sped back up the wilderness road to his brother.

🪱

THE BLADE CHEWED THROUGH the final row of money trees and the bounty toppled onto the ground. He stood and caught his breath, sucking in the high altitude air, sweating from the feverish last round of cutting. The garden had been taken down and the heist was nearly complete. He was glad he came back to finish the job. He was going to be rich—and his brother would thank him later when they were drinking piña coladas on the beach at some tropical resort, away from the infected splinters and angry insects, shading themselves under lavish palm trees and colorful umbrellas. He'd never drunk a piña colada before and he was eager to try one. Or ten—a hundred of them for that matter, flinging twenty dollar tips at the bartender with each round. Watch the ladies crowd around him. *I've got an attractant now—the most powerful one on Planet Earth.*

He couldn't remember ever feeling this good about himself. His mind was thundering with possibilities. He packed a chew and soared even higher. He slung his saw over his shoulder, pulled tight his work gloves, and prepared for the final haul. But then slowly, as if he could feel the presence of someone watching him in the forest, Jake turned his head and discovered a man with red-mirrored goggles over his eyes, pointing a gun at him.

"Toss that thing to the side," Ruben said.

Jake did as he was told. The saw landed in the matted marijuana leaves with a heavy thud.

"Now get on your motherfucking knees and put your hands on top of your head. Don't fuck around."

Ruben inched forward with his gun hand shaking.

"You dumb motherfucker," he said before kicking Jake in the face.

Jake's world went black and he lost consciousness for a glimpse. When he awakened, and lifted his dizzy head from the leafy ground, he could smell the beer on the man's steamy breath as a punch drove into his nose and his world went black again.

♣

THE FORD PICKUP FISHTAILED around a bend and spit dust and gravel into the forested canyon below. Caleb righted the truck and stomped back on the gas, both hands on the wheel, hoping that he was wrong, hoping that his suspicions were incorrect and that he'd run into his brother around the next corner, driving the wood truck back down the mountain, his face plastered with a huge stupid grin.

Lelah clenched the door handle and jerked forward in her seatbelt. It pressed hard against her breasts and burned into the skin of her neck. She could see the worry on Caleb's face and that was a rare thing to witness. He was not the kind to show worry, at least not since he got back from overseas, from the war.

♣

"WHO THE FUCK ARE you working for?" Ruben demanded, pressing the pistol barrel into the back of Jake's head. He slapped Jake in the ear with his free hand. "Who?"

"Nobody," Jake replied, his ear ringing. "I'm just a logger. I'm just up here getting firewood. I sell firewood."

"Bullshit. Who sent you up here? Who told you about this?"

"I swear. I swear it. Nobody sent me up here. I just found this place. I just found it. You gotta believe me. I'll put it all back. All of it. Just let me go."

Jake felt intensely alone, cold and shivering in the heat. His vision was already dimming and he was flinching in anticipation of the bullet that would soon drive through his brain. He was about to die and there was nothing heroic about it. He should've listened to his brother. His brother was right. He was going to leave the best friend he ever had.

𝕬

CALEB SHOT THE TRUCK off the wilderness road and bounced over the uneven ground. He turned off the engine and coasted to a stop.

"Stay here, Lelah."

Caleb limped over to the wood truck and grabbed the hunting rifle from the gun rack above the bench seat. He slid back the bolt and chambered a .270 round and moved up the rise toward the garden, cursing his prosthetic leg and the shrapnel in his hip for slowing him down. Through the trees he could hear his brother and another man speaking in loud and harsh tones. His brother was pleading and this quickened his pace. He'd heard such pleadings before and dormant senses came alive in him.

The rifle was now pressed into his shoulder and he slipped through the pine branches as he had been trained to kill. The soft pine needles and grass under his boots made his approach nearly silent.

"Please don't kill me," Jake said.

"It's too late for that," said Ruben.

Caleb pushed away the last branch and he was looking at the scene. The man with the gun had his back to him.

"Put your gun down," Caleb said.

Ruben startled and whirled around. There was a lack of resolve and experience in his movements that Caleb immediately perceived. But these were also the most dangerous people with guns—the frightened ones without real knowledge of murder and only the fantasy of it.

"Put your gun down," Caleb repeated in a measured tone. He limped forward with his rifle aimed on the chest of his target. "Nobody needs to die today."

Ruben held his .40 cal on Caleb and then pointed it back at Jake, nervous, shaking, unsure what to do, frantic and jumpy. Back and forth, who to put the gun on, who is the greatest threat?

Caleb remained calm and levelheaded and tried to reassure the man with the handgun of his peaceful intentions. He needed to take command of the situation and lead it to a safe resolution. Quickly. "Nobody needs to die today. Put down your gun." He continued sliding forward, closing the gap, thirty feet away now.

"I don't trust thieves," Ruben shouted. "You put down your gun."

"Don't do it," Jake yelled. "Shoot him, Caleb."

"Be quiet, Jake," Caleb said.

"Shoot him."

"Jake…be quiet."

But amid the swirling turmoil Caleb was struck with the image, ludicrous, absurd, comical—the man with the gun was still wearing those ridiculous red-mirrored goggles. He looked like a retarded bank robber, a criminal with special needs. It was impossible to take him seriously. But here he was waving a gun and you had to take him seriously. Caleb had seen men killed under the most benign conditions. That was the peculiar thing about war—you were never worried when you should be and by the time you started worrying someone was already dead.

"You're going to put your gun down and we're going to give you back your crop. Then we're going to leave and nobody will be the wiser. Okay? Does that sound like a deal?"

Ruben was losing a handle on himself, his faculties unhinging. The different voices, the conflicting orders, the cheap malt liquor in his blood, the rifle pointed at him, the crop destroyed, gone, everything ripped up—how would he explain it? He'd already fucked up more than once. More than twice even.

"Why should I trust you?" Ruben said.

"Shoot him, bro."

"Fuck you," Ruben yelled down into Jake's face. "Fuck you— and-shut-the-fuck-up."

"Be quiet, Jake…please be quiet." Caleb stared through Ruben's red-mirrored goggles and into his panicked eyes. *Just keep looking at me. Keep looking at me, kid.* "You have my word. Nobody needs to die today. Nobody is going to die. But I need you to put down your gun. It's that simple."

The stress had become unbearable for Jake and the frayed ropes that held his ragged nerves together finally snapped. He'd been looking for an opening, a way to get the gun barrel away from his pounding head, a way to break free from this son-of-a-bitch who was threatening to kill him—and found one. He spun and knocked the gun from Ruben's hand.

"No!" Caleb shouted.

Jake tackled Ruben and slammed his head into the ground. Then Jake lunged for the gun and snatched it off the forest floor.

"No—Jake—Don't!" Caleb yelled, pulling his bad leg behind his good one. "No!"

But Jake could hear neither sound nor wisdom, his instincts overriding all subtlety and discretion—he spun and squeezed the trigger in one furious motion. A flash of fire from the gun barrel and a spray of blood and Ruben caved from the blast. The bullet ruptured his heart and exited through his upper back and hurled a chunk of meat with it. He was dead by the time Jake lowered the smoking barrel.

The mountains rang with the killshot and the echo settled among the trees and became silent.

"It was self-defense," Jake gasped, doubled over, hands on his knees. "He would've killed both of us."

"Goddamnit, Jake. Goddamnit." Caleb shook his head and looked at the lifeless body on the ground and then back at his brother. "Goddamnit."

"It was self-defense," Jake said with thinning confidence. His legs and arms trembled and he looked to his brother for guidance.

Branches snapped underfoot and the forest floor rustled behind them as Lelah ran to the edge of the clearing and saw the young man dead on the ground and the blood seeping from the hole in his chest.

"Go back to the truck, Lelah...please, sweetheart. Go back to the truck."

Lelah stood paralyzed with her hands over her mouth. She could not take her eyes off the dead man. She'd never seen a dead body before.

"What are we gonna do?" Jake asked.

"Leave," Caleb said.

"What about him? Should we bury him?"

"No."

"We can't just leave him here like this."

"You should've thought about that before you shot him. How do you know there's not twenty more of him coming up the road right now?"

Jake looked down at the young man he had just killed. His throat clenched and he was unable to swallow. His shoulders sagged and he became terribly heavy and he wondered if he could take even one step right now when Caleb took him by the arm and commanded his attention.

"Grab your chainsaw and let's get the fuck outta here while we still can."

14.

CALEB RIPPED OPEN THE sliding aluminum door to the woodshed as Jake backed up the truck until the tailgate was flush. Then Caleb unlatched the tailgate and it dropped with a clang and the brothers began to drag the plants out of the truck bed and across the dirt floor to the back wall. The pungent leaves and ripe marijuana buds overpowered the dank odor of rotting grease and mothballed tools and stale work rags. The plants were the size of bushy Christmas trees and they had a surprising weight to them.

Lelah stood a few steps back from the doorway watching what she could not believe. What was supposed to be an innocent afternoon up on the mountain with her man, her fiancé, the father of her future children, the one she believed she was carrying inside her, the simple act of sharing a cold beer at the end of the day had now escalated into a capital offense in just a few hours.

In short order the truck was emptied in the dimming light and the plants were stacked to the roof in a bushy heap. The brothers threw a large blue tarpaulin over the plants and set a discarded truck axle and two greasy hydraulic car jacks on the edges to secure it in place.

"I'm going home, Caleb," Lelah said.

"Let's stay here tonight."

"No. I don't want to be here."

"I'll come with you then."

Lelah walked over to her pickup truck and climbed inside.

The veins in Caleb's neck were tense green ropes and there was a fierce edge to his voice when he turned to his brother and said, "Call your buddy and get this shit out of here."

Then Caleb pointed to the .40 cal Beretta tucked in Jake's waistband.

"And get rid of that guy's gun."

"Don't worry. I'm gonna set things right."

"You better. 'Cause you sure did fuck them up."

15.

THE SUN HAD DISAPPEARED behind the mesas and the prairieland was settling into the shapeless dark of a moonless night. The road was empty save the pickup truck and there were no oncoming headlights for miles ahead and they wouldn't see any for several minutes more.

"We should tell my dad," Lelah said. "He can help us."

"No. Not unless we have to."

"He's the sheriff, Caleb. He'll know what to do."

"Do you want to go to jail? I don't."

"It was self-defense."

"You have to prove that."

"There's a dead man lying in the forest up there."

"Yes. There is."

"How can you be so calloused?" she asked. "How can you say it like that?"

"I'm not worried about the dead guy right now. Those are the stakes when you walk around with a gun and pull it on somebody. He knew them. If he didn't, he should have."

"A young man lost his life."

"He did. And I don't want any of us to either. This may all blow over. Then again it may not. If I'm a betting man, the people he was working with probably won't report his death to the authorities. Maybe he was working alone. Pray that he was. Pray that he was some stupid kid up there trying to make a move all by himself. We don't know anything yet. And until then, we need to be patient and lay low. There's already been enough stupidity for one day. We need to stay calm and see how things play out."

"Be patient? Stay calm? Who are you?"

"I'm trying to keep all of us alive and out of prison," Caleb said. "It's that simple. What do you want to say to the police: Jake was stealing some guy's marijuana and then Jake shot the guy in self-defense—the guy whose marijuana he was stealing? And we just happened to be there but we weren't part of it? There's not a jury in this land that will buy that. Or a prosecutor for that matter. Or whomever. And guess what? We're accessories, whether we like it or not. Once we open our mouths and start talking we can't go back. That'll be it. They'll pit us against each other. Or me and you against my brother. Or any other combination that serves them and there won't be a damn thing your dad can do about it. And what if that guy was part of a cartel or something? They'll have our names. They'll know who we are. Nobody will be able to protect us from that. Not your father. Not prison. Nothing. At least we have a chance if we keep quiet. We have time. I just don't know how much."

They were traveling through the dark with only the headlights from the truck showing the way.

"I'm sorry, baby," he said. "I really am. But we can't go losing our heads now. Jake lost his head and look what happened. We can't take that back. We can't rewind things. And I figure the best we can do right now is let everything settle: our nerves, our emotions, and wait until we can think clearly again. The best thing to do right now is nothing."

Caleb looked across the cab and saw her staring at the broken yellow lines on the road, the glow from the dashboard reflecting off her wet face. He could see the anguish in her clenched features, the confused glaze over her eyes. Speeches did not work right now. He knew that much. What could he say that would do any good?

"I love you, Lelah," he said. "I'm sorry it's this way. I'm sorry that this happened."

"I won't be able to sleep," she said.

"Neither will I. But at least we'll be by each other's side."

Caleb pulled Lelah across the bench seat and kissed her and she set her head in his lap for the rest of the way to her house. When they pulled down the dirt driveway they were relieved that her father was not home. They walked through the back door and into her bedroom and held each other through the long night.

16.

SHERIFF GATES AND DEPUTY Sparks stood over Ruben's corpse sprawled in a puddle of glutinous blood, black against the shade of the forest. His face was burned a greenish purple from exposure and bloated from death. He was still wearing his red-mirrored goggles and the tissue around them had swollen up the sides and partially depressed them into his skin like a cookie cutter in a ball of dough. His mouth was agape in a mood of stupefied horror and his tonsils and gums had taken on the pruning texture of dried meat.

The chopped remnants of marijuana stalks and leaves were quickly withering from the rich green of the harvest to the ashen lifelessness of decay. Uprooted drip lines snaked across the decimated garden. It looked as if a pack of savage elephants had run riot over the place.

Gates kneeled beside Ruben and studied the bullet wound.

"Shot at close-range," he said. He surveyed the matted area and the erratic grooves carved into the soil. "Looks like there was a struggle and then boom. Bye-bye Ruben."

He stood and walked with his eyes on the ground and then bent down to pick up a brass shell casing. He read the numbers stamped into the base.

"Forty cal."

"What did he carry?" Sparks asked.

".40 cal."

"What do you figure happened?"

"I don't believe he shot himself."

They left the garden and found Ruben's ATV parked randomly amid the pine trees. There was a case of Mickey's with a plastic bag of melted ice over the top fastened to the rack by a bungee chord. Pockets of ice-melt pooled the edges of the plastic. Several beers were missing.

"Do you think he traded the marijuana for the beer?" Sparks asked.

"He certainly would've considered it."

They snooped around the ATV and then moved on. They fanned out and hiked over a rise and came upon an area where someone had been harvesting wood. Gates scooped a handful of sawdust and brought it to his nose.

"Fresh," he said. "A few days at most."

Sparks bent down and examined the deep tire ruts made by the wood truck.

"A big hauler," Sparks said. "Probably a six- or eight-ton. That's about as big a truck as could get up here."

Sparks moved on. He stepped through the soft tinder and over a fallen pine branch and stopped.

"Got another set of tracks here," he said. "Smaller vehicle. Looks like a standard four-wheel drive pickup."

Several yards away Gates squatted and studied the forest floor, pondering the situation. He stood up and his legs tingled and he grew lightheaded. A rush of vertigo came upon him and the earth wheeled and spun on its axis. He braced himself against a pine tree and closed his eyes. He took several deep breaths and before long his equilibrium came back to him with a pounding heartbeat.

Sparks hiked over to him.

"You all right?" he asked.

"Yeah, I just forgot how thin the air was up here."

"No shit. I feel out of shape."

"You are."

Sparks glanced at his growing paunch and then at his flaccid arms that lacked even a hint of muscle definition or a healthy vein to circulate his blood. "I guess so," he said.

They looked out at a break in the trees and the land fell off before them and they could see the arid valley way below stretching for some hundred miles.

"What do you think?" Sparks said.

"Dunno just yet."

"You think some loggers stole the crop?"

"It's unlikely," Gates said. "But greed is a peculiar thing."

"Maybe they stumbled upon it when Ruben was out grabbing his beer?"

"Certainly could've."

"But you don't think so?"

"We'll rule out dumb luck for now."

"What are we gonna tell Marlo?"

"The truth," Gates said. "The dumbass lush walked off the job like so many fucking times before and got our shit stolen and himself killed in the process. The fucking truth."

"He's gonna think it was an inside job."

"Maybe it was. We're not the only side involved."

"Maybe Ruben bragged about his dealings to the wrong people."

"Drunks have been known to do that from time-to-time. Lot's of *maybes* right now."

Gates lifted the bindle of cocaine from the shirt pocket behind his badge and tapped a power-stroke on the back of his hand and hoovered it up his nose. An instant Übermensch.

"Yola-bola-rockin-rolla. God bless Peru. Those little fucking llama riders. Lake Titi-caca." He sniffed and wiped, then said, "Machu Picchu. Now that's a high motherfucking city."

"How high?"

"Higher than this mountain."

"Can I get a bump?" Sparks asked.

Gates tossed him the bindle. Sparks snorted a bump and handed it back.

"Let's go grab Ruben," said Gates, "and throw his dumb ass in the trunk."

17.

ARLO STARED DOWN AT Ruben's corpse slumped in the trunk of the patriotic cruiser and caught his reflection in the red-mirrored goggles.

"At every funeral I have ever attended the deceased always wears a thin smile," he began. "As if they were now happily residing in a carefree place, lost in blissful slumber. It comforts the bereaved, or at least that is the belief of the Undertaker's Guild of America. But I've never seen this smile occur naturally. Clearly, Ruben is not smiling."

"He sure ain't," Gates said.

"But he will be smiling at his funeral. Trust me. Ruben will smile again. The undertaker will make certain of it. I have heard that freezing to death produces a smile on the face of the deceased."

"I've heard that too."

"Have you ever seen it?"

"Seen what?"

"A frozen man and his smile."

"No."

Marlo cocked his head to the side and pondered his nephew from a different angle. "I must say that this hideous pose isn't a very accurate characterization of the young man. The attitude of

Ruben's mouth, this gaping rictus of dumbfounded horror, makes him look much dumber than he actually was."

Gates didn't necessarily agree with Marlo's observation. Dead or alive, Ruben looked just as dumb as he'd always been.

Marlo turned around and motioned to three men who were standing in the doorway of the warehouse. Gates had never seen these men before. He'd seen plenty of other men at the compound, was familiar with their faces, but never these three. Maybe they were Marlo's lovers. Maybe they were his henchmen. Maybe they were both. But whatever they were, Gates thought them creepy. He couldn't exactly put a finger on it but he could feel it in a vaguely tangible way, like a faint odor.

Sparks was sitting inside the cruiser with the windows rolled up and doors locked.

"Could you please stick Ruben in the walk-in for now?" Marlo said to the three men striding across the gravel. "There should be plenty of room behind the ice cream. Thank you so much."

The man in the point position of the trio was wearing a black mesh top and a yellow Speedo. Two large nipple rings were visible through the mesh. He was muscular and athletic with long sculpted legs and Gates supposed that he was from some place far away. His hair was gelled into a faux-hawk and he appeared to be wearing eye shadow.

Gates studied the three men and then looked over at Marlo for some possible answer to the inscrutable way in which he lived out here. But Gates was no wiser after the searching. He figured he should just accept it. Whatever IT was. He couldn't tell if Marlo was forty or sixty.

The men lifted Ruben's stiff corpse out of the trunk and carried him into the warehouse. He looked like a giant baby curled in a napping position after a long drive with his parents.

Marlo shut the trunk.

"What percentage of theft is employee theft?" he asked.

"Is that an accusation?"

"No. It's a question. Don't you deal in those types of statistics?"

"I don't know the exact percentage. But it's high."

"Exceptionally high."

Marlo threw his hands toward the heavens with his palms turned upward and held them there. He looked around at his vast property and inhaled the flowery sage that was riding on the afternoon wind coming down off the mesa above. He closed his eyes and shook his head with ironic resignation. The universe was unfair.

"His mother pleaded with me for months: 'give the boy a job,'" Marlo said. "'Give him a job. All he does is sit around and play video games and get high and drink with his buddies. Please—please—please—give Ruben a job. Give him a reason to get out of the house and stop wasting his life. Something that will make him feel better about himself. Make him feel like a man.' And now she will undoubtedly blame me for his misfortune, for allowing him to be a man, or at least attempt to be one. Regrettably, Ruben always struggled with responsibility. He was like that as a little boy. People rarely take into account the pitfalls of an occupation. They only look at the potential rewards, the benefits. But as economists and the Devil are fond of saying: there's always a trade-off."

Marlo exhaled and admired Darius Gates in the slanting light that shaded the left side of his face, noting that he was handsome in a hard-lived, grizzled sort of a way, an old workhorse still carrying some of its virility. He wondered for a moment if the old cop had a big penis and concluded that he probably did not. He'd observed over the years that men with large penises had more easygoing dispositions. Most of them at least, there were always exceptions. He'd met several fiery sons-of-a-bitches with thunder cocks, even loved one of them for a time whose cuddle name was Hotspur. But they were defending other issues.

"Well, you know what needs to be done," Marlo said. "You're the sheriff of this fine county. You've been entrusted by these thousands of square miles of outlaw country and noble citizenry to find thieves and murderers and bring them to justice."

"We'll find them. Sure enough we'll find them."

"And when you do, we'll make sure to put great big happy smiles on their faces, won't we? Great big smiles so that when their mothers look down on them in their caskets they may take comfort knowing that they're in a better place, and that God does everything for a reason."

"It'll be my pleasure."

Marlo walked alongside the patriotic cruiser with his bare toes curling against the warm gravel. He traced his fingertips down the waves of red and white stripes that were coated with road-dust and knocked on the passenger window. Deputy Sparks jumped in his seat. Marlo blew him a kiss and waved with his fingers aflutter.

"I'll suck your cock for five dollars, Dep-you-tee."

Sparks turned away.

"How about ten? Fuckee suckee. Bang-bang-mee-assee."

Marlo bellowed and watched the metal flag pull down the dirt road until it turned left behind the mesa, still laughing into the prairie minutes after they were gone.

18.

THE MONOTONOUS DRONE AND cleave of the log splitter under the sun and windless sky. The maul plunged and split a pine log with a dry crack. Caleb tossed the halves onto a pile and set another log on the holding plate.

Chop. Toss. Stack.

Chop.

Toss.

Stack.

Chop. Toss. Stack.

              Chop.

        Toss.

Stack.

For hours he'd been doing this and the time was lost to the cadence of the pounding maul. The dead man. The gunshot. The body falling. Coming upon his brother with a pistol to his head. Starting to control the situation—and then the shattering of it. Forever. He never should have left his brother there with the marijuana garden—he should have forced him to leave, taken the chainsaws, whatever it took—even if he needed to resort to violence, to whoop his brother, cave in his face, to beat him into coming down the mountain after they'd found that curse. Jake would've been pissed for a little while but he would've gotten over it. He would've seen how stupid he was. He never should have left his brother behind. You didn't do that. *He* didn't do that. He'd gone soft on the situation and now he hoped that they would not pay for it—that Lelah and his brother would be safe. He could take care of himself.

Damnit, why Lelah? Fuck! Fuck! Fuck! Fuck you Jake! You dumb motherfucker!

Chop. Toss. Stack.

Pull the bandana off your head and wring out the sweat. Wring it out. Pack a lipper. The nicotine does nothing today. It's only there. In the fleshy pouch of your chapped bottom lip.

Chop. Toss. Stack.

Chop.

Toss.

Stack.

The arch of his right foot had been bothering him all day, a phantom pain in the foot that he no longer had. The foot that had been blown off and never found, leaving behind a flapping curtain of mutilated flesh and the fractured splinters of a shinbone. There was only aluminum and carbon down there now. But the pain running up his right calf and shin and along his sciatic nerve was real, very real, and he had a high threshold for pain. His lower back was cramping. He bent over and stretched his hands to the ground. He glanced at his prosthetic leg and the pain shooting up it.

It ain't no phantom.

When he had first lost his leg his body thought that he still had it. The brain took a while to get used to the leg being gone. For weeks he woke up and had to look down to see that it was not there. One night he forgot to look. He swung out of the hospital bed to take a leak and when he tried to step forward with his right leg he crashed onto the linoleum floor and broke his nose and chipped his front tooth. He still dreamed at times that the leg was there and oftentimes he ran in his dreams through the mountain trails and conjectured that it was no different than dreaming of loved ones that he had lost. Loss was loss. The brain sometimes remembered and sometimes it didn't as though it jumped back and forth in time where it wanted and when it chose. Time travel was real in the mind.

Chop.

Toss.

Stack.

Spit the tobacco juice in the dirt.

He thought about his days and nights in the hospital and the grueling hours of recovery, the months spent strengthening his muscles and learning how to walk with the prosthetic. He remembered how painful the rehabilitation was and how he'd felt sorry for himself at times but then he thought about the others and he was just glad to be alive.

He was one of the lucky ones. There were those who had lost both legs. Men and women who'd lost both arms and legs. Faces and bodies burned and melted skin that looked like stretched plastic. Young men and women that would need constant custodial care for the rest of their lives. Men who had lost the unspeakable.

He was more than lucky. Below the knee and clean with a kickass prosthetic that was stronger than any bone or muscle tissue or ligament bound by the constraints of human evolution. Yeah, he was more than lucky. There wasn't even a word for what he was.

He remembered how Lelah cried into his chest when she first saw him in the hospital and how he had cried too even though he had tried to hold back. He held her in his arms and she said that she was sorry and he told her that there was no reason to be and that everything was going to be all right. She had brought him flowers and she put them in a glass vase beside his bed and they ate brownies that she had baked for him and carried on the flight all the way from home. She stayed for over a month and pushed him around the hospital grounds in a wheelchair. It was early summer back east and very beautiful. She took him out one night and they got drunk and had sex in the wheelchair in the shadows of the hospital courtyard as the sun was coming up. He wasn't supposed to drink on his meds but he did anyway. He had a terrible headache that morning and puked all over himself trying to get out of bed and the nurse stuck him with an IV and his headache was gone in less than an hour.

He remembered looking at Lelah sitting in a chair next to the window and thinking how blessed he was to have such a wonderful lady and he wondered how the other soldiers made it through without such support. There were a few that never even had a visitor.

He remembered when Jake came out to see him and how Jake had never been out of New Mexico before or on a plane and how he'd missed his first flight because his driver's license was expired. He remembered how uncomfortable Jake was at the hospital, how nervous and anxious he looked, pacing around the room in his work clothes with his greasy baseball cap scrunched in his hands and craning out the door and down the hallway as if expecting some enemy to show up, and how after a week Jake said "I love you brother but I gotta go home." And Caleb understood exactly. He was grateful that he had come at all.

The log splitter chopped a piece of dwarf oak in half and the violent sound brought him back to the wood yard under the heavy sun and windless sky.

He looked over at his brother. Jake's face was drawn and pale and he appeared nearly helpless stacking the wood as though he'd forgotten the most basic of tasks. They'd been stacking wood since before he could remember. Little kids earning fifty cents a day from their dad. Two quarters. Stacking wood all day for a Snickers bar. You had to do very little thinking and arranging. The firewood almost fell into place. And his brother was lost right now. He was holding two pieces of the same log and staring at an impossible jigsaw puzzle.

Then Jake's phone rang and life jumped back into him. Perhaps this was the call he'd been waiting for all morning and into the afternoon. He snatched his phone from the hood of the truck and checked the caller ID.

"It's him," Jake said. "Kill the switch."

Caleb flicked off the splitter and the hammering echo faded. A hush fell over the wood yard and the prairieland that surrounded it.

Jake answered.

"Hey, buddy." There was a pause. "Yeah, that's right. I wanna show you something that I think you'll like." Jake listened and his face flushed with blood, with energy, with hope. "How soon can you come up here?" He listened. "Two days? You can't come no sooner?" He faked a laugh. He was nervous and trying to mask it. "I just had some plans, is all. No, that won't work. I'll be gone all next week and the week after that. Vacation. Hawaii... So, I need to see you this week. Gotta be this week... Two days is fine. See you in two days. You know how to get here?" He listened. "I'll text you the address. It's way out in the boonies but easy to find. OK. Cool. See you then."

Jake ended the call. His eyes were animated with the prospect of redemption and he couldn't hold back a smile. Everything was going to work out just fine.

"Two days, bro," Jake said. "He'll be here in two days."

Caleb spit into the dirt and hit the switch on the log splitter and went back to work. Jake waited for a nod of confirmation, a gesture of approval, a look, anything from his brother that said he'd done good. But it did not come.

The splitter droned away and Caleb wandered into the pounding monotony.

Chop. Toss. Stack.

Chop.

Toss.

Stack.

　　　Chop.

　　Toss.

Stack.

　　　　Lelah.

19.

ATES AND SPARKS IDLED the cruiser beside the truck of Park Ranger Ortiz at the mouth of a recreational road leading into Carson National Forest.

Ortiz flipped through the sheets of a yellow notepad on his lap. It was scribbled with hieroglyphics that only he could decipher—and then only sometimes.

"We appreciate you meeting us out here," Gates said.

"Any excuse to break up my day, I'll take," Ortiz said. He licked his forefinger and leafed through the coffee-stained pages. "Did anything untoward occur in the area that I should know about?"

"Nothing yet," Gates said.

"Expecting something to?"

"We're just looking into some complaints from a few nosy types."

"Right. They got nothing going on in their own life and so they gotta make trouble in someone else's."

"You know the kind."

"My ex-wife was one of them—the team fucking leader," Ortiz said. "She'd stir up shit in an outhouse. She and her boyfriend have sued me three times now for alimony and to make bullshit repairs on the house I bought for us when we were married and that they live in now. You imagine that? My ex-wife lives with her boyfriend in the house that I bought. I bought. But somehow she owns it. I don't even know how that happened. But it did. I lived in a teepee for a while, no kidding—thank God it was the summer. The lowness of some people just to take what someone else got. No shame. Well, I hope that bitch chokes on his black cock one night and then bites it off in a thrashing fit and they both die." Ortiz paused. "She's an epileptic you know."

"I did not know that," Gates said.

"Oh yeah, buddy. She's had seizures ever since her second pregnancy. Big fits. Flaps around like a dog after it's been road hit by a truck. You ever seen a dog right after it's been hit?"

"Too many times."

"Well, she looks like that. Yapping and squealing and spinning around. Hell, I like being single. Freest I ever been in my adult life. And you know why? 'Cause I ain't the dumb son of a bitch I was when I was younger. I can see things coming now. I know that a hangover hurts and that it don't get no better after the third beer." He found the sheet he was looking for and scrolled down with his finger. "Let's see. I issued over a dozen camping permits for the fall season. A handful of hiking permits as well."

"What about logging permits?" Gates asked.

"Issued five of them. But most people don't even bother with permits. Only the commercial outfits bother. Most of the people up there are just firewood poachers, trying to heat their homes for the winter without paying for it. Hell, I'm sympathetic. We don't bother policing it much, at least I don't. And even if I wanted to—we don't have the manpower. There's hundreds of thousands of acres and hundreds of miles of road up there and only three of us. Hey, to be honest, I buy my firewood from guys I know never got any permits. Anyway—"

Gates cut him off. Ortiz could flap for days. It was the curse of solitary employment.

"Can you email me the names on those permits?" Gates asked.

"I don't do email. But I can read them to you right now if you like. You got a pen and paper handy?"

♟

THEY PULLED INTO EAGLE Feather Timber Company at half past four o'clock in the afternoon. A monsoon had gushed through the mesa land and a flash flood had washed across the interstate, making it impassable for nearly an hour until the road crew showed up with a grader and scraped the silt and muddy clay off the asphalt.

Gates and Sparks had to redirect traffic and haul a woman out of her car after the torrent had pushed her into a ditch. When they arrived the car was nearly submerged and her lapdog had managed to swim out the window and find dry ground for a moment before the embankment collapsed and it was swept away. The woman was much too large and traumatized to swim through the floodwaters. So Gates waded into the churning brown current and tied the winch cable from the cruiser around the woman and hauled them both out, the woman screaming hysterically that the Second Coming had arrived and that her dog was its first victim, and heaven willing, its first Saint. After wrapping the bereaved prophet woman in a towel, and agreeing with her that this in fact might be the Second Coming, the ambulance finally arrived and carried her off to Hell, Gates hoped.

Gates changed his uniform and they continued the seventy-mile drive into Santa Fe. The sky was blotched with cotton swab clouds and the rain was now a thing for tomorrow. The ground was already dry underneath their boots as they spoke with Arnold Weston beneath stacks of milled wood.

"You guys are permitted for Carson, isn't that right?" Gates asked.

"Yeah, but we ain't been up there for months," Arnold said. "We were up in the Santa Fe Forest a week back. Just a few of us."

"Any of your guys doing any side work up there, you know, weekend or after work stuff?"

"They'd better not be. This equipment ain't cheap and I ain't known for paying much. It would be a check none of their asses could cash."

"What about other companies?"

"Might be," Arnold said. "But there's nothing but old snags and fells up there. A company like ours can't survive on that. We need the big timber for the vigas and corbels that all the rich Texans and movie stars want in their second and third and tenth homes up in the hills around here. Those Texans right now got more goddamn money than the movie stars, especially those assholes from Fort Worth. It's gushing out of the hair in their ears. They're trying to outspend Hollywood. Of course they try and pretend that's the last thing they care about, you know, making a showy display of wealth, them being humble Christians and all, but in reality, it's all those Texans care about. That, and making sure their wives stay blonde." He smiled. "But it's good for business. Go Longhorns."

"I appreciate your time, Arnold."

"Yeah," Arnold said, "Carson was a big let down this year. It just wasn't worth the time and the cost of the machinery to get up there. But the roads were in pretty descent shape. I remember we could hump it pretty quick."

"Adios," Gates said.

He and Sparks climbed into the cruiser. Gates took the notepad from the dashboard and crossed off Eagle Feather Timber Company from the list Ortiz gave them.

It was getting dark.

They drove to Buffalo Thunder Casino and gambled and drank Jack and Cokes and snorted a bluff of Johnny Yayo in the parking lot before riding home north on the interstate after midnight with blown eyes of flame like cod brought up from the deep.

20.

THERE WAS A NEW violence to their sex. Her back arched and she bit hard into his neck, suppressing a scream but commanding him—*Fuck me. Fuck me harder. Drive your fucking cock into me.*

She had clawed and scratched into his back till the skin bled and he had enjoyed the pain and she had enjoyed inflicting it. He came inside her from behind and slapped her ass. *You liked that didn't you—you little fucking slut.* The words rose up in him from some unfamiliar place and she liked being called that right now. Afterward, they didn't talk about it. But they thrilled at the carnal discovery and wanted to revisit the act with the same violent pleasure.

They curled in each other's arms, mingling sweat with sweat. It was early in the evening and neither of them had slept the night before. They hadn't eaten dinner and were not in a rush to leave each other's embrace. Food could wait. There was no sense of time, no schedule, all was nothing until the grim matter was resolved.

"I'm sorry for the other day on the mountain," she said. "I wasn't siding with your brother. I just didn't know what to do and say. I was confused and I didn't want you two to argue or get into a fight."

"I know."

"You sure?"

"Yes."

There was a candor in his tone and she knew that he meant what he said. So far as she knew he'd never lied to her and she believed that he never would. He kissed her softly and she felt warm and she could not help but smile so close to him.

The room was dark and humid and their words seemed to float through a shapeless dreamscape. Fluorescent light shafted through a slit in the curtains from the naked bulb on the woodshed roof where the marijuana lay heaped under the tarpaulin.

Caleb caressed her back and she thought about the pregnancy scare they had in high school, how they had talked about what they would do and how he said that he would stand by her, whatever her decision. Two weeks later her period came, and that was that. But now she hoped that this time was not a scare, but a blessing, that they would be welcoming a child late in the spring. And the vanity of having a perfect figure in her wedding photos? Oh well. It was just that—vanity. She had a great man. She could get used to a larger dress size. Or maybe slim down after the birth and get married then. *Stop. Wait till you see the doctor.*

"Can you come with me on Friday?" she said.

"What day is it today?" he asked, nodding off.

"Monday."

"Of course. I just gotta tell my brother... Of course I'll come with you."

Then she thought of the killing in the forest and wanted to scream at the image and remove it forever from her mind. The young man. Where was he now? Was he still up there alone on the mountain, cold and rotting, torn apart by the vultures and coyotes and maggots? Were his eyes open? Did he have a family? Was there a mother somewhere crying over her dead son?

But the most disturbing aspect about the whole nightmarish incident was that she had been part of it. No matter what happened, no matter if it just went away because nobody cared about the dead man or whomever he was involved with covered it up or a court of law cleared them of any wrongdoing. No matter what happened, the raw and simple truth, the irrevocable fact remained: it had happened. The nightmare was real. The nightmare would forever change the course of her life. It was changing it now.

Why are the bad images so much more powerful than the good?

Her blood pressure increased. Her heart rate jumped. Her pupils dilated and she could make out forms in the room where minutes before she could not.

Then she said, "I just don't want you to think that I would choose anyone over you on anything. Ever."

"I don't."

"Are you sure?"

"Yes. Now put your head on my chest and close your eyes and let's try and sleep a bit."

♌

IN THE OTHER ROOM Jake heard the low rattling and stifled moans and started to become aroused. He bent his ear to the flimsy trailer wall, spit in his hand, and rubbed one out. The going was quick. He didn't last as long as his brother. He had no one to please but himself.

He felt guilty afterward, but not for very long. He rationalized that his brother, most men for that matter, would've done the same in his shoes. So what the heck? It was only his mind at work and he wasn't thinking about *really* having sex with Lelah. The real object of his pleasure was some trashy-looking blonde chick with floppy tits he'd seen on the back of some dude's Harley a few weeks ago. A real road hag. Perfect whack-off material. Lelah's suppressed moans and the headboard rattle merely served to stimulate the creative process. They were the erotic soundtrack. The mood lighting. The mode of imaginative transport.

He put on his earphones and blasted *Appetite for Destruction*. He made himself a peanut butter and grape jelly sandwich for dinner and sat down on the company computer, an ancient desktop that he barely knew how to operate. It took a minute to warm up. He was a two-finger hunt and peck typist who hunted for every keystroke. He never understood why the keyboard wasn't in alphabetical order beginning with A at the top left corner and ending with Z at the bottom right corner. That would make sense.

But smart people always did stupid shit.

His research began with one word: *mariwana*, which Google miraculously corrected for him. The word opened an infinite corridor of possibilities and an overwhelming wealth of information. He was not a fast reader. He started with the Wikipedia page and before long he was swimming through a constellation of hyperlinks on the subject. He soon realized that there wasn't just one type of marijuana—there were countless strains of the stuff, with exotic and sensational names like California Skunk, OG Kush, Bob Marley Sativa, Grand Daddy Purple, Sour Diesel, Girl Scout Cookies, Early Misty, White Widow, Blueberry Yum Yum, Hawaiian Gold, G-13, Cherry Pie, Green Crack, AK-47, Alien Blues, Jagoo.

I wonder what kind we have?

He studied photos of numerous strains but they all looked about the same to him. He lacked the practiced eye of a connoisseur, of someone who smoked bud and rolled fatties every day, one of the stoned masses that worshipped the green leaf and adhered to the cult of cannabis. He knew firewood, could distinguish between oak and walnut, pine and fur, redwood and cedar, maple and birch, eucalyptus and ash, hard wood and soft wood, dry wood you could light with a match and wet wood that would never burn, long-burning woods and those that burned faster, what made for good kindling and what made for bad. Sure, he and Caleb would smoke the occasional joint or bowl if it was around. They had even taken a few bong hits at a high school party in Española. But they had always been nicotine and alcohol guys. It was the high they liked most.

About an hour later Jake concluded that all he needed to know about marijuana was that there was a lot of money in that green herb—and he had a bunch of it. A motherfucking truckload. Literally.

He scrolled through his iPod and "One in a Million" started playing and it triggered a cascade of positive thoughts.

Before long he was spinning fantasies again, fantasies about the riches to be made, the riches sitting out there in the woodshed. Make the big deal and ditch this dump of a life. Even take a little less to get the cash quick. He'd ask his brother and Lelah to come with him. Wanted them to. Thought it would be best. He loved them. They were his best friends, the only family he had. What was done was done.

No. Grow the firewood business for a little while. A year or two. Then hire someone to take it over and manage once the money rolls in. Take out ads. Get new trucks and equipment. More efficiency. Generate more money. Feed the cash back into the business. Grow it. Become a better businessman. View this cash as the big loan they needed. Yes. That was the right thing to do. Supply every house from here to Albuquerque with firewood. Then up to Colorado. Take over Denver. The big city. Thousands and thousands of homes. Millions of dollars in revenue. Yes. That was the plan. Brother Firewood. Get some. You're damn right.

The new money would also give him time to pursue other things, leisurely activities, hobbies. Isn't that what rich people had—*hobbies*? He'd take up chainsaw sculpting again in earnest, really learn the craft this time, hone his skills and carve some amazing pieces, redeem that humiliating chapter of his life in his early twenties when he had hoped to transition out of the firewood business and into the art game.

In the peak of tourist season he had trundled one of his sculptures around the square in Santa Fe, but nobody ever stopped to admire his work, not even a friendly inquiry: What's that? How'd you do it? How much?

Nothing. Just the random glance and then the casual turn away.

He compared his sculptures to other sculptures in the galleries and discovered that he had a considerable ways to go before climbing the ranks into the professional realm. His sculptures lacked personality. The problem was he could visualize what he wanted to carve but he couldn't quite *execute* his vision. The wood never seemed to cooperate.

The final humiliation came when he attempted to carve a standing grizzly bear out of a slab of redwood. He'd saved six months for that magnificent cut of wood, shipped from a mill in Northern California. For weeks he worked tirelessly into the night with white-hot passion to carve something great, true art, an expression of the beauty trapped within his soul. He was talented, even if nobody ever told him he was. But try as he might he was never able to coax the bear from its hibernation inside the burgundy slab. The sculpture never resembled a bear any more than it did a pudgy human pawing at the wind.

Sure, he could carve chains out of wood. But any half-decent woodsman could do that. The old wooden chain was a cheap carnival trick.

Chainsaw sculptures were old news though. Their heyday was over. Sales had peaked in the mid-eighties. It had been downhill from there. But Jake remembered hearing somewhere that *markets could always be resurrected.* What's old becomes new again. He'd bring back the demand with his newfound leisure time bought with the green gold outside in the shed.

He might even try and track down their father. They hadn't heard from him in over fifteen years. They had received one letter from him, about a year after he left. It was written on a torn piece of brown paper bag and said: YOU WILL BE A STAR. It was addressed to both of them.

Last they knew he had disappeared somewhere out there in the great people-swallowing pit of Los Angeles. He was probably dead though, some homeless man scraped off the street one morning and never claimed by his family, chilled in some stainless steel drawer at the county morgue until the policy for the body storage of unclaimed indigents expired and he was incinerated to bone ash and laid to rest with the other anonymous dead. Yeah, he might try and track him down. But what was the point?

Back to the good thoughts, the positive things in his life, marijuana and money.

M&M, he laughed.

But he had killed someone—no he hadn't. It was self-defense. That guy had probably killed other people in his life and a lot more would've followed. He was a dirty drug dealer. Better him than me.

21.

DARIUS GATES HAD A cleaver wedged into his skull. It was buried deep into the heart of his dehydrated brain. He was pale and frosted with a sweat that reeked of whiskey and cocaine. His nose had bled during the night and left a flaky black crust on the side of his face and a ruddy brown stain on his pillow, a monstrous cloud of it. The scene looked as though he'd been bludgeoned to death while he slept. God he felt like it. And the stench curling up from under his sheets informed him that he had in fact shit himself again.

When he swung his feet out of bed and planted them on the carpet a sledgehammer pounded the cleaver and chopped his brain in half. He saw a white flash and there was a terrible shrieking in his ears. He went blind for a moment. Then flitting sparks of light danced around his vision for the next few minutes.

He ran a hot shower and then vomited all over the tub and mildewed curtain. A violent green bile of abuse. It reminded him of the *chile verde* sauce they drench over enchiladas and the thought made him vomit again. He swirled the chunks down the drain with his fingers and then stood under the flowing heat with his head bowed like the *End of the Trail*.

It had never been this bad. He stared at his .45 on the nightstand and thought about blowing out his brains. End this filthy charade once and for all.

I'm tired of hiding. Always hiding. You smear yourself in shit when you sleep. Your own shit. You're a fucking ape.

You can't start over. Not at your age.

You've got no money. Nothing.

You're back in overdraft.

He'd blown it all. Literally. Every penny he'd ever saved, up his nose and on the table, that green and red felt thief, that cardsharping bastard. The bottle played a role too, of course. But that was a cheap addiction. It was more of an enabler, the catalyst that triggered the reaction and caused the nose to start sucking and the bets to start humming. The curtain of inhibitions rolled up and bound tight, the naked man dancing his dick off, abandoned of all cares, the future be damned, *this is the moment, the only one I'm alive. The only one I know for sure. Pour me a shot, chalk one up, throw down the bet—this one's a winner. You lose. No worries. I'll win the next one. Honk goes the rail. I'm a winner.*

Because that's what addicts did. They did what they were supposed to do. They followed orders. As predictable as time.

He took the gun into his hand. It would only take a slight bending of his arm at the elbow to raise the barrel to his temple and then six pounds of pressure against the trigger. Just go away, float into nothingness, no more shame and infantile helplessness. No more lies. No more hate. No more murder. Just one more. The murder of myself.

But one name stopped him: Lelah.

I can't leave her alone in this fucked-up world. There's plenty of other horrible creatures out there like me. They're all over the place.

Still in his towel he stripped the bed down to the mattress and threw the soiled clump into the trunk of his cruiser and discarded it in a dried out gulch that the Pueblo Indians used as a dumping place, ensuring that Lelah would never find the filthy incriminating evidence.

He called Sparks and told him to pick up some brandy on his way to the office.

Hair of the dog, he said as he poured several seconds of the bottle into his coffee mug. Then with morbid amusement: *But does he bite this morning? Yes, he does. He's a pitbull from the E&J farm of pain. Always reliable. A sweet bite after a sour night.*

"Why didn't we stay in Santa Fe yesterday?" Sparks asked on the drive back down the interstate.

"Because I like sleeping in my own bed."

Well, he thought. *Some nights.*

They pulled into Bud Allen Lumber shortly after lunchtime and started talking to the owner. It was over quickly.

"Carson is only good for firewood harvesting right now," Bud said. "We're not in that business."

"Thanks for talking to us," Gates said.

"I can sell you some vigas though?"

"Maybe next time. So long."

Gates and Sparks climbed into the cruiser. Gates took the notepad from the dash and crossed Bud Allen Lumber off the list, the third name to be struck. They had started with the permit holders that were farthest away and were now working back toward home. That morning they had hit up a company in Pecos and came away with nothing other than the strong impression that nobody at the company had been involved in the heist either. It was quite possible that the list wouldn't reveal anything of value. The most likely scenario was that Ruben had confided in the wrong people about his agricultural endeavor and the indiscretion had cost him his life. Random crimes of this nature were rare. The victim almost always knew the perpetrator on some level. You knew who robbed you. And you knew who killed you. Those were the odds. And they were stacked heavily along these lines. Moreover, there was almost always some level of premeditation involved in the commission of a high crime. So who had planned it and who had done it?

He drifted to other thoughts and ideas and words people had said to him and he became enraged in the instant. Marlo had brought up his daughter in conversation. It was a veiled threat, to be sure. His daughter! No wickedness, no invention of evil was beyond that cocksucking faggot. Beyond his people, whoever the fuck they were. Who was the top? Who did Marlo answer to? Probably some homosexual in Quito taking cock right now.

But such personal ramblings were a distraction: find the perp or perps and recover what was stolen and bring swift violence upon them. He was out hundreds of thousands personally. Marlo was too. And whoever was above him. They would demand retribution. Recovery and retribution. Those were the rules of the trade. The violence was the glue. Money was the king like every other business. But violence held it all in place. Violence kept the machine oiled and running. Violence made the trade valuable. Violence made you rich.

You did not shy from it.

And Marlo had brought up his daughter...

"Where to?" Sparks asked.

Gates took in a long breath. He exhaled and stared across the lumberyard and the vast rolling scrubland where it met a horizon of pearlescent sky. Somewhere out there he could see a coyote loping through the mesquite and high above the dark shape of a hawk following him, embroidering the heavens with its calligraphy, some mysterious ritual of nature millions of years ancient. He envied the unthinking virtue of pure instincts. He had fucked his in so many ways, perverted and contaminated them with counterfeit pleasures and foul-hearted lies. He could no longer trust them. His conscience lied to him. That's what tormented the most. His conscience had become a liar, a cruel and ruthless deceiver.

"Let's head back up to the forest, Lester," he said. "I want to look around some more. See if we didn't miss anything."

"You want me to drive? You look tired."

"No."

There was one more name on the list of logging permits Ranger Ortiz had given them: JAKE BOYD.

The ring was closing. Perhaps around nothing.

Jake Boyd?

That fuckup was too stupid to plan a heist. He didn't have the sand either. And there's no way Caleb would be involved. He was too good for this shit. Too good. He was marrying an angel.

Gates threw the cruiser in gear and turned onto the interstate. Several hours later they drove back up the wilderness road to the top of the mountain.

22.

CALEB PULLED DOWN THE potholed driveway and passed a flatbed semi leaving their place. He gave a friendly wave to the driver and wondered who he was and what he was doing there. They weren't expecting any deliveries, so far as he was aware. Then he squinted against the harsh sunlight into the wood yard and thought he saw Jake sitting in the cab of a brand new John Deere backhoe loader.

He drove closer and it was indeed his brother. Jake jammed the horn and revved the diesel. The stack thundered and spewed throaty black exhaust.

"Isn't she sweet?" Jake shouted, hanging out the cab with one hand on the steering wheel and a boot heel on the ladder. "She's got both AC and a heater for year-round comfort. The 310SK, bro. Our dream machine!"

Caleb stepped out of the truck and stared up at his brother.

"What are you doing?"

"I got six months free financing from Equipment Depot. No money down—not a goddamn penny. I wanted to surprise you for all your hard work. You've been working so hard. It's a gift from me to both of us."

"A gift?" Caleb's face creased around his eyes and the skin on his forehead and brow folded in ridges of frustrated bewilderment. It was hard to react to such remarkable stupidity with anything other than pity. "A gift?" he repeated, still trying to make sense of the yellow machine that right now reminded him of a hideous monster with a scorpion's tail. "A fucking gift?"

"Relax. You're always stressing. Put a little of me in you."

Jake jumped down from the loader. He scanned the prairie and mesa for snooping eyes and ears and then threw his arm around his brother and leaned in as if to reveal a secret. He could see no sign of two-legged life. There was a sun glare kicking off an aluminum roof several miles to the east. That was all.

"I've been doing some research on the Internet," Jake said. "Long and hard. Lots of reading, brother. Lots of it. You see, we got over two hundred plants in the woodshed—ten-footers, some eleven, and a few twelve. I measured them last night. Now, according to my research, there should be about three pounds per plant. At two thousand a pound, that's like a million dollars. Tax free." He pumped his fist into the air. "Millionaires, brother. Millionaires. Can you fucking believe it—I never thought I'd be able to say that word about us."

"Are you fucking retarded? I swear to god you must've been dropped on your head as a child."

But Jake was too intoxicated with their gold-plated future to hear anything beyond his own opinion. His research had endowed him with the misleading genius of newly acquired knowledge. In one evening of study he had become an expert. He cradled Caleb's face with both hands and kissed him on the forehead.

"It's money in the bank, little brother. Money in the bank. We're rich. Goddamn fucking rich motherfuckers. I feel like I'm dreaming. But I'm not. We're not dreaming. This is real. Do you want a beer?"

Caleb grabbed Jake's wrists and shoved him away from his face. "This is your problem. You don't think."

"Been doing a lot of thinking, actually."

"You're so damn impulsive. You're taking the loader back now."

"I ain't."

"Yes you are."

"It's staying put," Jake said. "This is the first tool of our expansion. We're going to build this little business into a big business just like we always said we would. Build it into an empire." He paced and gestured with prophetic certainty. "I can see it so clearly now. Brother Firewood is going to dominate New Mexico and then we'll move on up into snowy motherfucking Colorado and take over Denver. Brother Firewood: We get your fire raging. Now that's a catchy slogan. We'll shoot some commercials—hell, buy our own camera. Make some YouTube promos. Viral-fucking-videos. You know what that means—they go fucking viral, which is great for us. It'll get our names and faces out there. Hey, let's be real. We're a couple of good-looking young guys. People want to buy from good-looking people. It's true. They've done studies on it."

He paused and turned to Caleb for affirmation. But all he got from his brother was that same look of continued bewilderment.

"Hey, bro. If you don't appreciate what I've done for our business today by purchasing this acquisition, then I'll pay for the whole thing out of my share. A hundred percent."

"What share? What the fuck are you saying?"

"He's coming tomorrow. You'll see. Edgar is coming tomorrow. How many times do I gotta fucking tell you? He's gonna buy everything."

"You don't know that."

"Yes I do," Jake said. "These hills grow some great weed. Top-dollar. You don't know because you haven't been doing the research like I have because you don't believe yet. I've been studying."

"We're supposed to be laying low. Not drawing attention to ourselves."

"It's only a backhoe. It's not like I bought a Ferrari or anything fancy."

"It's a fucking hundred thousand dollar piece of machinery—you might as well have bought a Ferrari. You don't get it, Jake. You're like a fucking child." He was so thoroughly mystified and frustrated that all he could mutter was—"Fuck."

Caleb kicked the dirt and then glanced over at the woodshed. The door was wide open, the padlock hanging from the metal staple.

"Why the fuck is the woodshed open? It's supposed to stay locked and shut at all times."

"I know, but I'm working."

"What about that delivery guy that was just here? He could've seen the marijuana. Or smelled it."

"You think I took him inside? You think I took him over there and said look at our shit? You think I'm that stupid?"

"The shed is supposed to stay locked and shut goddamnit."

"You know what, you're the one who's lost his mind," Jake said. "You need to relax, little brother. I think the war got to your head. Seriously."

"You just don't get it, Jake. You really don't."

"'First they ignore you, then they laugh at you, then they fight you, and then you win.'"

"What?"

"Mahatma Gandhi."

Jake climbed back up the ladder and swung into the cab. Before closing the glass door he said, "It's got AC."

He throttled the diesel and spun into the wood yard and scooped a heap of firewood into the loader and carried it over to the splitter and dropped the load with a dry tumbling clatter. He spun the wheel and drove back across the yard for another haul. He was all smiles and discovery.

Caleb could only shake his head. What could he do at this point? Take a ratchet to the side of his brother's skull? He would just have to wait until tomorrow and see how it played out.

He exhaled and looked skyward and then down at the ground. He pulled his can from his back pocket and took a pinch of tobacco and tucked it into his bottom lip. He flicked the moist shavings from his fingers and put away the can. He spit and shook his head again and took a few steps toward the woodshed when he felt a prickling of his senses and it wasn't from the nicotine rush. He turned and looked over his right shoulder and stopped.

Two men were sitting atop horses at the head of the driveway where the dirt met the blacktop. A dog stood below them. The sun was directly overhead and their faces had no shape or features from this distance and if they were staring at him or looking in another direction he could not tell.

He studied them for a long moment and they put their heels to their painted horses and moved at a walk down the driveway toward him. He watched them the entire time and did not take his eyes from them until they slowed and halted at the end of the driveway where it widened in front of the trailer. They were both shirtless and had on jeans and tattered hightop sneakers with raven hair down to the middle of their backs and they looked full-blooded Native American. They were barrel-chested with long arms and he figured they were at least six feet tall when standing on the ground. The man on the right had a hunting rifle slung across his back with a length of nylon rope. The other man wore a large caliber handgun from a tan leather holster on a black leather belt.

Caleb searched his memory and tried to put them somewhere in it but he could not. He had never seen either of them before.

"How you doing?" he said.

They did not answer at first and looked around the yard from atop their horses. Their dog caught a scent and darted into the piles of firewood and then leaped atop the seam of two cords and then dropped from sight back into the labyrinth.

"Can I help you?" Caleb asked.

The two horsemen said something to each other in Tewa. The one with the rifle nodded to the other and pointed toward the woodshed. The horses were wet up to their bellies and dust clung to the wetness and Caleb figured that they had just crossed the Chama. They were riding without saddles and sat on woolen blankets and held leather-braided hackamores in their right hands.

"You sell firewood?" asked the man with the handgun.

"Yes, sir." Caleb waved his hand across the yard. "As much as you want."

"How long you been down here?"

"All my life."

They nodded and looked around without emotion.

"Where you guys from?" Caleb asked.

"The Pueblo."

"Which one?"

They exchanged a few words again in their native tongue and nodded as if in agreement and continued to look about the place.

"Where are you riding from?" Caleb asked.

There was a long pause and he thought they might not answer him at all.

"The mountains," said the man with the rifle. He adjusted himself on the riding blanket and set his hand on the rifle rope and adjusted that as well.

"Camping?" Caleb asked.

"Just up there for a time," said the man with the handgun.

They did not have any bedrolls or canteens or any of the instruments of a long trail ride.

"That's quite a ways," Caleb said.

"We have good horses."

"Where you heading now?" Caleb asked.

"Nowheres," said the man with the handgun, shrugging.

Jake spun the loader around and saw the two men on horseback towering over his brother and he did not like the look of them. He saw the rifle slung across the man's back. He drove the loader across the yard and jumped down from the cabin and interrupted the conversation.

"How's it going?" he said. "This is private property."

"Most homes and businesses are these days," said the man with the handgun.

The horsemen did not make eye contact with him. They continued to look around the yard as though they were taking inventory or looking for something they had lost and suspected it to be here.

"Where you get your wood from?" asked the man with the handgun.

"Lots of places," Caleb said.

"Locally?"

"Yes."

"Carson?"

Caleb spit tobacco juice. "Sometimes."

"Lots of wood up in Carson," said the man with the handgun.

"Sure is," Caleb said.

"It's good this year, no?" asked the man with the rifle.

"Good as any other."

"How far up you go to get your wood?"

"As far up as we need to." Caleb spit again.

"That's where we came from," said the man with the rifle. "Carson."

There was a pause and the brothers were looking up at them on their horses at a sharp angle against the sun and they could not see the whites of their eyes or any color whatsoever in the dark pools that held them. The silence was cutting and the brothers wondered if it cut both ways.

"You got any smoke?" asked the man with the rifle.

Jake took his pack of cigarettes from his pocket and offered them up.

"Not that kind," said the man with the rifle. He pinched his thumb and index finger together and raised them toward his lips in the universal joint sign. "The other kind of smoke."

"No," Caleb said.

"We don't smoke that kind," said Jake.

"You should." The horsemen looked at each other and laughed.

Caleb studied them. He watched their hands and he watched their guns. He wondered if these men knew more than they were leading on. He wondered if they were connected to what was in the shed. If the marijuana was theirs and the dead boy was associated with them. He looked at his brother and figured he was thinking the same.

Jake tapped out a cigarette from the pack and lit it with his lighter.

"We got beer," he said.

"We don't drink," said the man with the rifle. "Our wives won't let us."

"We just smoke." They both smiled. Perfect white teeth glowing from behind brown skin. "The other kind of smoke."

They continued to look around the yard. Their horses stood still.

Several pieces of split oak tumbled from a loose stack of firewood and their dog bolted out and ran with his nose to the ground across the dirt and through the open woodshed door and disappeared inside.

"Gwambo smells something," said the man with the handgun.

"Can you call your dog please?" Caleb said.

"Do you got cats?" asked the man with the rifle.

"No, we ain't got no cats," Jake said. "Call your dog."

"Can you please call your dog?" Caleb repeated.

Jake's eyes darted from the two horsemen and across to the woodshed. Caleb's eyes darted as well.

"You don't have to worry about him," said the man with the handgun. "He's a good dog."

"Are you sure you don't got cats?" asked the other man.

Inside the woodshed they could hear the dog yapping and its paws running across the tarpaulin and then the clang of loose tools and the thump of the dog pounding against the wallboards and more barking and then pawing and scratching and a general disorder of things.

"Gwambo. Get over here," said the man with the rifle.

"Gwambo," called the other.

"I'll get him," Caleb said, trying to stay calm and not give the incident any undue importance.

"No, he might bite you," said the man with the rifle. "I got him."

But Caleb had already started limping for the woodshed when the man with the rifle turned his horse and loped past him.

"No," Caleb said. "I'll get him."

But it was too late. The man and the painted horse had split the distance to the woodshed in three strides.

Jake had started toward the woodshed as well. He wondered what he would say if the horseman saw the marijuana pile or got close enough to smell it. He wondered what he would have to do to him and the other fellow. They had guns.

The horseman loped to within a few feet of the shed and was about to dismount when the dog shot out of the doorway with something in its mouth, startling the horse. The horse rose up and its back legs kicked out and nearly threw the rider as the dog scampered around the spooked animal. The horse bucked and reared in a cloud of dust and the rifle barrel knocked the rider in the back of the head and he tugged on the hackamore and clenched his thighs and read the horse's movements before the horse had made them. He finally gained control and caressed the horse's neck with his hand and leaned and whispered calm sentiments into its ear. The horse snorted and whinnied and stamped the earth. The rider continued whispering and smoothing his hand along its neck.

He turned and rode back through the dust and over to where they had parleyed. He rubbed the back of his head where the rifle had struck him. He winced and smiled good-naturedly.

"Already got a bump."

"That's gonna hurt tomorrow," said the man with the handgun.

The dog finally stopped running in circles around the horses and dropped a huge rat onto the ground and barked up at his masters.

"See. He's a good dog," said the man with the rifle, squaring his horse back up for conversation. "He's a helper. Good boy."

"You two brothers?" asked the man with the handgun.

"Yeah," Caleb said.

"That's why it's called Brother Firewood," Jake said, pointing to the sign and then back and forth at himself and Caleb. "Because we're brothers."

"That's interesting," said the man with the handgun. "I like that."

The once taciturn horsemen now appeared to be enjoying themselves and showed every inclination of staying for a while and a desire to talk. Caleb and Jake just wanted them to leave. Now.

"What are your names?" asked the man with the rifle.

"I'm Caleb. He's Jake."

"Why do you limp?" asked the man with the handgun.

"Because he's a pimp," Jake said on an exhale of cigarette smoke. "He's a goddamn pimp."

"A pimp limp. Funny." The horsemen laughed and rocked atop their horses.

"We're brothers too," said the man with the rifle.

"Good for you," Jake said under his breath. Either the horsemen didn't perceive that he was being condescending or they didn't care.

"How much you want for a cord?" asked the man with the handgun. When the brothers were slow to respond he said, "It says on the sign you sell by the cord."

"We do," Caleb said.

"How much?"

"Two hundred and fifty."

"How much for two cords?"

"Five hundred."

"You make us a deal for three?"

"Sure."

"How much?"

"Seven hundred," Caleb said. "That's fifty dollars off."

"You deliver to the Pueblo?"

"Why not."

"Free of charge?"

"Sure."

"You stack it?"

"Yeah."

The horsemen nodded.

"Gonna be a cold winter," said the man with the rifle.

"What days are you open?" asked the man with the handgun.

"Seven days a week," Caleb said.

"You got a card?"

"Yeah," said Jake, "I got one." He pulled his wallet from his front pocket and handed the man a creased business card with rounded edges.

The man with the rifle removed a phone from his jeans and punched in the number and gave the card back to Jake.

"You can use it again. Recycle it." He smiled and leaned over. "Gwambo?"

The dog looked up at his master.

"Grab your rat. That's your lunch my four-legged friend."

Gwambo picked up the dead rat and wagged his tail, waiting for the next command.

"Have a good one," said the man with the rifle. "We'll call you soon, brothers."

They nudged their horses and moved at a walking pace across the wood yard and into the prairie and their dog followed behind with the rat in his mouth. Jake had smoked two cigarettes and Caleb had discarded and squeezed the nicotine high from another dip before the horsemen and dog vanished into the mesa land.

"What do you make of those two?" Caleb asked.

"Just a couple of Indians out for a little ride, I guess."

"You sure about that?"

"It was their land before it was ours."

"I know the history, fucker."

Jake ground his cigarette into the dirt with his boot and began laughing as if struck with some humorous revelation that made sense of it all.

"You know what this is like?" he said. "This is fucking amazing. It really is. You remember that time I sent away for the ant farm when we were kids? The ones they used to advertise in the back of comic books? Well, when the ant farm arrived, all the ants were dead. Every little fucking one of them. Remember that shit? They all must've suffocated or starved to death or killed one another on the trip out here from wherever the fuck it is that ant farms come from. But you know what I did? I didn't cry. Nope. I didn't blame the world for getting ripped off. I didn't even call the company to complain. Hell, I didn't even tell mom and dad about my tragedy. Nope. Nine-year-old Jake went out in the yard, dug a hole, and held a funeral for the little fuckers. And then nine-year-old Jake went and caught him some alive ones. And I had me a thriving ant farm for a couple months until Dad knocked it over and the glass broke and the ants ran away. But you know what it was? It was a valuable lesson I learned then. It was like making lemonade out of lemons, only with ants. And that's what we're doing now."

Jake waited for some sort of recognition. He had just made a profound correlation between the past and the present and expected his brother to say something about it. But he wasn't surprised when he didn't.

"Let's face it, Caleb. I've always had the business mind between us. And you've always been, well, you know, the younger brother.

It's not an easy role. And I've never blamed you for being jealous of me at times."

"You see things that nobody else sees, Jake, that's for sure."

"You're still sour about our new machine, aren't you?"

But Caleb had nothing more to say to his brother. He opened his can again and packed another chew and retied the sweaty red bandana around his head. The afternoon wind was rising up and kicking dust over the mesa. To the south violet clouds tumbled before dark thunderheads casting rain into the low country. He could smell the fragrant sagebrush and the approaching moisture on the air and he saw the thin stripes of a rainbow arching out of the darkness toward a sunbeam throwing light onto the sandstone hills below.

Jake shrugged and walked back over to the loader.

"You'll see," he said. "Edgar's coming tomorrow. It's all gonna work out. We're gonna be millionaires."

He climbed up the ladder and swung into the chair.

"You sure you don't want to take her for a spin?"

Caleb turned his back and limped over to the woodshed and padlocked the door.

23.

THEY STARTED WIDE AND circled back through the forest. They hiked through the pine needle carpet and up the ridgeline and along the outcropping for perspective and squatted on their heels and gazed into the scorched grassland, the interstate a noiseless filament running the divide.

"They could've come up from Los Alamos and across the Valles Caldera," Sparks said, pointing up and down the land. "And then exited by the same route. It's only about twenty miles on a fast dirt road. Or they could've come in from the west and the long route from 550. Or up the old road from Española. Or north from Abiquiú off of eighty-four or ninety-six."

"What does it matter where and how they came?" Gates said. He winced and closed his eyes and rubbed his temples with his right thumb and index finger. His head was pounding. "That's all a bunch of extraneous details that only sound like investigative work."

"I figured it might be important if we knew the provenance of the thieves."

"The provenance?"

"Yeah."

"Do me a favor, Lester."

"Sure."

"Shut the fuck up so I can think."

Gates stared over the land. To the north the pinyon tumbled down the folds of the canyons and bled green into the ashen plain that stretched to the volcanic steeple of Pedernal, standing as a black witness to all that had ever traveled up and down the broad valley.

He shook his head.

You can't start over. Not at your age.

The numbers he'd lost kept running around his mind and leaping into his thoughts in the form of a harlequin trickster fanning dollars stolen from his pocket and howling in his face with crimson fangs from some fisheyed carnival world. Half of the profits from the marijuana haul were going to be his. That was the deal he had worked out with Marlo. A fifty-fifty split. Marlo had lined up a buyer in Denver who owned several dispensaries and would pay $2,150 per pound. Delivery was in six weeks. He would be back on his feet with close to $650,000 in cash. And then these thieves showed up and took his money and his future.

He wanted to stand and scream into the canyon: "YOU MOTHERFUCKERS!!!"

He closed his eyes and rubbed his temples again and he could see in the darkness the seared vision of the land before him. He reassured himself that he would find the thieves soon enough. Find them and take back what was his. Take back his new beginning.

He walked down the outcropping and they scoured the steep arroyo for clues they might have missed. A rusted and faded Pepsi can was half-submerged in the silted bottom. Gates kicked it loose. The can tumbled and the pebbles inside rattled. He moved on and the arroyo curved and his boots crunched on the gravel bed and then became soft when he stepped onto a sandy deposit. He bent down and picked up a fractured piece of obsidian that he imagined might have broken off inside a deer centuries ago or perhaps it was just an errant shot. He set it in his pant pocket.

They rifled through Ruben's trash and concluded that he drank even more than they had thought. He must have been making secret runs down the mountain all the time and arousing suspicion from the locals.

No wonder he was dead.

They fanned out and inspected the undergrowth bordering the marijuana garden and tracked their way back to where they had found the deep rutted tire tracks, stirring the ground with their black boots, attempting to find a story in the earth.

To their favor the recent monsoons that had washed out roads and muddied rivers and torn across the mesas had forked around the higher elevations of the mountain and focused their deluge on the lands below. There had been a few drops up here and little wind, almost no disturbance.

"I think I found another set of footprints over here," Sparks said. "Much smaller than the others. Tennis shoes, not boots. Like a kid's size."

"Or a woman's," Gates said.

He moved up the rise and through the trees, searching the tinder for the slightest deviation, slow and deliberate, when a metallic glint caught his eye near the base of a pine. He bent down to the exposed roots and picked up a bottle cap. He turned it in the sunlight. It was new. No rust. It was not faded from time and smelled of fresh beer. He read the emblem, LAGUNITAS IPA, and then repeated the name phonetically just like he had at Bode's a few days earlier.

Lah-goo-KNEE-tuss.

He rolled the bottle cap between his fingers and looked up at the wind blowing through the tops of the pine trees. Far off he could see a thunderstorm sweeping through the eastern mesas, dropping its dark tentacles and drenching the badlands in watery shades of charcoal and flashing lightning like some malignant jellyfish stinging the world.

He pressed the bottle cap ridges into his palm. A white sun with serrated edges.

"You hungry?" he asked Sparks.

"I could eat."

He dropped the bottle cap into his breast pocket where it tinked softly against the bindle of cocaine.

"There's too much goddamn land out here," he said.

"There's certainly a lot of it."

"That's not what I meant."

24.

"MY BOSS SAID THAT he could go as high as eight-twenty-five an hour."

"Did you wear your push-up bra when you talked to him?" Caleb asked, trying to lighten the mood. He looked down and smoothed the gravel of the motel parking lot with his work boot. He pulled on the cigarette and blew a stream of smoke into the twilight and passed the cigarette to her.

"I couldn't find the bra," she said, taking a drag. But there was no smile to match his. "He said you can start as soon as you like."

She blew out the smoke and handed the cigarette back to him.

Thus far, they had managed to avoid talking about the only thing that was really on their minds. A hatch of moths swarmed around a light on a telephone pole that had winked on a moment ago not far from where they were standing. As if the moths kept time with the electric schedule and not the sun that was still hanging on in the western skyline.

"I'll speak with him in the next couple of days," he said. "I figure it ain't half bad that I'll be getting paid to see you." He took a drag and grinned when he exhaled. "Maybe we can even sneak off to room seventeen every now and then?"

"That would be nice." She lightened. A little. A glimmer of it on her face.

"There it is." He touched the dimple on her cheek and she almost giggled. "Can you hold that smile forever? Just for me, please?"

"I can try."

He took the cigarette from her.

"I forgot. You don't get anymore of this."

"I forgot too," she said. "Sorry."

"It's not your fault. I'm the bad influence."

He rarely bought cigarettes any more and she had nearly quit but he had been craving one and stopped at the gas station on the way to see her.

"This will be the last pack," he said.

Her opal green eyes had a play of silver in the lowering sunlight and her strawberry hair almost appeared to flame as if she were a maiden in a Celtic myth and not real to him. How did he have such a beautiful woman? If this wasn't luck, he thought, there was no such thing on earth. He ground the cigarette into the gravel with his heel and nuzzled into her neck.

"I still smell good?"

"Always," she said. And she was not lying.

The humming of tires on the cooling asphalt came closer and then ran away as the first vehicle in a good while passed north on the interstate and across the bridge over the Chama, pushing along a sage breeze that spoke of a change in the season and tasted of autumn. The first bite of cold in the sunset, a blue fire.

"I'm scared, Caleb."

"I'm not going to let anything happen to you."

"What are we gonna do?"

"Wait."

"For what? I'm not like you, Caleb." She showed him her hands. "They haven't stopped shaking. I have no appetite. I can't eat. I can't live like this. I don't even know how long it's been—how long has it been?"

"Three days."

He rubbed his hands down her shoulders and took her hands prayer-like into his and spoke softly to her.

"There hasn't been any mention in the paper or on the news of anyone finding that guy's body."

"It doesn't make him any less dead," she said.

"No, but it gives us time."

"To do what?"

"To think. To come up with a plan."

"A plan?"

"Yes. A plan."

"This isn't war, Caleb."

"It might be. And we need to know who the other side is."

Another vehicle approached on the two-lane highway. It slowed and its tires crunched into the gravel parking lot, a gray-blue silhouette with pinhole headlights in the dimming sky.

The patriotic cruiser wheeled over and pulled alongside them.

"Howdy, lovebirds," her father said.

"Hey, Mr. Gates," said Caleb. "Hey, Sparks. Good to see you."

"Likewise, Caleb," said Gates.

Sparks nodded from across the cab and waved. "Yo."

"How's it going?" Caleb said, nodding back.

There was a sudden lull and an unusual pause of speech between them after the exchange of pleasantries. The low idle of the cruiser and the engine heat blowing from under the hood gave volume and temperature to the silence.

Gates looked at his daughter and then at Caleb and then back at his daughter, examining them as though he were performing some rehearsed procedure. He gave an easy smile and nodded.

"How was the beer party the other day?" he asked.

The question caught them off-guard and for a moment they had no idea what he was talking about. They had pretty much forgotten about the beer on the mountain.

"The one I wasn't invited to?" Gates said, refreshing their memories.

"Nothing like an ice cold beer at the end of a long day," Caleb said.

"Especially when it's a Lagunitas," Gates added.

There was another long pause in the evening stillness and Gates held his smile and his eyes on them. "Isn't that the beer you like, Caleb?"

"One of them."

"It's hard to decide these days, isn't it? There's so damn many of them. I think I liked it better when it was just Coors and Bud. But I haven't had a drink for a long time." He locked eyes with Caleb and then turned to his daughter. "Babe, you doing alright?"

"Yeah," she said.

"You sure?"

"I'm fine dad."

"She telling me the truth, Caleb?"

Lelah interrupted before Caleb could reply. "Dad, I'm just tired. That's all. Just tired."

"Planning a wedding can be stressful," Gates said. "You gotta make a lot of decisions. Have you decided on a location?"

Caleb looked at Lelah and she looked back at him.

"We haven't really talked about it yet," she said.

"Right," said Gates. "Take your time. There's no rush."

Lelah wanted to run inside and sit at the front desk and pretend it was last week. Her heart jumped and then pounded against her ribs and her empty stomach turned over and she became nauseous. Her upper lip quivered involuntarily and the faint chill in the air wrapped around her and constricted her breathing. She set her trembling hands in her pockets. There was a disturbing edge to her father's behavior and her thoughts sped into areas she did not want to think about, specifically, two chief anxieties: was her father using again and did he know.

DID HE KNOW?

But her father provided a reprieve without further ordeal.

"Well, we'll let you two get back to whatever it was you were talking about before we interrupted." He threw the cruiser in drive and was about to pull away when he shifted back into park. "Lelah, come here."

Her heartbeat pounded even louder and her entire body seized up and she was momentarily frozen in place. She thought she was going to throw up.

Finally she stepped forward across the gravel and placed her right hand on the roof of the cruiser above her father's head.

Gates craned out the window as if to whisper a secret into his daughter's ear and instead placed a kiss on her cheek.

"Remember," he said, "it ain't that important." He paused, then, "You can tell me anything."

"I know."

"You sure?"

"Yes."

She felt as though her father was staring into her thoughts and she smiled in hopes of ending the inspection.

"Catch you later my little Lovebug," he said.

The tires crunched the gravel again and the cruiser drove across the parking lot and onto the empty highway toward the lonely mesa land that was now without shadow against the coming night.

"How does your dad know what kind of beer we were drinking?"

"He saw me at the store when I was buying it."

"Did you tell him where you were heading?"

"I said I was going to meet you. I didn't say where."

"So he doesn't know we were up in the forest?"

"No."

"Are you positive?"

"I think so," she said.

"Either you are or you aren't."

"I'm tired. I can't really remember, but I don't think I told him—why are you raising your voice?"

"I'm not raising my voice." He placed his hands softly on her shoulders and looked into her eyes. "I'm just asking, baby. I'm sorry if you thought I was raising my voice. I'm just trying to keep us safe. I'm just trying to protect us."

"I feel like I'm betraying my dad by not telling him what happened up there. I feel like I'm in my parent's divorce again and that I have to choose between two people I love. I feel so horrible each time I see my dad right now, I can't even look him in the eyes for two seconds."

He wrapped his arms around her and pulled her tight. He rubbed her back and warmed her against his body and he could feel her trembling against his chest. She looked up at him with tears coming down her face.

"I never told you this before, but my mother had an affair," she said. "That's why they got divorced, that's why the marriage ended. Because she was selfish. It was her selfish desires that broke up the marriage and she gave up on my dad. She's the one that was selfish. She gave up on us just as he was getting sober, when he needed help the most." She paused and he continued rubbing her back. "I don't want to be selfish, Caleb. I just want to be good to you. But I don't want to lie to my dad. I love you so much and I love my father too."

He wiped the tears from her cheeks and stared down into her sad eyes with a tenderness that she could feel within.

"I ain't asking you to choose between me or your father," he said. "I would never do that to you. You know that, right?"

She nodded into his chest.

"I just think that not telling him right now is better than telling him," he said. "I'm confused too. But sometimes you gotta ride out the confusion with patience."

He kissed her on the forehead and she lifted her chin and kissed him on the lips and tucked her head back into his chest and nestled there with her arms around him.

"I'm nervous about going to the doctor," she said. "I'm pretty sure I'm pregnant."

"How do you know?"

"I just know."

He kissed her again and told her that he would be there with her forever and that she wasn't alone and they would raise beautiful children together.

"I'm just so nervous," she said. "It's like my brain is just going and going and it won't stop. Do you think they would take our baby away if this thing went to trial or something?"

"Who?"

"Child Protective Services, or somebody like that?"

"I don't know, babe. I don't know how that stuff works."

"If you had to guess?" she asked.

"I don't think it's good to think about that right now."

"They took away Jenna's baby after she was arrested for fighting with her boyfriend, and she was just protecting herself. She swore to me that she was just protecting herself and they took away her baby anyway."

"No one is going to take our child. OK?"

But she didn't say anything. He tilted her chin back and looked into her wet eyes.

"Nobody is going to take our child," he said. "OK?"

"The guy up there had a gun to Jake's head, didn't he?" she asked.

"Yes he did."

"And he probably would've shot Jake if you hadn't come back?"

"Probably." He nodded. "It was certainly looking like that."

"And your brother would be dead," she said.

"I don't know how else it would've worked out."

"I'm glad that you went back."

"So am I."

He looked across the two-lane highway. A vague stillness owned the twilight as the land settled into the arrival of night and the cliffs rose up to meet the birthing stars. There was wood smoke in the air. At their backs the muddy Chama silted against the willow and aspen in the monsoon swell and brought water to the farming fields along a plexus of irrigation ditches carved four centuries ago by Spanish settlers.

He thought about her father and the unsettling questions he was asking. He wondered if they were only unsettling because of the narrow scope of his mental vision right now, his preoccupation, his clouded prism. He was confused and his thoughts were jumbled. But he couldn't show Lelah. He had to stay composed. He had to maintain a level head for her. He could see the pain inside her and it hurt him to see her this way.

Perhaps her father didn't know anything about the situation and him stopping by with Sparks was just a coincidence. Her father stopped by her work all the time to say hello and bring her lunch or dinner or just something to drink. Perhaps it was nothing. Perhaps it was only paranoia playing tricks on Caleb's mind. Sheriff Gates was the law. If he needed to speak with them about the matter, if he suspected them, he would come right out with it. He would ask, perhaps even arrest. But why would he suspect them? His daughter?

You're looking too deep into things. You're being paranoid right now. You need to relax. This is when you need to relax most of all, not only for yourself, but for Lelah. Most of all for her. You're forming those cognitive distortions like the psychiatrist at the hospital used to talk about in the discussion circles. Remember? You remember that. You're jumping to conclusions without sufficient evidence. You need to relax and measure the situation in the light of reason.

He told himself that the body of the young man was an MIA from another kind of war whose soldiers would conceal the kill from any law enforcement agency or formal authority. They did not erect monuments for their dead.

At the end of his internal ramblings and rationalizations he reckoned that Sheriff Gates was ignorant to the whole grim affair. At least for now.

"I don't know how much longer I can do this," she said. "I just want to go back to the way things were."

"Moving forward is all we got now. And I need you to stay strong for us. I know you can do that, Lelah."

"I can."

25.

THEY PARKED THE RED, white, and blue cruiser on the mesa a thousand yards distant and surveilled the wood yard through the night and into the next day. In the late afternoon a blue sedan entered the long dirt driveway and stopped in front of the brother's trailer. Gates read the license plate with his Leupold Mark 4 spotting scope and Sparks ran the vehicle on the laptop.

26.

Inside the woodshed the brothers pulled back the tarpaulin and revealed the heap of plundered marijuana. Sticky vapors of ripe bud pushed into their nostrils and they could taste the cannabis perfume on their tongues.

Edgar Rivera owned the blue sedan and stood with a bottle of IPA in his left hand, cold from the brothers' fridge. His ass ached from the long drive and his knees were stiff. He pulled on the bottle and the beer provided comfort to his injuries from the road.

"How many plants you got here?" Edgar asked.

"A few hundred," Jake said.

"Big fuckers."

"Yes they are," said Jake, playing expert. He had asked Caleb to allow him to run the deal, to captain any negotiation that might ensue. Caleb had agreed without protest. It was Jake's show.

"Ten-footers?" Edgar asked.

"Yessir."

Jake threw Caleb a look of growing confidence. It was all coming together, just like he said it would.

"How long have they been stored like this?" Edgar asked. His rounded features and sloping shoulders belied a shrewd and cunning intelligence.

"About four days." Jake said.

"Why'd you do that?"

"Do what?"

"Store them like this." Edgar stepped across the dirt floor and bent down to inspect the health of the plants. He plucked a handful of serrated leaves and rubbed them between his fingers and dropped them to the floor. He pushed aside several thick stalks and peered into the middle of the pile. A mild steam rose from the organic mass and he could feel the moisture upon his face as he inhaled deeply through his nose.

"How else were we supposed to store them?" Jake said.

"Properly. It's still fucking wet. You guys have never harvested before, have you?"

"This is our first time."

"It's a shame," Edgar said. "You guys definitely have a green thumb but you sure as hell don't know shit about getting it ready to smoke. Why the fuck didn't you ask somebody?"

Edgar glanced at Jake and received only a blank stare.

"You can't just chop it down and pile it all in one heap like this," Edgar said. "You need to dry out each plant separately. It's probably already got mold and maybe even worms by now."

Edgar snapped the crown bud from the top of a plant and stepped over to the open doorway. He studied the cannabis nugget in the sunlight, the purple resin crystals and the fine red hairs, the tiny involutions and the stickiness of the pungent herb. The smoky smoke.

"This bud is all fucked," he said. "Look at it."

"What does it matter how it looks?" Jake asked.

"All that matters right now is how it looks. You fucking serious? Do you care how your steak looks at a restaurant? Yes, you do. If you ordered a filet mignon and the waiter brought you a stuffed squirrel with its eyeballs sticking out its butthole, would that bother you? Yes, it would. You'd send the shit back. You wouldn't pay for it. This ain't fucking Chinatown we're smoking."

Edgar smelled the bud again and his nose wrinkled.

"It's already molding. Smell it." He brought the bud to Jake's nose. "I don't even want to see how fucked up the plants are at the bottom of the pile. It's probably like fucking seaweed. Just a bunch of soggy decomposing shit."

"Can't we just trim off the mold?" Jake asked.

Edgar chuckled. "What, like the crust of molding bread? You fucking kidding me?"

"Or spray it with some sort of pesticide?" Jake asked.

"Yeah, a death joint," Edgar said. "People love smoking those. Where can I buy one? I wanna get so high I die."

"We need to sell it," Jake said. "We'll take half price, whatever you can give us for it."

"Sorry guys. Chalk it up to a hard lesson learned. It's worthless. I can't do shit with this pile of bushes."

"It can't be worthless."

"Yes. It can." Edgar sipped his beer. "It is."

"Do you know anybody that will buy it?"

"Worthless means worthless, Jake. Call me earlier next year. I'll help you build a drying room. Set you up right. Make sure everything is in place. I'm disappointed too. It's a damn shame. You got some good, big, tight buds here. Great color and crystals. I reckon you just blew close to a million dollars."

"We gotta get rid of this, Edgar."

"You're right. Burn it. It's a liability sitting in here. A worthless, illegal substance. I don't know nothing good that can come from that."

"You don't understand, Edgar."

"No, you don't understand. I mean exactly what I'm telling you. It's worthless and I can't do shit with it and I don't know nobody that can. Why would I lie to you? I want to make money just like you do. I drove all the way up here for nothing and now I gotta drive my ass back. I just wasted a whole goddamn day."

The farcical episode had taken an unsettling turn. The bungling brothers no longer amused Edgar. There were darker implications working through the situation that were now troubling him. If you were intelligent enough to grow marijuana and see it safely through to harvest, overcoming blights, mites, diseases, mold, voracious insects, a host of horticultural afflictions, set up an efficient irrigation system and not kill the plants through overwatering, cull the first sign of a male plant and extirpate him before he turned the entire crop sterile, prune along the way for maximum growth and yield, enhance the soil with fertilizer and carefully administer nitrogen and other nutrients and numerous other considerations— if you had the knowledge to survive and prosper in the face of this terribly capricious agricultural odyssey, you damn well knew the basics about cutting it down and drying it. These were fundamental considerations of the grower's trade. You could always hire some ladies with nimble fingers to trim and manicure the buds.

Edgar took a swig of beer. He swallowed and then asked a question that he should've asked earlier.

"Just out of curiosity," he said, "what strain is this anyway?"

Jake fumbled for a response.

"It's uhm…"

"Indica, Sativa?"

"Yeah, Indica," Jake said. "It's Indica."

"Indica, what?"

"What do you mean?" Jake asked.

"You know, Green Crack, OG, Triple Diesel?"

"Yeah, that's it."

"What's it?"

"The last one you said."

"Triple Diesel?" Edgar said.

"Yeah. Triple Diesel. That's the one."

"But you said this was Indica."

"It is."

"Triple Diesel is a Sativa strain," Edgar said. A smile opened his lips. It was a smile of anger. "It's not Indica."

There was a hard silence and Edgar could see that the line of pointed questions had produced a baffling effect. Jake stood rigidly with his hands out from his sides and his mouth partially open. He had the telltale look of someone caught in a lie.

"This ain't yours," Edgar said.

"Of course it's ours," said Jake.

"No. That's not what I meant." His head was tilted back and his chest was puffed toward the brothers in an attitude of bold challenge. His warm and unassuming aspect had changed and he showed the commitment and courage of a hardened trader in a violent and ruthless business. "You didn't grow this shit."

There was another long silence and the undercurrent of tension closed the walls of the aluminum shed around them.

"You fucking stole this, didn't you?" Edgar said. "You ripped off a million dollars of weed and called me to take it off your hands? Fuck you. I'm not here. I never was here."

Edgar strutted toward the doorway and turned back around to face the brothers before he exited.

"When you steal this much from somebody in my business people turn up missing. They end up in holes in the desert around here. My advice to you is burn this shit. Immediately. Make it go away and pray that whoever you stole this from doesn't find out. And don't ever call me again. Or word might get out what I've seen. You motherfuckers. Fuck you, Jake."

Edgar cocked across the yard and hurled his beer bottle at a pile of wood where it shattered. He ripped open the door of his blue sedan and kicked up a tail of loose dirt and rocks as he sped down the driveway and onto the county road.

♌

FROM THE VANTAGE OF the mesa the cruiser watched through binoculars. Gates put the vehicle in gear and drove down the spine and turned onto the county road and they took their time until the land flattened out and the road was deserted in front and behind the blue sedan.

27.

JAKE STOOD IN THE doorway and watched the blue sedan recede down the long driveway in swirls of dust, shaking his head, refusing to believe the terminal diagnosis. He took the pack of cigarettes from his jeans and sparked one with his lighter. He inhaled and blew a thick jet of smoke into the chilling air that rolled under and around the bald sun low on the ridge.

"Well that sure was a waste of time," he said. "Edgar has always been full of shit. I knew he wouldn't come through. He's just a big fucking talker, is all. A big bragger. Fuck him. Pussy. He doesn't have vision. Pussy ass bitch. He's lucky I didn't swat him in the face getting all bold like that."

He inhaled and blew another jet of smoke up and around the falling sun.

"I got other leads," he said.

Still inside the woodshed, Caleb stared at the rotting heap of marijuana. The deadly circus had played long enough. It was time to close the show—run the fucker out of town.

Without a word Caleb brushed past his brother in the doorway and limped across the yard and up the ladder of the new backhoe. He climbed into the cab and gassed the engine over to the woodshed and kept the diesel running. He limped through the doorway and grabbed a bushel of plants and hauled them outside and threw them into the shovelhead. He returned to the pile and grabbed another bushel.

"What the hell are you doing?" Jake asked. But he knew.

"What we should've done in the first place."

"Let's get a second opinion."

"Don't need one."

Caleb did not slow and limped back through the dust that was now rising from the dirt floor and clouding the shed. "I'm burning this curse right now." He punched his hands into the pile and latched onto several hefty stalks.

"Edgar was probably just lying to us so he could get a lower price," Jake said, striding alongside his brother and trying to get his attention. "He's a drug dealer."

"And I'm not going to become one."

Caleb stuffed the armload of plants into the shovelhead and pressed them down with his palms and snapped branches to make more room.

"Take it easy, brother," Jake said. "Slow down and think about what you're doing. Don't go getting all huffy."

Caleb limped over to Jake and seized him by the shoulders.

"Listen to me," said Caleb. "We're going to burn this right now and you're going to help me. You got us into this fix and now you're going to help get us out of it."

"Burning it ain't gonna make it go away," Jake said in a defeated tone that was moving toward despair.

"No, but it will get us closer to where we should be."

Truth kicked Jake in the teeth again. He'd banished the reality for the last couple of days, since the incident in the forest, and now it had returned to crash the party of his delusions. His work-hardened muscles ran slack and empty as a punishing regret came over him—he could see the face of the man he killed. He wasn't even a man. He was a boy, maybe twenty, more like eighteen or nineteen, a teenager. A teenager. For what?

For what?!

The question shouted at him as he stared far beyond the painted distance, his cigarette passing between his lips and back to his side in unthinking draws, and there was nothing that he could find, no foothold which to grasp onto in the horizon of his thoughts or the horizon of the darkening land. He was out there searching and there was nothing that came back to him that would reconcile the future with the past.

He dropped his cigarette into the dirt and grabbed a bushel of plants and hauled them across the shed and packed them into the loader.

♊

THE MARIJUANA HAD BEEN piled in a large heap in the barren field beyond the wood yard. The brothers doused the heap with gasoline from rusted aluminum jerricans as the sun died in the western sky and brought light to another part of the world.

Caleb struck a wooden match and the pile went up in a whoosh. The brothers stood back and the hungry flames ate wildly across their faces and upon the watery surface of their eyes and licked the yellow moon already watching through the fast black smoke.

28.

THE ACHE IN EDGAR'S ass increased with the thought of his ˙colossal misadventure into the northern wastelands of the state where dumbfuck yokels stole marijuana crops and drunk-howling Indians shot and stabbed each other over casino sluts and two-dollar bets.

Albuquerque had never shined so holy and bright.

One road into this shitville county and one road out and he was cruising at the speed limit with a half-eaten bag of *chicharrones* between his legs when the unmistakable blue and red lights of authority flashed in his rearview.

"Fuckin' pigs," he said and pulled onto the shoulder. Black prairie encircled a tunnel of broken yellow lines vanishing into the asphalt strip. Not even a distant ranch light could be seen so remote was the stretch of road.

Sheriff Gates and Deputy Sparks stepped out of the cruiser and walked forward through the swirling red and blue. Gates approached on the driver side of the sedan and Sparks on the passenger.

"Howdy, Edgar," Gates began. He raised his flashlight and blinded Edgar with the beam.

"Howdy," Edgar said.

"Edgar the Bandito Burrito."

"Do I know you?"

"No, but our computer sure does," Gates said. "It knows all about you. You haven't exactly been a law-abiding citizen."

"Those days are behind me."

"I doubt it."

"If it's not absolutely necessary officer," Edgar said in a tone of mild respect. He was used to police harassment and the law always won. "Could you please take the light out of my eyes?"

"It's necessary." Gates wiggled the beam mockingly across Edgar's face like a strobe light at the club. "What are you doing up here?"

"Just going for a drive."

"A drive, huh?"

"Yep."

"Where to?" Gates asked.

"Up here."

"Where up here? It's a big county."

"This town."

"We're not in a town right now," Gates said. He grinned. "Edgar the Bandito Burrito."

"Did I break the law?"

"Don't know yet."

"This is harassment."

"Who you visiting?"

"Like I said, I was just going for a drive is all."

"Who?"

"Nobody."

"We're a long ways from Albuquerque," Gates said.

"I like to get away."

"You know what I hate, Edgar?"

"Hemorrhoids?"

"A cocky felon."

Sparks leaned in from the passenger side. "I smell alcohol."

"So do I," Gates said. "We're gonna need you to step out of your vehicle, Edgar, and take a look inside. Bandito Burrito Comosito."

"Fine by me. I ain't got shit. I'm clean."

Edgar stepped out and placed his hands behind his back in a compliant manner. Gates handcuffed him and sat him on the shoulder of the road.

Sparks began to search the vehicle. He looked under the seats and opened the center console. He rifled through the glove box and produced a handgun without surprise.

"What do you know, Sheriff." He displayed the 9mm. "Edgar's packing."

"That ain't mine," Edgar said. "You know that ain't mine. You just fucking planted that."

"A felon with a handgun," Gates said. "Bad, bad, news."

"Very bad news," Sparks added. "You got any kids, Edgar?"

"You crooked motherfuckers. Fuck you."

Sparks whirled and kicked Edgar in the kidney with his steel-toe boot. "Of course you got kids, Edgar. You're Mexican."

"He asked you a question, Edgar. Bandito Burrito."

"Two," Edgar said, gasping. He coughed several times. The intense pain keeled him onto his side and he felt as though he might pass out. "I got two kids."

"How old?"

"Three and six."

"So much for enjoying their childhood," Gates said. "By the time you get outta prison this time, they'll be your age, grandpa."

"You never know what you're liable to find on a gun until you run it," Sparks said.

"You're absolutely right, Deputy. That weapon could be tied to a murder or two. Or three."

"If that's the case he ain't never getting out, Boss."

"No he ain't. Just another dead beaner in a prison jumpsuit." Gates stepped around Edgar and squatted down until their eyes met in the flashing darkness. "Do you want to die in prison, Edgar? It's a lonely place to go. Some two-bit wannabe doctor-in-training guts you like a fish and pulls out all your insides, and then they set you out in a cardboard box for your family to pick up at the front gate."

"They do all kinds of nasty experiments to a prisoner's body once they're dead," said Sparks.

"That's right. 'Cause we own you."

The cruiser lights swirled red and blue all around as Edgar stared across the road and into the night prairie that was blurred by the liquid pooling in his eyes. He could only shake his head weakly. He thought about three year-old Lupe on the carpet with her coloring books and crayons and six year-old Rosa playing princess with her dolls and about his wife frying empanadas right now and his mother who spoke no English and his *abuela* who wasn't even a citizen. He thought about what would happen to them if something were to happen to him. He supported them financially and what would they do without his livelihood? What hardships would they endure? How would his children fare without their father? Who would raise them, another man? He grew angrier with each thought and all he wanted to do was get out of the handcuffs and back to his family. He thought about Jake, the very reason for coming up here, and he told himself that he should have trusted his instincts. He knew better. He had made a rookie mistake. He had no business being up here and now he was certain of it.

"So, once again, who were you visiting, and why?" Gates asked. He could see Edgar's resolve breaking down. He could see the mounting fear in the prisoner and that he was weighing everything with only self-interest and survival in mind. "We already know. We just need you to confirm a few things, is all."

"I'm not a snitch," said Edgar.

"Tonight you are."

29.

WHITE GLOVES FLARED AT Marlo's wrists and his back was turned in the silence of the studio. His hands rose up from his sides and he began snapping his fingers in that signature Fosse style of absolute precision and physical articulation, every movement meticulously choreographed with magisterial intention, nothing wasted, nothing arbitrary. He whistled along with the soundtrack and then doffed his pilot's cap to his dance partner. When she returned the gesture they began the performance.

He had flown his dance partner in from New York. Last year he'd seen her on Broadway in a Fosse revue and was impressed with her grace and lines and technical facility. He was paying her $15,000 for the day plus agent fee, first class flight, and two nights' hotel with an eighty minute deep stone massage at Ten Thousand Waves in Santa Fe. She was nearly six feet tall and mostly legs with perfectly round petite breasts and if he were sexually attracted to women he thought that he would most certainly be attracted to her. He had brokered similar deals with her agent for over a decade now and the agent was always happy to take the call from the retired dancer and art collector out west who always paid upfront and never haggled over price and amenities and who always had town cars waiting for his dancers to take them to and from the airport.

They had worked all day modifying the choreography of the ensemble piece without compromising the integrity of the original. The props were in place, the scaffolding had been assembled, and she was lying atop the varnished plywood on her side, playing the central role.

She rose up swanlike and fell into his arms.

He eased her onto the dance floor and laid her flat on her belly. Resting on her elbows she placed her white-gloved hands on her cheeks and continued the lyrics and then Marlo lowered his right hand down to her and helped her off the floor and they hip rolled in a diagonal line across the studio.

Marlo's movements were masculine and powerful in accordance with his physical composition and artistic sensibility. There was nothing effeminate about his style. In fact, there was a complete absence of it. He considered it a moral violation for some queen to corrupt the form with accentuated femininity. It was a gross stereotype and one that he loathed in many American dancers. The form should be pure and loyal to the discipline and betray nothing regarding one's sexual orientation. The very nature of dance itself was a force of sexual expression. It didn't require additional ornamentation, especially from those with poor taste.

The cymbals clanged and the piano dropped and Marlo lost himself in the performance and his mind reflected on his early days in the trade, the cowboy days, the screaming-disco-fuck-yeah and the glitter-rock-oh-yeah before all the telephony wizardry and the DEA super-jet task force and paramilitary outfits hunting drug runners. When the players were so far ahead of the authorities in trade and craft. When America was blown white from its first cocaine blizzard and wanted more-more-more at fifty-five grand a key. When you could flip bales of Thai Stick out the cargo bay of a Cessna in an Illinois farm field or stroll onto a TWA flight bound for JFK with

162 ~ LOGAN & NOAH MILLER

twenty chickens packed snug in a Samsonite suitcase without a single uptick in blood pressure. The analog freewheeling foot-chasing load up and roll in the night flight commercial or private and score a huge payday in old hundreds without the Big Brother watermark. When you could buy a ranch in NorCal after one score and grow organic produce for the rest of your days rolling joints of your own outdoor and nobody would ever know that you came and went in the exotic trade. When you could drive semis of brick-hard Columbian as seedy as a watermelon from Miami to Forest Knolls for $250 an elbow and flip them for $400. Thirty-five thousand pounds of it in one haul and celebrate the coup with bottles of Louis XIII, swilling the cognac directly into your mouth from the Baccarat crystal like upstart kings without pedigree. When you could redline your eighteen-wheeler across the Deep South past the redneck Mississippi and Louisiana and Texas troopers and not get pulled over so long as you had a Confederate flag draped across your grille—just another good ole boy—or a real shrewd hippie fucking those crackers in the ass all the way across I-10. When you could pilot a fishing vessel with a bellyful of tar straight across the Pacific and pull into Seattle or San Francisco or little Albion with counterfeit credentials that only had to deceive the scrutiny of imperfect or indifferent eyeballs.

From there the trade went this way and that way and he had begun back then. He had lived all over and been here for some time.

Because how did one get into the trade of mass murderers and money printing kings and the earthly princes of darkness?

He had started small while on tour with his dance company in Europe, a young smuggler with big balls and cutthroat acumen. He could buy a kilo of Moroccan hash in Paris and triple his profits on the other side of the water. And it wasn't long before he made new connections and met new people and he grew and they grew with him.

The music paused.

They concluded the first piece and during the interlude he turned off the lights save one strip overhead that cast the studio in dramatic shadows. He turned on the smoke machine and grabbed two vintage Sportsman chrome flashlights from atop the sound system and clicked on the beams. He held the flashlight with both hands just below his chin and shined the beam on his face and she did the same with hers.

They welcomed their imaginary passengers aboard Air-rotica and promised to fly them anywhere their fantasies wished to take them.

He pulled off his gloves and slid off his pants and unzipped his shirt and tossed the articles to the side so that only a dance belt girded his genitalia and he wore nothing else. His lithe musculature held a gleam of sweat.

When the music changed she climbed back atop the scaffolding and stripped down to a black crop top and black thong. She pulled off the crop top and unsnapped her lace bra and flung them with a dramatic wave of her arm and her breasts were naked in harmony with the original piece.

"My name is Zola," she said.

"My name is Marlo."

The piano played slowly and his movements reflected the cadence, elongated and graceful, the momentum building. The drums came in and the tempo grabbed hold and his mind was off again, speeding across oceans to images long ago, dirty, foul, misguided, loud and cacophonous, and he saw the ruffled plumage and the blood spray as roosters fluttered up and crashed together and sliced and stabbed one another with Philippine long knives. He could see the dusty smoke veiled arena and hear the yelling and the staccato Tagalog shouting of bets. He saw the nobility and the colorful plumage of the roosters and in their danse macabre he saw himself and the bloodletting and the raging vibrancy of the spectacle and the beauty and the courage in the roosters' heaving breasts. He saw the twitching of the vanquished lying in its shredded feathers on broken wings, its eyes trying to comprehend the gash ripped across its throat and the blood pooling in the dust. The avian victor held aloft and the crowd seething in the blood sport. His bird. His victory.

He fought roosters in the Philippines and in the states with the Oakies and then the sport took him to Mexico and opened up business for him on both sides of the border.

He was in a *palenque* now in the state of Guanajuato, the cerveza and tequila vapors hanging in the stagnant breath of the place, the cigarillo smoke, the peanut shell floor, the raucous crowd and the wailing music.

He saw the handlers bring the roosters together in the center of the pit and let them peck each other so that each may know his adversary. He saw the handlers draw the roosters behind the long score lines, and when the referee signaled, the handlers released the roosters and they scurried toward each other with inborn truculence and flew up and stabbed and slashed neck and breast in combat old as the species with weapons harnessed on them by a much younger species more savage than they.

And on those same travels he had swam in ocean waters that felt of liquid dreams against his skin, gliding along the emerald blue surf, the smooth waves and the gentle curl descending and rolling him under its caress that was warm and forgiving and carried him along with beatific grace. He could smell the tropical flowers along the shoreline and feel the white sand of the finest powder and there was perfume in the air that made him lightheaded from its beauty. He had met gorgeous brown-skinned boys and traveled on scooters around island roads with them holding him around the waist and the blooming current that ran its fingers through their hair and upon their faces, the universe wonderful and alive with rum-soaked epiphanies. He had seen the world as a young adult from a boyhood without privilege and a manhood that knew wealth and violence and understood that they were one and the same.

The drums, the piano, the keyboard, and the tambourine rallied into crescendo and then all went silent at once.

Marlo exhaled and stood erect. The droplets of sweat slithered down his graceful limbs and crested the blue and green ridges of his veins and blotted the wood along the circuitous path of saline coins that traced his movements across the studio. He exhaled again and stared at a thousand mirrored phantoms of himself alone in a thousand phantom worlds.

She was holding her final position atop the scaffolding with her back arched and breasts pointing heavenward, spread eagle to the opposing wall as if offering herself up to some primitive god of eroticism, her hands clenching each of the metal poles and waiting for the deity's phallic deliverance.

Marlo concluded Fosse's piece and spoke out loud the final lines of taking you everywhere and yet getting you nowhere. And he thought at that moment: *Yes. Yes, indeed.*

He helped her down from the scaffolding and kissed her on the cheek.

"You were magnificent."

"Thank you," she said. "I had a great time today. I really appreciate the work." She looked down his legs and said, "You have such beautiful feet. I wish I had your arches."

He flexed his calves and lifted his right foot and pointed the toes. "A blessing of my birth, I suppose."

"I'm so jealous. They're perfect."

He blushed and then motioned to the doorway across the studio. "There's a bathroom at the end of that hall with fresh towels if you want to shower before heading back to Santa Fe."

She said that she would like to rinse off and he told her that the driver would wait for her as long as she liked and that there was a bottle of champagne on ice for her in the car. He told her that he was stepping outside and that if she needed anything to press the intercom and he would be right there.

He opened the side door and walked into the night air with his body steaming. He caught his breath and stared into the wild darkness. The moon was rising behind the mesas and the slopes and caprocks were aglow with electric silver as though a vast city sprawled across the uninhabited plains beneath them. He thought about what he had and what was at stake in this hour of his life. He thought about those that had stuck with the business and died bloody, stuffed in the trunks of their cars, a head full of bullets. He thought about those languishing in prison cells on five continents. He thought about luck, fate, and chance. He thought about other things but mostly his mind turned from the past and into the current drifting now. Gates had become a disappointing name. A disappointing face. A disappointing idea. He had become a problem.

30.

THE NIGHT PASSED WITHOUT sleep for Jake and he found himself on the couch smoking a cigarette when the prairie sky flushed red against the dawn and the mesas rose out of the blackness and took form.

He had come out to the living room around midnight to see if the television would help carry his mind away so that he could rest. But the people and the shows seemed excruciatingly remote and only made him feel more depressed. They were so far away, on a planet and life he would never touch—the successful, the rich, the famous, the people who had made the right decisions in their lives and the world envied them. He turned off the television and sat against the tattered cushions and muffled his crying with a pillow so that no one would hear. But there was only his brother sleeping in the back of the trailer with Lelah in his arms.

It was 7:00 a.m. when they stepped into the living room freshly showered.

"I won't be back until this evening," Caleb said.

Lelah could see Jake's bloodshot eyes and disheveled appearance and so she said goodbye to him and walked outside to the truck and waited. She could tell that the brothers needed to talk and besides she hoped that the morning air would lessen her anxiety.

"I'll just be working around the yard today," Jake said. "Cutting up some wood and old timber. It should be nice and dry by now."

"What about the backhoe?"

"I'm gonna call Equipment Depot when they open and see if they have a return policy. I'm pretty sure they do. I hope." Jake took a drag on the cigarette and blew the smoke out the window notched open above his head. "I'll get rid of that guy's gun as well."

"The gun?" Caleb winced. "You're kidding right? Please tell me you're kidding. You were supposed to get rid of it that night."

Jake looked down at the carpet and shook his head.

"I know," he said.

"Where is it?"

"I hid it."

"Where?"

"In the woodshed. In the bottom drawer of the tool chest. I didn't know what else to do with it."

"In the bottom drawer of the tool chest?"

"I didn't know what to do."

The impulse to lash into his brother had never been stronger but Caleb hesitated and then halted entirely. Sitting on the tattered couch in day-old underwear and grimed with yellow-brown sweat he saw a broken child. A broken down child of a man with a cigarette. He saw their father. His brother had become that withered man and he pitied him. He pitied both men. He had lost the anger toward their father when he was overseas staring into the blue desert twilights of a foreign land and he now lost the anger that moments ago had raged toward his brother. Speaking his mind would only wound his brother further. And what good would that do right now?

"Smash the gun apart with the log splitter and then scatter the pieces in the Chama far away from each other." Caleb spoke firmly and without reproach. "Far away and in the deep pools, not the shallow parts that dry up in the summer. One piece here. Drive several miles and drop another piece there. And so on. Can you do that? I don't have time right now."

"Yeah... I can do that." Jake took another drag and he could not raise his head to look at his brother. "I've never been good at the little things. I've always had big ideas. Always had things that I thought that I could do and now I know for sure that I can't. I won't ever."

Caleb stepped over to his brother and set his hand on his shoulder. His brother looked up with a penitent frown and eyes veined red and graceless with fatigue.

"I'm sorry, Caleb."

"I know...I know you are."

"Drive safe."

"See you this evening."

"Love you."

"I love you too, Jake."

31.

THREE HOURS LATER CALEB and Lelah sat in the adobe décor waiting room when a nurse opened a door from behind them.

"Miss Gates?" the nurse asked.

Caleb and Lelah stood from their chairs and held hands.

"Right this way," the nurse said, holding open the door for them. She escorted them down a beige linoleum hallway and into a room with a blue medical gown sitting on the examination table.

"Please disrobe from the waist down and Doctor Sherry will be with you shortly."

&

BACK AT THE WOOD yard Jake had finally talked himself into feeling better. He ate two pieces of white toast with grape jelly and washed it down with a glass of milk. He brewed a pot of coffee and drank a cup on the front steps with two cigarettes before retiring again to the couch where he napped until ten.

Finally some sleep.

The sleep was heavy and without dreams and there was an oppressive energy about it as though he hadn't slept at all and only silenced his mind against the onrushing world. When he awakened he turned on the television and surfed the channels and decided that there was nothing worth watching but he kept the television on anyway and fell asleep again. By noon he picked himself off the cushions and headed outside to get some work done.

Shit.

He needed to get rid of the gun. He'd nearly forgotten. Again. He'd call about returning the backhoe afterward. Equipment Depot was open late.

He packed a lipper of Skoal and walked across the yard and turned on the log splitter and then walked to the other end of the yard through the corridors of stacked firewood and into the shed. The scent of marijuana still clung to the place. He pulled on the string hanging from the ceiling and the bulb flickered and then cast light onto the standing Craftsman tool chest against the wall. He spit tobacco juice onto the dirt floor and then opened the bottom drawer.

He pushed aside a greasy collection of second- and third-generation screwdrivers and ratchets and vice grips and wriggled his hand to the back of the drawer. He felt the rag and the hard object wrapped inside.

He pulled the rag from the drawer and unfolded it and stared down at the .40 caliber Beretta. His stomach wrenched with a flash of heat and he slouched under the weight of sorrow and regret. He felt terrible about himself again. His eyes became bleary and his lower jaw began to quiver as the inescapable reality thrust itself back to the forefront. He had killed a man. A boy, really. But then he reminded himself, as he had countless times already, that the boy had pressed this very gun into the back of his head with the intention of blowing out his brains. The boy was no angel. He would have grown into a very bad man.

He told himself that he would eventually come to terms with this crazy episode in his life. Time heals. He was on a new path now, a path of redemption. But first he needed to get rid of the evidence. That was the first step. His brother was counting on him.

He turned and was about to step into the sunlight with the .40 cal and shatter it to pieces in the log splitter when the sheriff's cruiser nosed down the driveway.

He froze. His stomach turned again, sharper and more intense. His entire body flushed with adrenaline and another wave of heat and it was hard to collect his thoughts.

Be cool. You haven't done anything wrong.

He rewrapped the gun in the rag and stuffed it back in the bottom drawer and closed the tool chest. He took several deep breaths and then walked out of the shed and over to the log splitter and turned off the noisy machine.

He removed his gloves and set them on a stump.

"How's the firewood business going?" Gates said, walking over.

"Burning along," Jake said, taking a stab at humor.

"Must be," Gates said. "I see you got yourself a new backhoe. She's a beauty."

"I got a really good deal on it."

"I bet."

Jake shook hands with Gates and Sparks.

"Is it gonna be a cold winter?" Gates asked.

"That's what they're saying."

Sparks stepped over to the log splitter and admired it. "How does this thing work? Can I try it?"

But Sparks did not wait for permission. He hit the power switch and the log splitter roared back to life. The industrial machine reminded him of a medieval interrogation device. He set a pine log on the holding plate.

"You put the wood here?" Sparks asked. "Is that right?"

Jake nodded slowly.

The maul drove down and halved the log with a thundering whack of machine-powered steel.

"Efficient," Sparks said. He took another log from the pile and repeated the process, amusing himself with his new violent toy.

The prelude had produced the desired effect: Jake was becoming visibly nervous. His eyes were darting from Gates to Sparks and his hands were clasped at belt level and his fingers were fidgeting with each other. He shifted his weight from one leg to the other and swallowed with noticeable discomfort. He reached for his cigarettes and shakily removed one from the pack and realized that he still had the dip in his mouth. He tried to press the cigarette back inside the pack and the cigarette buckled and the rolling paper tore and tobacco shavings curled out.

"Caleb and Lelah ain't here," he said, tossing aside the broken cigarette.

"We didn't come here for them," Gates said. "We came here for you."

The maul drove down and halved another piece of wood. Sparks chuckled at the destructive power. What a clever tool.

Gates smiled. But the smile was cold and it frightened Jake. He wondered what they knew.

"Our system is so fucked up, Jake," Gates said, speaking loudly over the clamoring log splitter. "I'm not sure how well-read you are—you don't strike me as someone with a library card. Frankly, I've never met a lumberjack who liked reading more than he liked drinking beer and scratching his ass watching *Duck Dynasty*. But in Saudi Arabia, that backwater of fundamentalist shit, those sand gorillas got thieves figured out."

The log splitter fell like a guillotine and whacked a log in two.

"And in America, well, we've gotten soft on criminals. We might put a first-time thief on probation. A habitual fuckup might serve a few years in the joint. But only the most notorious face long-term imprisonment. Hence the reason why this country has so many fucking thieves. And don't get me started on Wall Street. Those white collar faggots steal billions everyday without ever being core-bored in prison by some Cho-mo serving consecutive life sentences for sodomizing an orphanage. So you know what I say? The fucking sand gorillas got it right. I mean, when you have to pause every time before you take a shit to ponder the fact that the hand you used to wipe your ass with is gone—well, that's a powerful deterrent."

"I'm not a thief," Jake said.

"Sure you are. But a murderer to boot? I never would've suspected that. I always knew you were a first-rate fuckup. But the commission of a crime is a peculiar thing, Jacob. It has a way of creating its own weather system. Things tend to escalate and evolve into something way beyond one's control and initial intention."

"I want a lawyer."

"A lawyer? What the fuck for?"

"Are you going to arrest me?"

"I'm confused, Jake."

"So am I."

The maul drove down and shattered another log.

♆

DOCTOR SHERRY LUBRICATED THE ultrasound wand. Caleb held Lelah's hand, her back on the examination table, knees bent.

"When was your last period?" Doctor Sherry asked.

"About six weeks ago."

Doctor Sherry nodded and then sat down on a stool. She wheeled over to the examination table. "This will feel a little cold at first," she said. Doctor Sherry moved between Lelah's open legs and inserted the wand. "The image will come up in just a moment. How are you feeling today, Lelah?"

"Fine."

"I remember delivering you. Time flies. Boy does it. How's your mom like Lubbock?"

"She says it's flat."

"I need to give her a call."

"I'm sure she'd love to hear from you."

"How's your father doing?"

"He's doing really good."

❧

THE MAUL HAMMERED THROUGH another log. Splinters exploded from its dry core.

"Did you know a turd named Edgar Rivera?" Gates asked.

Jake stood several feet away from them. He wanted to run. But where would he go? He had a strong urge to piss.

"I'm not talking," Jake said. "I want a lawyer."

"Goddamnit, Jake. Stop saying that. You're not under arrest. No fucking lawyers. Only the truth. Lawyers get involved and the train of lies starts rolling on down the track. And before you know it the train has derailed and everything is spilled all over the place and pell-mell. I only want the truth right now. We only want the truth right now, you and me. We're cowboys in the same rodeo. Can you nod in agreement to that?"

But Jake made no response, not even a slight nod.

Gates sighed. He bent down and picked up a piece of split wood and flicked off a scab of bark with his thumb. There was a worm trail on the flesh of the wood that ran like a white river on a map. He tossed the piece onto the pile beside the log splitter and continued.

"You see, last night Edgar caught himself on fire. Yep. Burned himself to chorizo grease in the front seat of his lowrider just off Interstate 84. A freak accident. Some sort of electrical malfunction in the fuel line. Wasn't that what it was, Lester?"

"Sure was," Sparks replied. "Yes indeed. That's what the firemen said this morning."

"Well, shortly before Edgar became a Mexican marshmallow, we had a very interesting conversation with him, one in which he informed us that he was up here looking at what he figured to be several hundred pounds of marijuana in your woodshed."

"He was lying."

"Do you want to take us over there and show us? Or are we going to have to kick down the door."

"I don't know what you're talking about."

"I believe you do."

♊

THE TELEVISION MONITOR DISPLAYED Lelah's uterus as the transducer bounced sound waves through her and read the echoes.

"You see the egg and the sperm there?" Doctor Sherry said, pointing to the tiny spheroid sack on the monitor. "The beginning of life. You're pregnant. Congratulations."

Lelah squeezed Caleb's hand and they smiled at one another.

It was their first real smile in days. Tentative, but a smile nonetheless.

♊

ACROSS THE YARD SPARKS walked out of the woodshed and shook his head at Gates, who had sent him over there to have a look.

"It's empty," Sparks yelled.

"Told you," Jake said to Gates. They were still standing beside the log splitter.

"But it sure does smell like something was in there," Sparks said, making his way back over to them. "A lot of something."

"Where is it, Jake?" Gates asked.

"I don't know what the hell you're talking about."

"We could be friends, Jake. All you have to do is try."

"I am your friend."

"You're not acting like one."

Gates strolled over to the cruiser and removed his bindle of cocaine from the shirt pocket behind his badge. He dabbed a hit onto the star-spangled hood and chalked the line with his business card.

"You like cocaine, Jake?" he said.

"What do you mean?"

"You know. A fat rail every now and then. To improve things. To get you out of a funk. To pick you up. To make you macho."

Jake did not answer.

"C'mon, Jake. I can't arrest you for your thoughts—I ain't Jesus." Gates ran the edge of his business card up and down the line several more times and made sure it was orderly. "You mean to tell me you've never partied with Johnny Yayo? Snorted a little snowball off a girl's nipple out at a mesa party? C'mon, just a little snowball atop a brown señorita nipple?"

"No harm in that," Sparks added. "No harm at all."

"Along with some Viagra—you can fuck all night, party boy. Party Boy Jake."

Gates bent to the hood and snorted the rail off the flag. He stood and gathered himself in the burning light and exhaled with brilliant satisfaction.

"I mean, c'mon, Jake, just a little?" Gates made a small measurement with his thumb and index finger. "You don't like cocaine just a little? A little bit of coke?"

"What, you don't think cops do drugs?" Sparks said. "You don't think we like to party—Party Boy Jake?"

"You never answered my question, Jake," Gates said. "Do you like cocaine?"

Jake could only mutter a frightened and timid, "I guess... Well, sometimes."

"How about now-time?" Gates said.

"It's go-time," said Sparks. "Now-time. A little boom-boom time."

"Step on up, Jake. You'll feel better. I promise."

"Go time. Now-time. Party Boy Jake."

"Party Boy Jake. Go-time. Now-time. Yeah!"

Gates knocked a line on the hood and beckoned Jake to come over.

Jake took a step toward the cruiser and halted.

Gates slapped the hood and the force of his hand against the hollow metal scared Jake even more. The line of cocaine bounced up and lost its shape and scattered flat across the hood. There was a fierce intention behind the slap. An implication of violence.

"C'mon, Jake," Gates said, straightening the scattered coke with his business card. "C'mon now."

"It's boom-time," said Sparks.

"Now-time. Go-time."

"Boom-time."

"Now-time."

Boom-time. Now-time. Go-time. Yeah!

Jake glanced at Gates for approval. Gates nodded with flaming hunger and a smile all teeth and wide-eyed and coke-charged.

Jake hesitated once more.

"C'mon, Jakey Snakey. Take a little boom-time honker. It won't kill yah. It'll just make you better."

Jake took a deep breath and then leaned over and snorted the rail off the hood. He staggered backward, his nose stinging, eyes watering. It was a sloppy hit. His upper lip and nostrils were dusted with white powder as if he'd been pounded in the mouth with a dry snowball.

"You're a monster," Jake said.

"I suppose I am."

Gates pulled his baton and clubbed Jake in the knee with a hideous crunch of cartilage and bone. Jake screamed and dropped in the same moment.

"Where is it, Jake?"

"I don't know what the hell you're talking about," he said, writhing in the dirt and clutching his kneecap. "Why do you want the marijuana anyway? You're a fucking cop. I'm gonna report you."

"To who? The other cops? That's probably not in the cards today. Hey Lester, what are the odds of that?"

"About a million to one."

"I'd say you're correct deputy. A million to one. We're the only law for a hundred miles." He thumped his baton against his palm and his eyes glanced over the wood yard and up to the sky and back down. "Goddamnit, Jake. God-fucking-damnit. All you need to do is turn over what you stole. Either that or the money you've made from it."

"I told you," Jake said. "I don't know what you're talking about. I swear."

Gates and Sparks hooked Jake under his armpits and dragged him over to the log splitter.

"I'm gonna ask you one more time," Gates said, "and if you don't tell me the truth, you're gonna be in a whole lot more pain. Now, where is it?"

"I burned it. I burned the fucking weed. It went bad. It was molding. So I burned it. I swear to God."

"I guess you're gonna have to learn to wipe your ass with your left hand."

Gates and Sparks stretched Jake's hand across the holding plate. But Jake struggled and wrestled his hand away from them. So Gates cudgeled him with furious swings that shattered forearms and shins and ribs until Jake crumpled to the earth in a broken heap.

Again they lifted Jake and set his dangling right hand on the holding plate. All Jake had left in him was a pleading scream.

"Please God—NO!"

The maul drove down and Jake's bloody hand tumbled onto a pine log and then came to rest on the splintered ground with a shallow thud.

♣

DOCTOR SHERRY SET THE ultrasound wand on a blue medical towel atop the counter and removed her latex gloves and threw them in the trash. She washed her hands in the sink and soaped up to her elbows.

Lelah sat up on the examination table and wiped herself off with a sterile towel the doctor had given her. She pulled on her underwear and Caleb handed her jeans to her and she slid into them.

"You're bringing a new life into the world," Doctor Sherry said, drying off her hands. "Congratulations."

Lelah forced a smile and then said, "Thank you, Doctor."

Doctor Sherry looked at Caleb.

"Are you nervous?" she asked.

"I think I'm ready." He paused and then nodded. "Yeah, I'm ready."

"Just remember," Doctor Sherry said, "and I tell all my young and older couples this, there's never a perfect time to have a baby. As long as you two love each other and the child, you'll do fine." She smirked. "Reverse the order. Love the child first. Then yourselves." She glanced absentmindedly in the mirror above the sink and brushed her bangs off her forehead and then returned to them. "Wow. Two generations. Does that make me old, Lelah?"

"Lucky, I guess."

"Yes it does. Very lucky. I'll see you back here in a month."

She hugged Lelah and was about to shake Caleb's hand when he moved in for a hug instead.

32.

THEY HAD LUNCH AT Tomasita's and picked up toothpaste and a few other things at Target before heading north into the wilder lands where the afternoon gusts yawed the backend of the truck across the lane as if they were traveling in a small boat on a whipped up lake. They climbed over the plateau and the flesh-colored badlands ran along the east and west of them beautiful in their bleakness that held its own tragic romance of barren cascades where rains once fell.

"I'd like to get married before we have the baby," Lelah said.

"That's probably best."

Her head was resting in his lap.

"Once the baby comes," she said, "I got a feeling that we're not going to have time to plan a wedding. There's a little adobe church up in Chama that I always had thoughts about getting married in. The scenic railroad train goes right past it, you know, the tourist one with the old smokestack."

"The steam engine."

"Yeah, the steam engine. Anyway, we could rent out the train so that people can drink and not have to think about driving."

"Sounds good to me."

He smiled down at her and she smiled up at him. He blew her a kiss and she blew one back.

"I'd ask my dad to help us out with the costs but he's broke, I think. He'd never tell me he was broke but I opened a letter on accident a few months back from a mortgage company in Phoenix saying they were foreclosing on some houses he'd bought."

"I got a few dollars saved. We'll make it work."

The truck tires thrummed against the asphalt and the wind hissed through the narrow gap in the driver's side window.

"Did Jake sell the stuff?" she asked.

"We burned it."

She sat up from his lap and faced him. "What?"

"We burned it."

"When?"

"Last night. Before you came over."

"Why?"

"It was nothing but trouble."

"I thought the plan was to sell it? Why didn't you tell me?"

"I just did."

"What if I hadn't asked?"

"I would've told you."

"We've been together all day and last night and you never mentioned it."

"I didn't want you to worry about it before seeing the doctor. I know how stressed out you've been and I didn't want to get into an argument about it."

"Yeah. Not telling me until later—that was a great idea. I can't believe you, Caleb."

Lelah's phone started ringing in the console. She leaned over and checked the caller ID and then sat back against the seat without answering.

"Who is it?" he asked.

"My dad."

"Why don't you answer it?"

"I don't feel like talking to him right now. Is that OK?"

"It might be important. Maybe they found something."

Lelah glared at Caleb and then answered her phone.

"Hey, Dad." She listened. "Just driving back from Santa Fe with Caleb." She listened and then lied. "We were just looking at wedding locations." She glared at Caleb again. "I'll be home in a few hours. Why? What's up?" A pause. "Sure. I'll see you then."

She ended the call and set her phone back in the console.

"Everything cool?" Caleb asked.

"He said he needed to talk to me about something when I got home."

"He didn't say why?"

"No."

Lelah placed her hands on top of her head with her fingers laced together and stared at the road.

"When do you want to tell him you're pregnant?" he asked.

"We could've used that money, Caleb. We really could've used it."

"At what price, Lelah? We got a child on the way and you're sounding like my brother."

"I didn't get us into it," she shot back.

"Neither did I. But I was protecting us by getting rid of it. I was thinking of you. I was thinking of us. I was thinking about the family we're making." He turned and looked at her but she turned away. "You'll thank me later. And you'll be glad that I did what I did."

They drove in silence for a few miles. Lelah stared out the window at the cloud shadows upon the sun-bright earth.

"It was self-defense, wasn't it?" she asked.

"Yes."

"You sure?"

"Yes."

There was another pause.

The tires thrummed and the truck cut through the crosswind.

"I just can't believe it," she said. "Why did I have to tell you guys about that tent? Why did I have to see it? I just don't understand. We're good people. I'm so stupid."

"It's not your fault, baby. Please don't blame yourself. You didn't do anything wrong."

"I don't want anyone to take our baby, Caleb."

"Nobody is going to take our baby, sweetheart. Nobody."

He reached out to her and rubbed the back of her neck and massaged with his fingertips the delicate strips of muscle that ran from her shoulder blades to the base of her hairline. She closed her eyes—and his touch was calming. It gave her conviction in what he was saying and she believed him now even more than before.

"It's all right. Whatever you're feeling is all right," he said. "I'll talk with my brother tonight. We should just come clean and tell your dad. I think that's best. I think it's the right thing to do."

He could feel her muscles relax all at once and her face had brightened when she turned her eyes to him and said, "My dad will help us. He won't let them take our child."

And she believed it. They both did.

"Yeah, it was self-defense," Caleb convinced himself. The more you said it, whether lies or the truth, the more you believed it. "The law is on our side."

33.

CALEB PULLED THE TRUCK down the dusty drive and stopped in front of Lelah's house. It was long since dark and Lelah had fallen asleep on his lap.

For the last fifty miles his thoughts had drifted in and out of memories from long ago and the future that would forever be marred in a way that he could never have anticipated. He was hopeful though that Lelah's father would be able to turn it all around or at least put them on the path to some sort of constructive resolution. They were the only witnesses and none of them had any prior offenses. Well, Jake had a couple of DUI's but never any violent infraction, which he presumed would help in the final course of things.

He thought about the various outcomes and then his mind wandered in the darkness of the road and he remembered the day before he left for Iraq, swimming naked in the Chama with Lelah and how her skin glistened golden brown and how perfect she looked and how he remembered wishing—that if he'd had just one wish—that he would come back alive so that he could swim naked again with her in the summer river and hold her tight under the night sky afterward and make love to her trembling body.

And now they were bringing a child into the world.

It was sleeping right beside him. A tiny embryo. Growing every second. Crying soon enough. He wanted their world to be in harmony when their child came into it. He had nine months to make things right. Well, eight.

"We're here, baby," he said. He caressed her face with the back of his hand. She rose from his lap and rubbed her eyes. He kissed her. "I'll be back in a few hours, after I talk to my brother."

"What if your brother says no? That he doesn't want to tell my dad?"

"He won't. I'm not giving him any choice."

"I love you so much," she said.

"I love you too. See you in a few."

The rumble from Caleb's truck faded down the long dirt driveway into the night prairie as Lelah stepped inside and turned on the light. She startled and gasped. Her breathing eased when she recognized the two silhouettes. Her father and Sparks were sitting at the kitchen table in near darkness. She turned on a second light directly above the table and could see their features now, heavy with fatigue. They blinked and squinted as their bloodshot eyes adjusted.

"Hi, honey," Gates said. He stood and kissed her on the cheek. She thought she smelled a trace of whiskey on his breath, fleeting and then gone.

"You really scared me, Dad," she said. "Why are you sitting in the dark?"

"We were just resting for a bit. It's been a long day."

"Well, next time let me know. It's creepy. You really scared me."

"I'm sorry, honey. We just fell asleep and didn't hear you drive up."

She set her purse on the table and opened the refrigerator and took out a soda.

"Either of you want one?" she asked, holding up the can.

"No, thanks, honey."

"Sparks, you want one?" she said.

"I'm fine, Lelah. Thanks for asking."

She sat down across from them and opened the soda and took a sip.

"What did you want to talk about, Dad?"

"Is Caleb on his way home?"

"Yeah. Why?"

"Just curious."

"Do you want me to turn on the AC?" she asked.

"No, honey. It feels good in here. It's just right."

"You're sweating."

Gates wiped his brow with the back of his hand and smiled at her.

"I guess I am."

He was slow in recognizing the sweat and he continued to smile at his sluggish perception. Like the drunkard who falls and only realizes after touching his bleeding skin that he has hit his head and is amused by it.

She sipped her drink and studied her father. She looked at Sparks and studied him.

"How was your day?" Gates asked.

"Good," she said.

"You went looking for wedding locations, right? Did you find any you like?"

"Not really."

"You were in Santa Fe?" Sparks said.

"Yeah."

"I like it there."

"Me too," she said.

"It's one of my favorite places."

She took another sip of her soda and she could hear the sound of the carbonation inside her mouth. She swallowed.

"How's the soda?" her dad asked. "Nice and cold, huh?"

"Dad, are you using again?"

The question pierced the room and instigated a thrashing silence. To be sure, Darius Gates was coming down from the high, nose red with irritation, distant and remote, an oppressive muddle and depression setting in. He could feel that he was in a bad place but it wasn't any bad place he hadn't visited many times before. He was confident that he still possessed enough threads of psychic composure to convincingly lie and deceive, even if his appearance betrayed him. He knew above all else that he could always play on the heartstrings of a daughter's love for her father and the denial that is born with it, the longing to believe only the best in a parent. No matter what.

"No, darling. Why would you even ask me that? I haven't had anything in over three years," he said in a wounded tone, a tone that he knew would inspire both pity and regret in his daughter. "You know that."

"Do I?" she asked. "Have you been telling me the truth?"

"Of course I have, sweetheart. I would never lie to you."

"We've just had a real long day, Lelah," Sparks said, "that's all. It can be a crap job sometimes. You gotta do things you don't wanna do."

"It's a real downer, sweetheart. And it takes a toll on me sometimes." Her father dropped his eyes to the table for effect. Like most addicts, he was a great actor. "Because I care and I'm human. Sometimes we see things that nobody should ever see. Horrible things. Unimaginable things. Things that you want to forget."

"It's a thankless job," Sparks said. "Absolutely thankless. The only time people want to see us is when they need us. Sometimes I feel like I'm not even part of the community around here."

Gates pushed himself out of his chair and grabbed his hat, his movements sluggish and weary. His breathing was labored.

"Well, honey, we gotta get back to work," he said.

"Now?"

"There's an accident out on the interstate. A big rig flipped over and they need us to help clean up the wreckage and direct traffic."

"I thought we needed to talk, Dad?"

"We did. But then this crash thing happened and now we need to go. We'll talk about it later tonight or in the morning. There's no rush. It's no big deal. You're staying here tonight, right?"

"Yes."

"The morning, then. We'll talk about it in the morning."

"Let me brew you some coffee before you go."

"That's all right, sweetheart. We don't have time for that." Gates kissed Lelah on the forehead. "I just wanted to make sure my little girl got home safely before we headed back out."

34.

CALEB OPENED THE TRAILER door and turned on the light.

"Jake," he called out, "where you at?"

He moved through the living room and down the narrow hallway of warping linoleum and faux wood paneling and into his bedroom. He took off his shirt and tossed it on the bed. He turned on the stereo and stepped into the bathroom and cranked on the hot water. The showerhead sputtered and then shot thick streams into the bottom of the tub. The trailer lacked many things but water pressure was not one of them.

Caleb pulled his belt from the pant loops and hung it on a nail in the wall.

"Jake," he called out again, "where you at?"

And still there was no answer.

He called Jake's cell phone and heard nothing but the empty ring on the other end until the voicemail picked up.

Light from outside spilled around the edges of his bedroom curtain and he pulled back the half-rag and looked across the wood yard to the shed. The door was cracked open and the light was on inside. He slid open the window and yelled.

"Jake? You out there? ...Jake?"

He stuck his head out the window and leaned his ear toward the shed. But there was no response. He pulled his head inside and slid the window shut. The shower steamed from the bathroom and the stereo consumed the space with loud rock music.

Caleb limped shirtless through his bedroom and back down the hallway and out the front door. He continued across the wood yard and his breath made clouds in the air that was cooling and would grow colder for many months forward. The night was without scent, crisp and fresh with the season's change, no bloom of sagebrush or sweetness of harvested wood, the land folded inward and dormant in rural silence.

He called out again and his pace quickened without conscious thought.

"Jake? You in there?"

He looked down and saw a dark trail of liquid on the gray earth, viscous and black like used motor oil. It was leading inside the shed.

"Jake? Where you at?"

There was an angry desperation in his voice and he exhaled great plumes and sucked in heaves to feed his rapidly beating heart. He reached out with both hands and yanked open the rusted aluminum door with a grating screech.

He stood in the doorway and the light cast off the pale skin on his chest and he saw his brother slumped against the back wall in a gruesome and contorted state. He limped forward and fell onto the dirt floor in front of him.

His brother's face was now cold white ash where it was not draped and smeared with caked blood. His eyes were open and the whites were now black. He'd been shot through the forehead and his dismembered hands were nailed to the side of his head as though he were shielding his ears from some deafening sound overrunning all of nature.

He cradled his brother's broken corpse and rocked him in his arms and told him that he loved him and that he was sorry, when an impulse awakened him and he remembered that he had to protect the living. He had to protect Lelah. From whom he did not know.

He laid his brother down gently on his side and closed his eyes. He staggered to his feet and hurried across the yard and into the trailer and grabbed his cell phone off his bed and called her.

The phone rang five times and then went to voicemail. He hung up and limped out of his room with the stereo blaring and the shower steaming and down the hallway and front steps and into his truck and gassed it down the driveway. He turned onto the asphalt without braking and called Lelah again. The phone spiraled for a connection and then the first chirp rang in his ear.

"C'mon baby, pick up. Pick up."

On the second ring he heard the sound of her phone ringing inside his truck. He looked down at the console and saw the glow of her screen against the plastic walls of the drink holder. The caller ID flashed with: MY WUV AND ONLY.

"Fuck," he said.

He called her house phone. But before it could ring the call dropped abruptly as he hit the dead zone that ran along the canyon between the two mesas.

𝄢

LELAH SEARCHED FOR HER phone. She rifled her purse. The kitchen table and the countertop. She went into the bathroom. She retraced her steps since she had gotten home but nowhere could she find her phone. She went back into the kitchen and dialed her cell on the house phone. But the call went straight to voicemail. She tried calling Caleb—and that call also went straight to voicemail.

Something bad was going to happen. She could feel it. The bizarre episode with her father had been terribly unnerving and only managed to heighten an already fraught set of circumstances. She just wanted to be with Caleb right now. She didn't want to be alone. Not even for another second.

She took her keys from her purse and hurried out the front door and motored down the long driveway in her Ford pickup and into the night. Far in the distance her brake lights flared and she turned onto the interstate as her house phone rang and rang and rang as Caleb left the dead zone and regained service.

35.

*H*AS IT COME TO *this?*

Of course it has.

Everything in my life always drives to the worst possible conclusion.

Oh, well, you're in the shit. So put on your game face and let's get it done. Your daughter will be better off in the long run with these two thieves out of her life. It will be hard for a while but she'll get over it. Plenty of other guys out there.

The cruiser's dashboard lights illuminated the interior in a wash of pale green as they rolled down the lonely asphalt toward the wood yard. The surrounding land was hidden in darkness and the stars were so thick they appeared more a luminescent cloud from north to south than distinct bodies of light.

And we won't have to worry about Marlo. That crusty cock-sucking faggot. Blood for blood. Faggot-ass-faggot-ass-pillow-biting-fuckhead-faggot.

Gates sniffed and wiped the powdery leftovers from his nostrils, once again refueled and recharged with the fantastic bravado of Johnny Yayo. He took another key-blaster and the brilliant orgasmic phantasm mortared up from his bowels and his ballsack and made him unquestionably invincible. *IN-FUCKING-VINCIBLE YOU ARE.*

"Give me one more hit before we go on duty," Sparks said.

"Help yourself, Lester."

Sparks dipped his key into the baggie and choppered another rocket up his nose.

A mile away Gates killed the headlights and they glided down the asphalt like some stealthy winged serpent of the night.

"Make sure your phone is off," Gates said.

"Already done."

Sparks placed their phones inside the glove box.

They turned down the driveway and rolled along the rutted track, the tires crunching against the sandy grit and worn stones. They stopped halfway down and concealed the cruiser behind cords of stacked firewood. They opened the doors slowly and stepped out and left the doors slightly ajar to avoid the loud steel bite of closing them.

They withdrew their firearms and crouched below the stacks of wood and stepped around the pool of light from the porch and made the front steps. The music was coming loud from the back room. It would muffle their entry. Perfect.

Gates craned his neck and looked down the side of the trailer and could see the steam on the bedroom window. Caleb is in the shower. Even better.

They climbed the front steps and slipped inside. Gates took the lead and Sparks trailed, staggered in formation so that each could fire. The music grew louder with each step and steam flooded out the bedroom in billowing clouds as thick as tule fog, steady and increasingly heavier as it met the cold air rushing down the hallway from the open front door.

❧

CALEB BARRELED DOWN THE driveway toward Lelah's house, a dome of light in the distance. The prairie was dark on all sides and his truck rocked and bucked over the ruts and water-eroded creases. He was thinking only of protecting her and he hoped that she was still home with her father. They were both there thirty minutes ago. But why hadn't anyone answered the house phone the three times he called? Had the killers come to her house? Who were they? Where were they? If they could do that to his brother, what would they do to her?

They were somewhere out there in the darkness.

Her father would protect her though. She'd be safest with him.

He prayed that her dad was still there. That Lelah was still there with him. Maybe they had turned off the ringer on the house phone and forgot to turn it back on. Her father turned it off during the day sometimes after working all night.

Then he saw his brother's mutilated body, his dead eyes. The image flashed in front of him. He tried to shake it out of his head.

He looked down at the steering wheel. His hands were still red with his brother's blood and his knuckles were coated with a stiff coagulated crust. He grunted and yelled to keep from wailing. *Your brother is dead. You need to stay calm. Keep your wits. Lelah. Focus. Focus on her.*

He skidded to a stop in the gravel turnout in front of her house. Her truck was gone—or maybe it was parked out back. The sheriff's cruiser was gone too.

What to do? Where did they go?

The lights are on. She might be inside.

I gotta check.

Please be inside, baby. Please.

He jumped out of his truck and left it running and hobbled up the front steps. The door was locked but he had a key and opened it.

"Lelah?" he called out as he limped through the house. The light was on in her bedroom. He moved down the hallway and peered inside.

"Where are you baby?" he muttered to himself.

He was breathing hard and sweating and the house was empty.

Where are you?

He didn't want to at first. But now he had to. He called her father. The phone went straight to voicemail.

He jumped back in his truck and sped down the long driveway that cut across the dark prairie. He made the asphalt and raced back to the wood yard.

♟

IN THE APPROACHING DISTANCE Lelah could see the faint glow of the trailer and the various halos of scattered lights the wood yard made against the night. When she drove closer she thought she could see her father's cruiser parked amid the silhouetted humps of firewood and heavy equipment that gave shape and outline to the featureless void.

When she left the asphalt and pulled down the driveway her suspicion was confirmed. She rolled past her father's cruiser and squinted to see if he and Sparks were inside. But they were not. Her anxiety had increased on the drive over here and was now compounded by the unexpected scene.

What are they doing here?

Why didn't my dad tell me he was coming here?

I thought there was an accident on the highway?

Did Caleb call them? Did Jake?

Has there been an accident here?

She'd never wished so strongly for her cell phone.

He's using. He has to be using again. None of this makes any sense right now. But it all makes sense if he's using again—then anything makes sense and nothing makes sense. Dad. Why? Why? You've come so far and now it's back to this. Back to the beginning. We'll start over. We can do this together. We will do this together. Father and daughter.

Settle down. Breathe. Perhaps there is a reasonable explanation.

She parked her truck and got out. She looked around for Caleb's truck but it was gone. Or maybe he parked it behind the shed. Maybe it's back there. She walked slowly toward the front steps and called Caleb's name. Then Jake's. Then: "Dad?"

ℒ

GATES AND SPARKS STALKED through the bedroom and the veils of steam toward the bathroom where the shower was running a loud torrent. Gates glanced down at Caleb's bed and saw the discarded shirt. Sparks saw the article of clothing as well. The music and the steam amplified the tension for there was little sight and only the noise from the speakers thumping off the walls and thumping in their ears.

They moved with knees bent and thighs flexed to absorb their weight so as not to shake the flimsy trailer flooring and give up the element of surprise. They led with their guns, both hands firm on the weapon, right hand on the pistol grip, left hand cupping the base and fingers supporting the outside of the right. Their eyes were blazed open and their concentration was intensified from the deadly situation and the peaking cocaine high. It was like hunting in a smoke machine–choked nightclub or the misty depths of some far-off cacophonous jungle warzone.

Sparks loved it. The music, the steam, all dressed up in cop gear with guns and a license to kill. Wow. This was the very essence of law enforcement. It was moments like these where he truly appreciated Gates and all the opportunities he'd given him. If not for Gates, where would he be? He didn't want to think about it. He'd do anything for the man. Anything.

Gates stepped inside the bathroom, the space tight, more steam in here, thick, hot, and wet, the walls sweating. He could smell the mildew from the shower tub but not the perfume of soap. The shower beat steadily against the hard surface, unusually steady, not broken from human contact.

Gates let Sparks slide in behind him.

Sparks sidled to his left and positioned himself in the corner above the toilet so that both men could fire at the same time without fear of shooting each other.

Gates nodded to Sparks and then reached out with his left hand, right hand pointing the gun, and ripped back the shower curtain— ready to murder.

But there was no one there—

—an empty tub

—a torrent of rushing hot water

—billowing steam.

Was the shower a ruse? A decoy? A cunning trick?

They spun around to cover their backs and crept out of the bathroom and into the bedroom with the music pounding from the speakers.

LELAH STEPPED ONTO THE front porch and called timidly through the open front door.

"Dad?"

She looked around, confused, unsure. The music was blaring from Caleb's bedroom.

"Caleb?"

She stepped forward and entered the trailer, each step cautious, fearful, slow, entirely its own. The living room light at the front of the trailer and Caleb's bedroom light in the back were the only lights on inside and in between those pockets of light there was darkness.

She stood in the living room and called down the hallway toward the music and steam. She could barely hear her voice and assumed that if someone was down there at the end of the hallway they could not hear it either. She stepped forward out of the light and toward the bedroom and into the dark. Then she thought she saw someone moving in Caleb's bedroom through the steam and she stepped faster and with heavier feet and called out louder.

⚘

DRUG-ADDLED AND PARANOID THAT they had been deceived, confused and raging with the noise of manic alertness and a desire to kill and settle the score—Gates and Sparks felt the dull vibration in the flimsy trailer floor—footsteps approaching—

—when simultaneously a streak of movement startled them in the steamy mirror—a vague form—a figure striding through the living room toward them—

—Lelah slowed and then she could make out her father and Sparks pointing their guns at her through the mist and she tried to call out over the music and she shuddered and her heart jumped and she thought, *my-god-why-do-they-have-their-guns-out-and-what-is-happening-and-where-is-my-Caleb*—

—Gates wheeled around and reflexively fired down the hallway through the steam and pockets of darkness, certain that the approaching figure was Caleb—

—The bullet struck the victim in the chest and their feet flew out from under them and they dropped from view behind the couch.

Gates crept out of the bedroom and down the hallway with his gun leading the way through the veils of steam, the hallway a corridor of darkness and opening to the light of the living room where the victim had landed on the other side of the couch, perhaps dead, or only wounded. Dead, he hoped.

Sparks followed over his shoulder, tactically staggered in the narrow hallway in the same manner as when they had approached the bedroom.

Gates stepped from the warped linoleum and onto the living room carpet, tense and ready for a surprise, tense and ready for another ruse, tense and ready to finish off the wounded Caleb. Just like he'd finished off his brother.

He stepped around the couch and his gun fell from his hand and he collapsed beside the gasping victim.

Blood frothed out of Lelah's mouth in scarlet bubbles. She was paralyzed and pinned to the ground as if by a heavy iron stake, a bullet hole ripped through the center of her chest, blood seeping in a great bloom across her shirt and out her back and onto the carpet. She made a gurgled choking sound and her pupils were convulsing and flitting around the whites of her eyes.

"Daddy," she gasped, barely able to find the oxygen and strength as she drowned in her own blood. "Daaaddy... Help me... Daaaghddy," she coughed.

Daddy.

Help me.

Gates placed his hands one over the other and pumped into his daughter's delicate chest, which only made the blood clog her windpipe and choke her more severely.

"Hang in there, sweetheart. Hang in there. Daddy's here."

He searched the room for help, for an explanation of some kind, a frantic jumble of nerves and thoughts that were all racing together and then speeding away faster than he could grab them. He had suddenly forgotten his name. He did not know where he was only that his daughter was beneath him and dying. Someone had shot her, but who? He ran over and snatched a pillow from the couch and set it beneath her head. He brushed the hair out of her eyes and tried to wipe away the blood leaking out her mouth and down the sides of her neck. He went back to pumping her chest but her heart had already stopped beating and her head fell limp to the side and she turned away from him.

Sparks looked down at Gates who was now cradling his daughter and whispering to her between violent sobs.

"We gotta go," Sparks said. "We gotta get outta here."

But Gates couldn't hear him.

"My baby. Lelah. My God, who did this to you? Why did you come here? Why?"

Sparks staggered through the blood on the carpet and the tread of his boots tracked the blood onto the front porch and he took one step more and saw a fiery explosion of light in the darkness in front of him and then nothing else ever again—

BOOM!

A 12-gauge shotgun slug tore a mangled hole into his stomach and hurled him back against the porch railing and then dead on the ground.

Inside Gates heard the blast and stumbled instinctively to his feet, vaguely conscious, a grieving zombie indifferent to the consequences held for him outside. His vision was bleary and swimming and he stepped onto the front porch with his gun dangling from his hand, wearing his daughter's blood.

He shielded his eyes against the porch light shining in his face and tried to see beyond it. He yelled something incoherent and slobbered out another threat and then fired wildly into the darkness and emptied his weapon in a sobbing wail. The gun blasts echoed and then rolled off into nowhere and brought silence.

He stared into the night and could make out nothing until a gunshot flashed light over a line of armed men in front of him and obliterated his face.

Marlo stepped barefoot out of the darkness as eight men materialized with him. They were armed with an assortment of automatic weapons and shotguns.

Marlo looked down at Sparks and contemplated the steaming hole in the deputy's stomach. Marlo sighed and walked over to the porch and stared down at Gates. A quarter of the sheriff's skull was missing.

"How did we get here?" Marlo said.

He climbed the porch and stepped inside the trailer. He could feel the wet murder cooling under his feet. The vital warmth was gone. A dark pool seeped across the floor from the young woman's corpse. He stood over her and looked into her lifeless green eyes and bent down and closed them.

36.

NINE MINUTES LATER CALEB whipped the truck left across the asphalt and floored the gas down the dirt driveway toward the wood yard. He caught the sheriff's cruiser in the corner of his eye and his mind rippled with confusion and he wondered why it was parked there and he became even more concerned.

He sped past without slowing and saw Lelah's truck parked outside the trailer and jerked to a stop beside it. He jumped out and hurried toward the front porch and saw Sparks dead on the ground in a black stain. Then he nearly stepped on the death-twisted body of Gates.

He called out, "Lelah?"

He limped inside and the nightmare he feared more than any other was confirmed. He stumbled forward and kneeled beside Lelah and his head fell onto her blood-soaked chest. He caressed her face and kissed her bloodied lips and pulled her into him without any thought or care of what to do next because all was now gone and he was numb and lost completely until a voice rose out of the shadows.

"A man must always put things in perspective."

A table lamp clicked on in the corner and revealed Marlo sitting on the couch with a sawed-off shotgun crosswise on his lap. Three armed men stood against the faux wood paneled wall. Two more huddled in the hallway leading to the bedroom. Three more stepped inside the front door from the night.

"A man needs to know what he's dealing with, what he's looking at," Marlo said.

"Why did you have to kill her? Why—"

Caleb lunged across the living room for Marlo.

Three men immediately tackled him and struck him with rifle butts and a barrage of boot heels and pounding fists until Caleb was twisting on his back in a semi-conscious haze, his vision a whirling kaleidoscope of faux wood paneling and cheap ceiling paper and grinning remorseless faces.

"I did not kill her," Marlo said. "Her father did. I don't believe that will provide you with much comfort, but at least you should have the facts of the situation so that you may form an accurate opinion amid the chaos."

Caleb's mouth was awash with blood and powdery fragments of chipped teeth. He blinked and tried to sharpen his focus. Everything was blurry.

He rolled onto his stomach and crawled feebly across the carpet back toward Marlo. He felt a wrenching on his prosthetic leg and then he was twisted over and dragged backward. His prosthetic unhinged and the man dragging him crashed onto his ass and knocked over the coffee table. The man flushed with bewilderment at the prosthetic leg now clutched in his hand. He raised the prosthetic into the light and showed the other men in a gesture to justify his clumsiness. There was a momentary silence until the room made sense of the fake leg and then the men laughed for some time.

Marlo rose from the couch and walked over to a dusty side table. He lifted a framed portrait of Caleb in his Marine Corps dress blues and looked at it.

"Without perspective, things are distorted," he said. "There's no order. No scope. No value, no understanding, no definition of what is and what is not. The world is populated with nothing but Humpty Dumpty's where everything is whatever anyone wants it to be."

Marlo set down the portrait and then removed the lid from a small wooden box. He lifted a Purple Heart from inside, held it by the ribbon, and spun the medal in the light.

"For instance, I am a homosexual. I make love to my own kind. The female genitalia does not arouse me whatsoever. But an engorged male organ, throbbing with sexual anticipation, excites me very much, especially if the man has a well-sculpted physique. I don't sound like a fag when I speak, but I assure you, I am a thoroughgoing butt-fucker."

Marlo placed the Purple Heart back inside the wooden box and inspected another war medal sitting on the table. He lifted the Navy Medal of Honor by the ribbon and blew off the dust.

"Let's say you and I had met at a bar or a sporting event, or some mindless testosterone-fueled extravaganza like a monster truck rally, and over the course of our conversation a beautiful woman sashayed past us, and you began speaking about the carnal pleasures resulting from intercourse with her, the taste of her supple breasts in your mouth, the scent of her well-lubricated pussy, your finger probing her airtight asshole during coitus, the drunken lust dripping from your words. You would assume throughout this salacious digression that I shared the same affinity for the female form as yourself—and all because you lacked perspective."

Marlo swept his hand through the air, gesturing to the room.

"The dead strewn about here, the carnage of this evening, were the consequence of foolish people lacking perspective for the grave stakes at hand. Ignorance writ large. Did they think I was a man of trifles? It appears so. But then again, that is only my perspective."

Marlo stepped over to the window and pulled back the curtain with the shotgun barrel. He looked across the yard at the woodshed and the light hanging above the doorway and let the curtain fall back into place.

"This situation fascinates me, you see. Am I to believe that a couple of noodle-heads hiking through the forest stumbled upon the marijuana crop and decided to steal it? Did you value your life so cheaply?" He paused as though he were trying to answer the question for himself and then carried on with his thoughts. "I would never stroll into a Chinese restaurant, see that it was temporarily deserted, kick on the fryer and start peddling wontons. For several reasons: one, I don't know how to cook wontons. Two, they're not my wontons to cook. And three, I'm not in the wonton fucking business."

He sighed and shook his head.

"Every living being in this room right now, the fierce-looking men surrounding you, are all in danger of losing their lives in a most gruesome fashion because of your foolish thievery. Yes. All of them. Me included. The million dollars in product you stole is a pittance to our bosses—they make hundreds of millions a year. Perhaps even billions. But they are fussbudgets. They are like Jewish accountants with violent balls. The mere principle of thievery is toxic to them. It is intolerable. As soon as there is even the remotest inkling of suspicion, one must dispatch the suspicious in this business. No matter whom they might be. Which leads us to you."

Marlo stood directly over Caleb now.

"There are only two ways to cure the situation for me and my men: you can return the marijuana that was stolen from us or deliver the million dollars it was worth. Now, do you have the marijuana?"

Caleb wanted to spit the tooth fragments and blood at the man towering over him but he was too weak. His nose was busted and he could not breathe through it.

"Do you?" Marlo asked.

"No."

Marlo lowered the barrel of the sawed-off shotgun from his shoulder and pointed it at Caleb's head. "I didn't think so. What about the money?"

The wide barrel trembled inches above Caleb's forehead. He stared into the black tunnel and thought of death and the thought had no emotion one way or the other. Life had no pull or luster, no magnetism drawing him toward its source. Everyone he loved was gone. But then a force unconscious and unbidden reared up and compelled him to struggle a little while longer and offered a quick reply.

"It'll be here tomorrow," he said.

"Tomorrow?"

"Yes. The money will be here tomorrow."

A skeptical grin changed Marlo's expression. How many times had he heard desperate pleas and lies in a human being's *final moments?*

But Caleb noticed a brief hitch in the man's composure, an unexpected pause, as though the man had mentally stumbled. The pause was telling enough and Caleb filled the breach with conviction. "If you kill me now, you'll never see the money."

"My years of experience tell me that all this bloodshed here tonight was the result of both the product and the money being absent—people rarely shoot each other when expectations are met. But now you want me to believe that the money is in fact forthcoming?"

"The guy left us a hundred thousand up front."

"Where is it?"

"Outside. How do you think we got that new backhoe?"

Marlo stared down at him and studied his beaten face, his eyes, searching for a look that would betray his statement, a look of doubt, a physical tell. He could find none.

He raised the shotgun barrel and set it back on his shoulder and stepped through the wet murder and over to the doorway. He peered across the yard at the John Deere backhoe, the fresh yellow paint glowing in the moonlight. He had to admit that the new machine was a convincing piece of evidence, especially for a couple of wood-mongering paupers.

"He's bringing the rest of the money tomorrow afternoon," Caleb said.

Another look of doubt appeared to wash across Marlo's face and his posture stiffened with a question and he squinted, but only for a moment, the briefest of moments. But Caleb could feel the shift in energy. He'd been on the other side before, the one asking the questions, the one doing the interrogating, the one with the loaded gun.

"And what is the name of this mysterious philanthropist?" Marlo asked.

"I don't know him. He's my brother's friend. They made the deal."

"Why should I believe you?"

"Because it's the truth."

Marlo pondered the young man's assertions. Perhaps he was telling the truth. It would certainly make Marlo's life a whole lot easier if he was.

"In less than twenty-four hours you'll have your money," Caleb said. "It's either that or a bunch of dead bodies. My corpse ain't worth much."

"I'll call your bluff and give you twelve hours. The only lawmen for a hundred miles are now dead. There's nobody left to save you." Marlo motioned to the two men huddled in the hallway. "Victor and Rhodes. Stay here with him. If the money does not arrive by noon tomorrow—put a bullet in his head. As many as you like."

Marlo paused beside the dusty table and stared down at the small wooden box.

"You can interpret your war medals in one of two ways, sailor— as either the commendations of an intrepid warrior or the garish trinkets of a clumsy bumpkin." He turned his head and his eyes fell on Caleb. "I have been to war many times, and as you can see, I still have all my limbs."

Marlo stepped through the cold blood and halted at the front door.

"Give him back his leg. You fucking barbarian."

37.

E STAYED ON THE floor with her in his arms the way that he always did in the early morning darkness when he held onto a few more minutes of her before going to work. His face was wet with her blood and his tears but the tears had stopped coming for now.

He heard several vehicles start up outside and then move into the night. His prosthetic had been thrown across the room. He heard it land and flip a few times and then thud against the wall. He heard the two men that were left behind step into the kitchen and open the refrigerator. He heard them push aside some beer bottles and then sweep things out of the refrigerator and onto the linoleum just to be destructive. Because they could. Because there was nothing the one-legged man on the floor could do about it.

Caleb sat up slowly and looked across the room at them. They were standing in the wedge of light from the open refrigerator door. One man had a compact military shotgun, flat black with a pump action. The other man carried what looked like an MP9 or some other kind of machine pistol. The man with the shotgun had a bottle of beer in his hand.

Caleb started crawling—

"Hey," the man with the shotgun said. He pointed the barrel at him, resting it on his forearm, his other hand occupied with the beer. "What do you think you're doing?"

"Can I put my leg back on?"

They chuckled.

"Sure," he said. "You can put your fucking leg back on."

"But do it slowly," the man with the machine pistol added. "You move too quick and we'll shoot your other leg off."

He impressed himself with the threat, a bona fide comedian. His partner thought it pretty funny too. They found another beer in the refrigerator and opened both bottles and tossed the caps at Caleb. One of the caps struck him in the ass. This gave them a good laugh.

Caleb crawled over to his prosthetic and sat with his back against the wall. He slid his fleshy nub into the carbon fiber sleeve and worked the flexing action of the ankle joint. He tried standing, but the leg gave out and he fell down onto his right side. The men laughed again.

"You should do stand-up."

"But first he has to learn how to stand."

They tapped beers in honor of their humorous talents.

Caleb took off the prosthetic and examined it in the dim light. He worked the ankle action back and forth. He slid back into the sleeve and pushed himself off the floor and braced himself against the wall. When he attempted to put his full weight on the leg it gave out again and he tumbled onto the floor a second time.

This really set them howling. Beer exploded from nostrils and mouth.

Caleb sat on the carpet and continued working the ankle action. He checked the screws and wiggled the joints.

"I need to go to the woodshed and get my tools," he said to them.

"What for?"

"To fix my leg."

"What's wrong with it?"

"It's not working."

"Why not?"

"Your buddy stripped out one of the screws when he pulled my leg off."

"Are you pulling our leg?"

Again they laughed.

Caleb raised the prosthetic and moved the ankle joint back and forth.

"Do you think we're fucking idiots?" the man with the machine pistol asked. "You think we're going to let you go out there by yourself?"

"No. I figured you'd come with me."

"Take his leg, Victor," the man with the machine pistol said. "He might try and use it as a weapon."

"Hold my beer."

Victor walked out of the kitchen and snatched the prosthetic from Caleb's hand.

"Get up gimpy," he said. "I want to see you hop out there."

Caleb crawled over to the end of the couch and lifted himself up and onto his left leg and started hopping across the living room. He steadied himself against the front doorjamb and then hopped onto the porch and down the front steps. He made the soft dirt and nearly fell, bracing himself on the ground with his left hand and then his right, like a sprinter in the starting blocks. He pushed himself up and found his balance and hopped toward the woodshed some thirty yards ahead, leaving the glow of the porch light and into an area of dark shadow.

The two men followed behind him with their guns at their sides.

"Little Bunny Foo Foo hopping through the forest—"

They laughed.

"Where do one-legged people eat?" He made the sound of a drum roll. "I-Hop."

Caleb ignored them and hopped across the yard. He was almost to the woodshed when the man with the shotgun kicked out his leg from under him. It took Caleb by surprise and he crashed so suddenly that he was unable to shield his face from the impact. Gravel cratered into his cheek and forehead and he saw a white flash and there was an explosion in his eardrum from the collision of his jawbone with the ground.

He sat up and tried to gather himself in the spinning darkness. For a moment he felt as though he would vomit. He took several deep breaths and fought to keep from tipping over. After a while the night stopped whirling and flattened out again.

He stayed in the dirt for a short time longer and caught his breath while his captors' laughs trailed off into the vacant prairieland.

And as they laughed he said to himself, *Keep it up, you're about to die.*

He pushed himself back onto his left leg and hopped into the woodshed and toward the red Craftsman tool chest that stood nicked and dented against the far wall. He could see his brother's mutilated body in the corner of his eye, but he would not look over at him. The sight could only distract him now, cloud his thinking, disrupt his composure. He needed to be as levelheaded as he could.

He made the tool chest and rested against it and caught his breath. When he reached to open the top drawer a loud bash startled him as the man with the shotgun hammered the metal tool chest with the butt of his weapon.

"Hold on," he said. "Slow the fuck down."

The man opened the top drawer, which was still rattling, and looked inside. He pushed tools out of the way, metal scraping against grit and metal, checking for a weapon of some sort. He opened the second drawer and the third and the fourth, more metal scraping against grit and metal. Nothing but scattered tools smudged with grease.

Satisfied, he stepped back. He didn't bother checking all nine drawers.

Caleb removed an Allen wrench from the second drawer.

"Can I have my leg back now?" he asked.

It clanged against the tool chest and thumped beside him.

"Can I grab that stool right there?" Caleb asked.

One of them nodded.

Caleb pulled the stool over and sat down and started wrenching on the ankle joint. The two men were standing near the door and from that distance it must have looked like he was really trying to fix things. He sure was selling it well.

But there was nothing wrong with his prosthetic.

"Can I get a screwdriver?" he asked.

The man with the shotgun nodded.

Caleb opened a lower drawer, testing the boundaries, the vigilance of his captors. But they had already dropped their guards and reassumed their funnyman roles.

The man with the machine pistol nudged his buddy and pointed with amusement at Jake's corpse.

"Why is your brother covering his ears?" he asked. "He can't hear shit."

"That's cold."

"No. He's cold."

The men howled at the gruesome barb.

Keep it up, Caleb said to himself. Keep it up.

Caleb set the screwdriver atop the tool chest and reached down for the bottom drawer, betting it all, betting his life that the .40 cal Beretta was still there, that his brother had stayed true to form and once again been neglectful of his duties. He slid open the drawer and reached inside. He felt the grease rag and he could feel the gun wrapped within. He turned his back slowly to the men. They were still laughing and pointing and mocking his brother.

They did not notice that he had opened the bottom drawer but it probably wouldn't have mattered anyway.

Caleb unfolded the rag, took the gun by the handle and slid back the action halfway. A brass shell winked at him. One in the chamber.

He swiveled in the stool and killed the men in mid-laughter with four rapid gunshots to the face and chest before they could even raise their weapons or register that they had been fooled.

38.

THE TEETH OF THE backhoe carved into the earth on the mesa near the edge of their property line. The eastern sky was growing pale and the far western horizon was a thin sheet of the deepest night.

Lelah and his brother were in the shovelhead and he was nearly finished with the second grave. He had pulled out the nails fastening his brother's severed hands to the side of his head. He wouldn't bury him in that mocking pose.

The teeth plunged into the grave and he raised the bucket and emptied the load into the pyramid of soil to the left of the machine. He turned off the diesel and stepped down from the cab and the chill wind from the north ruffled his pant legs and nipped at his bare chest. In all this he hadn't even thought about putting on a shirt. He didn't even know he was shirtless and he did not feel the cold of the wind.

He walked over to the shovelhead and rolled his brother into his arms and carried him down the earthen ramp into the grave. He laid his brother down and climbed back up the earthen ramp and retrieved his brother's severed hands from the shovelhead. He placed his brother's hands where they belonged as best he could. He climbed back up and took a bucket of water and a rag from inside the cab and went back into the grave and washed his brother's face.

He kissed him and laid his head on his chest. The wind blew and he stayed there beside him until he had strength enough to move on. He kissed his brother on the forehead one last time and walked back up the earthen ramp with the bucket of water and the wet rag.

He stared at Lelah reposed in the shovelhead, pale blue and beautiful, his gorgeous angel, their unborn child now sleeping inside her forever. She looked so young in death. He only needed to nudge her awake.

Death did not look real.

Where was her lovely voice now?

He took her into his arms and noticed how heavy she felt. She had never felt heavy in his arms. He carried her over to her grave and walked down the earthen ramp and laid her inside. He walked back up the earthen ramp and retrieved the wet rag and bucket.

He wiped the dried blood from her face and the blood that had washed down her neck, dipping the rag and wringing it out until the water in the bucket had taken her color. There was so much blood that it smeared her skin and left a pinkish veneer as though it were bringing life back to her. He continued dipping and wringing the rag and washing her skin until the veneer was gone.

When her lips were clean they held the chill of the winter sky. He kissed them and rode out into memories of the future that were supposed to happen but would never arrive. He thought he could still make out traces of blood on her skin in the early light and so he wiped her cheeks and lips again.

He said goodbye to the unborn child inside her. He said goodbye to the tiny life that would forever swim in the darkness. He said goodbye to the spirit that had only just been chosen and that would never have the earth to walk upon.

He placed a blanket over Lelah so that she and the baby wouldn't get any colder.

After laying with her for minutes that had no hour and smoothing over her hair and kissing her one last time on the winter of her lips he climbed back up the earthen ramp and into the loader and began filling the graves.

♁

HE DRAGGED THE DEAD men from the woodshed across the yard and stacked them inside the living room with the death-twisted corpses of Sheriff Darius Gates and Deputy Sparks. He took the lawmen's key rings and clipped them to his belt loop.

Then he moved through the trailer with a jerrican of gasoline and doused the interior with the combustible liquid, the ratty carpet and the warped linoleum, the stained mattresses and blankets, the cheap couch, the faux wood paneling, the objects that would flame high and crackle loud with their own blackened destruction.

He drenched the heap of corpses and trailed the gasoline across the carpet and down the front porch and onto the ground outside. He struck a wooden match and the fire danced and jumped along the gasoline path into the living room and ran through the trailer.

He watched the fire burn and rage and devour what used to be his home.

When the first rays of dawn touched his eyes he turned away and drove the patriotic cruiser down the dirt driveway and onto the paved road.

39.

HE NEVER THOUGHT HE would have to go to war again. He never thought he would have to kill again either, especially not in his own country. He figured that was thousands of miles behind him in a land and memory that he had hoped he would lose one day but knew that he never would. There were things that he had never told anybody. Things that he'd done that he never even told Lelah or his brother. They were secrets that he kept inside and now he felt guilty for never telling them. He had always figured he would tell them one day.

He wasn't proud of the things he'd done. But he'd had a job to do and he'd done it well. He'd done it better than he thought he ever could have. And he surprised and horrified himself only afterward when he thought about the doing. He'd killed twenty-seven men in Fallujah. Six in one building. They were holed up in the third floor of a bombed-out apartment. The first two never woke up. The last one had time to reach for his weapon but his hand never made it that far.

He had no regrets about killing the men while they slept.

꙳

TWENTY MINUTES AFTER HE drove away from the wood yard Caleb steered the patriotic cruiser into the parking lot and pulled in front of the squat building that stood on a stamp of concrete in the unincorporated prairie. A lone outpost for lawmen.

He swung out of the cruiser. A large brass key ring clattered in his hands as he approached the front door. The sun had barely crested and its slanting rays held little heat. There were no birds in the sky. He heard the faint tire thrum of a big rig on the interstate miles away. He looked over the scrubland and could see for a great distance the emptiness and stillness only.

He slid the key into the lock and pushed open the door.

He limped into the sparse office. Two desks a few feet across from each other. A bathroom in the back corner. No detention facility. When they had prisoners they drove them seventy miles south to Española.

He moved over to a storage closet and tried a few keys until one worked. He opened the double-doors and found several uniforms pressed and hanged. He lifted one off the rack and read the size. It would be a little baggie up top and he figured the pants would be a tad short. But they would do. So far as he could tell there were only two different size uniforms in the closet, which would make sense because Gates and Sparks were the only lawmen that worked out of this place.

He limped over to another storage closet. This one had a padlock for extra security. He found the right key and opened it. He took stock of the arsenal. Two AR-15 automatic rifles. One with a silencer attached. Three Remington tactical shotguns. Several spare clips already loaded and two boxes of 12-gauge shells.

A Smith & Wesson .44 magnum revolver caught his eye, an old-school handheld cannon. Dirty Harry. Plenty of shells for this one too.

A few minutes later he stood naked in front of the bathroom mirror. His beard and long hair were matted with blood that was nearly black and clotted in tangled clumps. He had swollen bruises under his eyes and his left temple had a lump the size of a quail egg under the skin. He touched the lump and felt the sensation of physical pain, but mostly he was numb to it right now. The purple was starting to darken his bruises and would deepen in color over the coming hours and days.

He lost himself in the mirror. He was the image of what he had been through. No less.

Hair clippers buzzed in his hand. He raised them to his scalp and cut a swath down the middle of his crown and thick tufts of hair tumbled onto the tiled floor.

The clippers cut swath upon swath and the hair piled around his bare feet until there was only white scalp. Then he took the clippers and removed his beard down to the stubble. Then he ran the hot water and lathered his face with soap and ran the razor down his skin until his lean jawline was shaved clean and fierce with clarity.

He washed his face and then showered.

He dried off and sat on the bench and slid his prosthetic into its sleeve and made his leg whole again. He stepped into the pressed pants and strapped on a bulletproof Kevlar vest. He buttoned the black shirt over the vest and pinned a gold star to his chest.

He limped into the other room and loaded the shotguns with 12-gauge slug loads. He ran the action and chambered rounds in each. He took the AR-15 clips and slammed one into each weapon and pulled back the slides and they were ready to roll. He pressed six hollow points into the .44 magnum and then spun the stainless steel cylinder and it hummed with a smooth-ticking rattle. He thrust the revolver into the holster on his right hip. A fully arrayed gunbelt: handcuffs, pepper spray, nightstick.

A few minutes later he exited the building and stocked the cruiser with two AR-15s, three combat shotguns, and a black sea bag with boxes of shells and loaded clips and a back up Kevlar vest. There was no coming back and so he was taking all of it with him. All of it.

He sat in the driver's seat and paused.

One last touch.

He set gold-rimmed aviator shades onto his bruised face and looked at himself in the rearview mirror. Big metallic fly-eyes and remorseless as a biblical locust.

Yeah. That'll do. If you ain't a cop then there never was one.

He backed up the cruiser and turned onto the empty blacktop, the road open to the horizon. It was just past 7:30 in the morning.

40.

SHERIFF CALEB HUDDLED OVER his coffee and pancakes in a booth near the back of the truck stop diner. A big cop breakfast for a big cop day—his first one on the job. His current persona was unrecognizable from the longhaired and bearded woodsman of yesterday.

He figured he had about eight hours before the heat came down on him. And by that time, he would either be dead or wounded and dying in some gully out in the badlands or his mission would be complete.

There were no local police in the conventional sense. There was the sheriff and the state. He reckoned if there was an emergency that demanded local law enforcement this day, well, the sheriff would never respond and eventually the state police would be called to resolve the matter. Once resolved, the state cops would start investigating where the hell the sheriff was—hours would have passed by then. And where would the state police begin their investigation? First, they'd go to the station and find it empty. Then they'd ride out to Gates's house and find it empty as well. Then Sparks. Same thing. Cell phone calls unanswered. He'd torched their phones along with their corpses. There would be nothing but utter bewilderment. When would they wander down the back road to the wood yard and find the burned ruins of his place? And why would they? Then they would need to identify the bodies that were incinerated to charcoal and ash. Moreover, he had removed the transponder from the cruiser. It could not be tracked. He had a small window of time unless he was very unlucky or did something really stupid. And if he survived, well, he'd worry about the consequences and what to do next with his life, if he even chose to go on living. For now, it was all about the mission. It was about not running. The mission was omnipotent.

Brooding behind his aviator sunglasses, the metallic surface reflected the world around him. His pancakes were buttermilk and the syrup had soaked the bacon. He took a strip into his mouth and chewed the salty sweet pork without taking his eyes off the four men on the other side of the diner, the true nature of his presence. They had been remarkably easy to find and when he walked past them into the diner they had barely noticed him, only that a lawman had entered. But what did they have to worry? As far as they knew, their boss owned the law in this desolate backwater, operated with impunity.

They might have noticed his limp but they never made the connection, if they had noticed it at all.

The waitress approached with a pot of coffee and refilled his mug.

"Can I please have another stack of pancakes ma'am?" Caleb asked.

"Long day ahead?"

"Real long."

"You new?"

"You could say that."

"Where are Gates and Sparks?"

"Retired."

"Both of them?"

"Yes."

"How do you like that?" she said. "They been coming here for twenty years, well, Sheriff Gates has, and don't even have the courtesy to let me know."

"I guess it's a sign of the times."

"I guess it is."

He ate the second stack of pancakes and drank his coffee and when the four men exited he exited right behind them.

♍

THEY PILED INTO A mud-caked Chevy Tahoe and pulled onto the interstate. He let a car pass in front of him and followed about a half mile behind. The blacktop was wide open and he could see across the basin of the broad valley for thirty or forty miles in every direction.

They traveled north for fifteen minutes, passing beneath the high bluffs of Ghost Ranch and the ancient road to the Monastery of Christ in the Desert, and then turned onto a rutted strip that cut across barren mesa land with columns of melting clay hoodoos.

He pulled onto the shoulder and watched the Tahoe until it disappeared over a rise. Then he turned onto the rutted strip and rolled through scrubland and scattered stands of pinyon and bur oak until he was looking at a doublewide trailer below an escarpment with an apron of cedar trees.

The Tahoe was parked out front next to a Ford Taurus and a Honda Pilot. He watched the trailer for twenty minutes from the front seat of the cruiser. The curtains were drawn shut on every window and nothing moved outside.

He watched the dashboard clock and listened to the police radio. The land was quiet and so was the radio.

And as he sat there listening to the soft morning wind through the dry grass outside his mind wandered into strange and commonplace things. He thought about how long he'd been alive and that his heart had beaten every second since then, and before then, in the womb when it had miraculously formed and pulsed for the first time, whole, the rhythm and sound of his genesis, and how this had continued and never ceased throughout his life, and how all of his organs had never failed him, not for a moment, ever, not even when he was unconscious after the blast and in a coma, unaware whether he was alive or dead, pure sleepless oblivion, but his body knew that he was still alive and never failed him. His heart had never failed him, not even for a beat.

He unbuttoned his shirt and slid his right hand underneath the bulletproof vest and tried to feel the life inside his breastplate. He sat there and listened, straining his ears. He readjusted his hand and thought that perhaps his heart had stopped, this one time when he had actually tried to feel it working without instruction. He listened a while longer for the elusive beat and then brought two fingers up to his neck and felt his pulse in his carotid artery. His heart hadn't failed him. It was still there.

He saw Lelah and his brother lifeless in the shovelhead and then he saw himself washing the blood from their faces and then he was burying them in the earth again. His breathing went shallow and his heart thundered in his ears. Every muscle and joint seized up and he managed to hold back a sudden convulsion, a fit of wailing. He was more alive now than he'd ever been and riddled with more sorrow than he'd ever known, exhausted and supercharged at the same time.

"Stop thinking," he said. "And go."

He put the cruiser in drive and rolled up to the trailer and parked. He killed the engine and stepped out with the shotgun and walked casually up to the porch.

He pulled back the screen and knocked on the white vinyl door. To his right, someone slid back the curtain and looked out the window. Then the door was ripped open. An average sized man with a big attitude stared down at him from the raised entryway. He wore jeans and a blue Pendleton buttoned to the collar.

Caleb recognized his face from the night before.

"This is private property," the man said.

"You think I give a shit?"

"What?"

"I said: 'You think I give a shit?'"

This paused the man. He responded with the only cliché he could think of. "You got a warrant?"

"Don't need one."

Caleb swung the shotgun level with his hip and fired a slug into the man. The gut shot hurled the man back inside the trailer where he crashed onto a folding table and twisted onto the floor, broken and dying.

Inside the trailer there was a yelling panic. The clatter of men scrambling and common objects knocked over.

Caleb pumped the shotgun and stood on the porch. The window curtain to his right was pulled open again. Huge eyes stared out at him for the briefest of moments until Caleb fired a slug into the center of the man's face and the man disappeared in a plume of blood mist and head fragments and shards of glass.

Caleb chambered another shell and stepped inside. On his left a man turned to run toward a back room when Caleb fired and the man crashed to the floor and skidded dead on his belly like a walrus on ice.

Another man jumped up from a table with a wad of hundred dollar bills in his hand. A money-counting machine in front of him.

Piles of cash. He reached for a pistol on the table and got hold of it. He tried to raise it but Caleb shot him first. Thousands of dollars exploded into the air and then fluttered to the carpet.

The bathroom door rattled ajar.

Caleb whipped around and fired. The slug tore apart the flimsy paneling and there was the impact of a body slumping onto the toilet and then onto the floor. Then a choking gurgle. Then quiet.

He stood and listened as smoke curled out of the shotgun barrel, the room thick with the acrid tang of burnt gunpowder.

He waited there for several moments and watched the smoke dissipate until he heard the floor creak in the back of the trailer and turned toward the sound with the butt of his shotgun grooved into the front of his shoulder.

He ducked.

A man fired two shots at him with an automatic pistol from the end of the hallway and then darted out the back door. Caleb held his fire and limped down the hallway and stood just inside the shaded interior. He could hear the man's fleeing footsteps and gasping breaths across the prairie grass as he made for the safety of the cedar trees a hundred yards distant.

Caleb leaned the shotgun against the wall and drew the .44 magnum from his hip.

Using the doorframe to steady his arm, Caleb placed the fleeing man in the stainless gunsights, the neon orange bead on the front sight dead in the middle and flush with the rear white. The man turned and fired a panicked shot over his shoulder that cracked twenty feet overhead when Caleb squeezed the trigger.

The hollow-point ripped into the man's spine and tore a bloody exit out his chest and he face-planted into the spidery roots of a cedar tree.

Caleb holstered the magnum and limped back down the hallway.

He stepped over to the money table and picked up a cell phone and scrolled through it. There were no entries in the address book. There were some recent phone calls but no names associated with them. Just the ten digits. There was no music or photos and he figured that the phone was used only for business and then only for a short time and then discarded. He continued searching the device and found a phone tracker app and opened it. Three red dots lit up in the valley. One red dot indicated his current location, the device in his hand. The second red dot appeared to be moving down I-84. And the third red dot was stationary at the end of a long dirt road between I-84 and I-96 about fifteen miles from where he was at right now. He figured it was a residence. He was familiar with the area but could not recall ever being down that particular dirt road. He'd hunted in the hills above when he was younger and remembered that there were a few scattered ranches in the valley below.

He looked around for something to write with. He found a pen and wrote down the address on a hundred dollar bill from the table and then set the phone back down where he found it.

He tucked the bill in his shirt pocket. He grabbed his shotgun from the wall and headed out the front door and drove the patriotic cruiser down the rutted track and across the scrubland and out to the blacktop.

41.

LOCKA-BLOCKA-BLOCKA BURPED THE EXHAUST pipes as the two men idled stripped-down choppers beside the smoldering carcass.

The trailer had been reduced to a twisted, charred, reeking mess of worthless debris. Wisps of gunky smoke rose from the remnant flames hidden deep in the heart where unexhausted material lay burning.

For a moment the men questioned if they were at the right place. The only thing they recognized from the night before were the piles of firewood.

One of them kick-standed his bike and walked over to the woodshed. He looked around and then walked back over to his bike and climbed into the saddle.

"No sign of anyone," he said into his phone. "The whole place is burned to hell. Not sure what to make of it." He listened. "We're on our way."

From atop the mesa Caleb watched them through the windshield of the cruiser.

I guess my twelve hours are up, he said.

He watched them ride back down the driveway and turn west onto the blacktop. He shifted the cruiser into drive and pulled slowly down the ranch road. He would catch up with them soon enough.

And he did.

He saw them up ahead on the road like wheeled apparitions across the rippling vapors of the desert. Shovelhead full-throater bucket rattlers with ape hangers and bazooka pipes, cherry bombs sparking hot dragon breath on down the squealing asphalt, real diamond-tumbling rumble machines, coarse putrid grease metal and rough leather, jagged steel chains and flare whip pom-poms.

Blocka-Blocka-Blocka-Blocka-Blocka-Blocka-Blocka.

He floored the cruiser and the augmented ponies under the hood hurtled him along at 110 miles an hour, sucking up the road, the broken yellow lines streaking under the chassis in speedy yellow blinks.

They saw the sheriff's cruiser approaching rapidly in their rearview mirrors and thought little of it. Only: *do they paint every fucking cop car in the flag around here?*

The patriotic cruiser slowed and then stalked behind them, ten feet from grille to chopper tire, a soulless death-machine of the windswept mesa land, gliding at an easy sixty-five miles an hour.

The choppers rode on the metallic surface of Caleb's sunglasses, thundering across the liquid mirror world within and the hot asphalt without. They were all he saw. A close-up in his eyes. A psychedelic image from a seventies grindhouse flick burned into the celluloid frames shuttering through his mind. Two bikers alone on an empty road out west and Johnny Law coming up behind them. Trouble in front. Trouble in back.

He rolled down the passenger window and gassed the cruiser and pulled alongside the choppers. They were riding abreast.

BLOCKA-BLOCKA-BLOCKA.

They glanced over and didn't know what to make of him driving in the empty stretch of oncoming traffic.

Sheriff Caleb smiled behind the aviator sunglasses and raised the shotgun off the front seat and rested the barrel on the open window space. The rider nearest him saw the shotgun and looked blankly at it. Then the shotgun barrel flamed and blew him out of the saddle where he flopped and flailed and broke apart on the blacktop. His chopper fishtailed and highsided and then shattered, littering both lanes of the road and the grassy shoulder with chrome accessories and fractured steel. All this took about a second or two.

The remaining rider tried to brake—but he didn't have time before Caleb shot him as well. The rider and his chopper launched off the side of the road and down into a red rock ravine where the bike collided with the bottom of an arroyo. The forks and front tire catapulted from the wreck and the riderless chopper continued to twist and cartwheel across the scorched clay.

Caleb drifted back across the yellow lines into the northbound lane and headed up the desolate stretch of highway.

Five miles ahead he approached a stop sign where the road came to a T. He turned left and headed north. In the distance he could see a vehicle parked on the shoulder. There was a woman standing beside it. She waved at him for help. But he drove past her.

"Don't even think about," he said. "Don't go getting caught up in something extra."

He watched her in the rearview mirror. She was alone on the empty road and he figured she'd been there for some time and would be for a while longer. He wondered who would eventually stop and help her and who had already passed her by. He watched her grow tiny and drop her waving hand to her side and give up.

"You are one stupid man," he said. "Watch this come back and bite you in the ass."

He turned the cruiser around and drove back toward her and then crossed the centerline and parked behind her car. He got out and walked over to her. The woman was round and short, very short, under five feet. He guessed that she was in her early fifties, about the same age as his mother if she were still alive.

"*Gracias,*" she said and smiled with great respect, clasping her hands in prayer and bowing to him. "*Muchas gracias.*"

Her two front teeth were silver and she had the appearance of an indigenous person from Central America.

"*¿Habla inglés?*" he asked.

"*Nada.*"

"*Mi español es poco,*" he said. "*¿Cómo es la problema?*"

"*Gasolina.*"

He thought about the situation here and what he could live with. He thought about what kind of man he was, and that he would never stop being the man he believed that he should be, even if he only had a few hours to live. *You are one hardheaded fool,* he told himself. *A goddamn fool.*

"*Venga aquí,*" he said, motioning toward the cruiser. "I'll give you a ride."

The center of her smile was a glinting silver square and she said, "*Un momento por favor,*" and rolled up the windows to her car and locked the doors and hurried over to him with a small black purse clutched across her chest with both arms.

He opened the passenger door for her and she climbed inside. She looked at the shotgun and the AR-15 in the back. From the way her curious eyes roved cautiously around the interior he figured she'd never been in a police car before.

He climbed behind the wheel and reached across the seat and pulled the seatbelt from over her shoulder and buckled her in. She was so short that her worn sneakers dangled above the floor and from behind one could not tell that there was a passenger in the vehicle. He put the cruiser in drive and pulled back onto the highway.

She set her purse in her lap and folded her hands atop it. They rode in silence for a few minutes and then she began speaking to him in Spanish, at first haltingly and then easing into what she had to say. She was soft-spoken and her mannerisms were humble and deferential. He figured she was telling him the story of how she came to run out of gas alongside the road but there seemed to be a great deal more to it than he would have expected. He thought he heard her voice crack a few times when she said the name Edgar and he thought nothing of the name until she removed a wallet-size photo from her purse and handed it to him.

"*Es mi hijo,*" she said. "My son."

It was the same Edgar that had come to visit them at the wood yard and he sadly concluded that Edgar had not come back home the evening that he had left. Given all that had happened he was not surprised to hear that he was missing. He did not know the how but he guessed at the why. He lied to her and said that he did not know him.

"*No sabe. No sabe.*"

He gathered from her story that she was up here looking for him and he felt terrible pity for her. He knew that her son was never coming home.

Fifteen minutes later they turned into a gas station. He handed her two twenty-dollar bills and told her in broken Spanish to *pagar el mercado por gasolina. ¿Comprende?* She nodded and said, "*Comprendo.*" Then he spoke in English and tried to explain to her that she also needed to purchase a container to store the gasoline. After about thirty seconds of the charade she said that she understood and went inside.

He would've gone inside and paid for the gasoline and the jerrican himself but he was pretty sure he knew the guy working the counter and didn't want to be recognized. About a minute later the woman emerged with a jerrican and he filled it with gasoline at the pump with his back turned to the cashier and they drove back down the highway.

He thought that he had never seen anyone so appreciative as her.

They drove across the low scrubland and neither of them said a word for several minutes. The road twisted out of a gorge and climbed a hill where the land flattened out along a broad plain.

She touched his arm and he turned and she was handing him a tissue. At first he was confused and then she touched her cheek just below her eye and pointed to his and said, *"Lágrimas."*

He felt his face and it was wet with tears. He took the tissue from her and said gracias and wiped his skin but the tears kept falling until they reached her car and he stepped out. He took the jerrican from the trunk and walked over to her car and pulled the gas cap and started filling the tank.

He watched the road in both directions. In the opposite lane two trucks crested the rise a mile distant and behind them followed a dark sedan. He studied the sedan and what he thought was something on the roof. After a few more seconds he made out the emergency lights of a state trooper.

The trucks passed and the trooper slowed and then turned across the centerline and parked behind the cruiser.

This is gonna bite you in the ass, Caleb said to himself. *You are one stupid son of a bitch.*

He could see the trooper speaking into his radio. When the trooper was done he stepped out of the vehicle and approached on the grass shoulder. Caleb studied him and the trooper smiled and stopped at the rear bumper of the woman's car.

"How's it going?" said the trooper.

"Just fine," Caleb said.

The trooper turned to the woman and nodded. "Ma'am."

She raised her hand in greeting and smiled. "*Buenos días.*"

Caleb figured the trooper couldn't have been a day older than twenty-five. His face was baby-skin shaved and there wasn't a stain of living on his white teeth.

"I reckoned you had it all covered," said the trooper. "I just wanted to stop and introduce myself. Name's Taylor Skaggs. Just got hired on last week and I'm heading up to the Pueblo to introduce myself to the tribal authorities up there."

"Nice to meet you, Taylor."

"It's my off day but I figured I should take the opportunity to acquaint myself with the county and some of its residents and such. I spoke with Sheriff Gates yesterday and told him I was coming on up. Is he nearby?"

"He retired."

"Retired? Get out of here. I was looking forward to meeting him. He didn't say anything about retiring yesterday."

"I'm just messing with you…rookie."

The trooper chuckled. "Tell me about it. The troopers have been messing with me all week. I met a group of them for lunch yesterday. They were ordering all kinds of food. Some of them even ordered things to go on top of their meal, but I didn't think much of it. So after we finished eating, one by one they walked outside to make a phone call, or have a cigarette, or disappeared into the back to use the restroom, and before I knew it, they'd all drove off and stuck me with a three hundred dollar lunch bill. You believe that?"

"Cops."

"No kidding." The trooper chuckled again and searched for something more to say. Then he remembered. "Seriously, though, is Sheriff Gates nearby?"

"He's on the other side of the valley, about thirty miles from here."

"Thirty miles?" He looked around and thought about it.

"Give him a call," Caleb said. "You got his cell number?"

The trooper thought some more. He labored over the decision.

"That's all right," he said. "I'll just see him next time."

The trooper leaned forward and squinted. Caleb thought he might be looking for a nametag on his uniform but he wasn't wearing one. The trooper smiled and his posture hunched slightly in an act of request. He pointed. "Hey, uh, I hate to ask, but can you spare a dip? I forgot my can at the house."

Caleb looked down at his shirt and remembered that his can was in his pocket, the unmistakable circular outline pressing against the fabric. He fished out the can and tossed it to the trooper.

"Keep it," Caleb said. "You got a long drive."

"You sure?" He pinched out a chew.

"I got a fresh can in the car."

"Well, I really appreciate it." The trooper tucked the tobacco in his bottom lip and slid the can in his back pocket. He spit and flicked the shavings from his fingers. "I'll buy you lunch one of these days—just you though. My wife is gonna shit when she sees the credit card bill. Take it easy."

"Have a good one."

The trooper turned and took a step toward his vehicle and then swiveled back around.

"I never got your name," he said.

"I never gave it, Rookie."

The trooper smiled and shrugged. He had been fucked with all week and this was just a little bit more of the fucking. The guy had given him a can of chew and he figured that was welcoming enough for one day.

"See you around," the trooper said over his shoulder.

"I doubt it."

The trooper chuckled again and then waved to the woman, who had been watching the exchange.

"Good day, ma'am," he said.

"Buenos días."

The trooper climbed into his vehicle and turned across the centerline and accelerated north on the interstate.

The jerrican was now empty.

Caleb jiggled the spout and the last drops trickled into the tank. He looked over at the woman and her careworn face. She was staring down at the side of the road and shaking her head and talking to herself. He figured she must be heartsick and terrified but she had somehow found the courage to drive up here and search for her son, a tiny woman who spoke no English in a country that wasn't hers to be born in, a country that was alien and at times hostile to her for being from somewhere else. She lifted her head and stared out at the inscrutable landscape as if lost, and he could only suppose that she was wondering where she would even start to look for him, searching the vastness with her eyes and calling out with her soul for her son to tell her where he was out there. But only her echo would return to her breast. For the rest of her days the nights would be long and the sunrise would bring sorrow, and always, she would be wondering.

You know what you gotta do and she ain't a part of it, he said to himself. *So stop thinking about her.*

He placed the jerrican in her trunk and told her that he must be going. He wished her luck and apologized that he could not help her anymore right now. She thanked him many times and tried to offer him money from her purse but he said no. He waited for her car to start and watched it sputter and chug away and disappear over the rise before heading back up the road.

42.

A N HOUR LATER MARLO stepped inside the trailer and surveyed the one-sided aftermath. Blood spattered walls and dead men, the flies planting their eggs in the drying eyeballs and mouths, the oozing 12-gauge wounds like meaty potholes, cash tumbling across the floor from the wind blowing in through the open doors and gunshot windows.

He had three men with him. One of them felt the need to editorialize.

"I knew it. We should've killed that cripple right away. I don't want to play armchair quarterback, but I fucking knew it. Gimps, retards, mongoloids, they're all slick. Need to be in order to survive. Their parents fill out paperwork, know how to game the system. Or else they die. It's Darwin."

Marlo was not listening. He squatted and picked up a spent shotgun shell. He brought it to his nose and smelled the discharged gunpowder.

"And that fucker gamed us," the man continued. "We should've killed him. I'd say he's up by at least two touchdowns right now."

Marlo stepped between a pair of bodies and over to the table. There was a loose stack of hundred dollar bills sitting beside the Ribao currency counter. He set the stack in the top tray and the machine rifled the money through. The green digital display read:

100. He reached into a plastic bag of red rubber bands and snapped one around the stack.

The man continued to carry on with his side of things. Marlo still hadn't heard a word. But now he did.

"I sure hope you didn't let the guy live because you thought he was cute or some other weird gay homo reason like that."

Marlo lifted his chin and swiveled his head. His right hand drew up from his side.

"Earl?" he said.

Earl turned. "Yeah?"

A gunblast shook the trailer and Earl dropped to the floor with a heavy whump.

Marlo lowered his Glock.

"Every organization, no matter what the profession, has at least one inveterate dumbass with the special talent for saying the wrong thing at the wrong time. Earl here, was just that man."

♁

THEY LEFT THE TRAILER with the money and the Ribao currency counter and locked the bodies inside. They would dispose of them later. They drove down the dirt road and padlocked the gate where it met the pavement at the end of the property.

Marlo sat in the backseat with his handgun resting on his thigh.

You never would have made this mistake twenty years ago, he said to himself. *Not even ten.*

He had underestimated the woodchopper and reproached himself for the miscalculation. Things had been too good for too long. He hadn't faced any existential threat, or any threat of considerable magnitude, in quite some time. He had remained at relative peace, his operations that is, for a longer period than he ever could have hoped for in this business. He thought that perhaps he had become complacent.

Well you have, more than a little. The proof is here right now. It's boiling across the valley. Like the kings of old, decadence has crept into the court, and now it's laughing all around you in naked fountains of flesh and gold.

The formative emotions and drives, the rapacious lust, the attitude that had propelled him to his princely throne seemed to be waning. If he was honest with himself, truly, deeply, philosophically honest, if he searched his acquired knowledge and erudition, the thing that he wanted most now was irreconcilable with the present. A rational and honest inquiry would ring back the truth, unalloyed and undeniable.

You can't have both in this business. You know that much.

But why had he underestimated the woodchopper? He already knew the answer.

For the first time in recent memory he did not know what his next move was.

The thought almost provoked laughter in him. He did not harbor any personal resentment toward his adversary. Nor was he seething with any particular anger or outrage. They were simply antagonistic forces converging in a fable of their own making.

In a dream. In an illusion.

And one of them had to win.

One of them had to prevail.

He puzzled over his next move and could only draw a straightforward conclusion.

He made a phone call and without disclosing the details of the present situation he merely asked for some friends to come northward and fish with him on his property. The man on the other end informed him that the boat would leave this evening and that the fishermen should arrive early tomorrow morning. That was the best he could do on such short notice.

Marlo ended the call and decided to go home and wait there.

He did not know where the woodchopper was at the moment or where he would show up next. But the woodchopper had shown formidable intelligence and bloodthirsty skill thus far. He had shown that he was deserving of his military medals and trinkets.

Marlo stared out the window at the white jet trails traversing the sky and felt vaguely indisposed. He felt ungrounded and unconnected to the planet's energy. He felt outside the vortex. When he got home he would close his eyes and light some incense and meditate on the sound of the water curling over the smooth rocks and rebalance himself.

It had been many years since he had been to war.

When the men arrived in the morning they would set forth and hunt down the woodchopper.

43.

HE WAS STANDING ON the rim of a great promontory looking over the rusted country that fell below and beyond and he searched the gradations of color in its weatherworn statues of rock and the arid plains drawing to the horizon. He asked the land, would it know him when he walked upon its ancient sands millennia from now and his spirit soared above and would the land trace his memory and embrace his homecoming or would he only be forgotten?

He told the land that he was its son and brother and the image vanished and Lelah was standing before him holding their naked child in a landscape unfamiliar to him. Her eyes were closed and her hair was wet and slack and her face was bloodless. Her shoulders were slumped and her arms cradled the child but there was no life to her posture and when she opened her eyes to him they were the sunless waters of a lake entombed in the earth. When she spoke her words frosted the air.

"You were supposed to protect us," she said.

"I'm sorry."

"Why didn't you protect us?"

There was sadness infinite in her voice, infinite from a darkness that made no refuge for the lost.

"I'm sorry," he said. "So sorry."

He reached out to hold her and their naked child but she held out an arm to stop him and the arm was horribly longer than hers in life and he could not touch them.

"You promised," she said.

He fell to his knees before her and she stared down at him from the pits of her eyes that held no color, no forgiveness, only an angry sadness. He professed his love to her and told her that he was sorry again and again.

"You promised, Caleb."

"I know."

He stared at her and she was pulled backward with the child in her arms as if on an invisible current and the land around receded with her until he was on his knees alone in the darkness and the light where she had been standing was only a pinhole on the horizon and he heard her whisper from that great distance, "You promised us."

His eyes shot open and he was staring into sunlight. He couldn't remember how or when he had fallen asleep. For a moment he couldn't say where he was and what he was doing behind a rifle. His amnesia was total. He blinked and tried to gain his bearings. He could smell the familiar sagebrush and saw a whiptail lizard scamper down the face of a rock and then slide underneath. And then his memory came back to him and he knew where he was and what he was doing there.

It was now late in the afternoon and he was lying prone on a mesa several hundred feet above and two hundred yards to the east of the address he had written on the hundred dollar bill.

He peered through the riflescope and noted the adobe walls and the cactus garden and rows of cholla and then out to the pinyon stands to the north across a pocket of scorched grass and broken earth. He counted two men standing guard. They were posted at opposite ends of the compound. A tall and lean mestizo with shoulder length hair stood at the backdoor with an AK-47. From behind an outcropping of black lava talus the other guard watched the approach of the dirt road that wound through the saddle of mesas before spilling unseen into the prairieland.

Caleb repositioned the barrel of the AR-15 on his coat that was rolled up tight and resting on a flat rock. A natural bench as sturdy as one at the rifle range and only slightly less comfortable. He checked the crosswind and figured it about five to seven knots. He also figured that the high-velocity .223 round would cut through it just fine from this distance. Another hundred yards and he might need to recalibrate the rifle settings. He placed the mestizo in the crosshairs and exhaled and squeezed his right hand and the rifle recoiled. The man's upper body jolted from the silent punch of the bullet and his knees buckled and he fell without notice onto the ground.

Caleb tracked the crosshairs over the adobe walls and cactus garden and found the other guard squatting in the black lava talus and squeezed the trigger. The bullet struck the man in the center of his back and he tripped forward and flipped over the crown of the outcropping and rolled down the jagged talus to the base of the gravel driveway.

Caleb walked down the backside of the mesa where he had parked the cruiser in a pocket of mesquite. He set the AR-15 on the front seat and drove down the spine and concealed the cruiser inside the pinyon grove. The crosswind had picked up and it would help muffle his approach. He slung the AR-15 over his shoulder and lifted the chainsaw from the backseat and then walked through the trees and crouched low across the grassland toward the compound.

He came to the oaken backdoor and looked down at the man he'd just shot. He was still dead. He checked the brass doorknob. It was locked. He ripped on the starter cord to his chainsaw and the engine spit-fired exhaust. He revved the throttle and the grating scream roared through the compound.

Inside Marlo and his two surviving men were meditating in the lotus position on tatami mats in his new age Zendo. A trickle of water fell over mossy rocks into a pool with marbled orange and white koi. Votive candles and incense burned on a jade altarpiece. Over the last twenty minutes he had cleared his mind and felt reconnected again with the universal energy source, the powerful magnetic forces, the timeless and the perennial. He could feel the vortex streaming white light up through the crust of the earth and gathering in his navel and radiating out to his limbs. He could feel the reduction in the beta wave activity across his cerebral hemisphere and he felt at peace with his consciousness now.

And then the screeching howl of the chainsaw disrupted the meditative journey and Marlo's eyes took in the world again. He picked up an MP9 machine pistol from his tatami mat and he and his men left through different doors and vanished into the compound with rehearsed efficiency.

Caleb shredded through the round oaken door and kicked it open. He killed the throttle and slung the saw over his back. He shouldered his AR-15 and stalked down the hallway, his tactical training and combat experience resuming authority, guiding his actions with the unthinking precision of long conditioning. His eyes were blazing with the alertness that had kept him alive in the door-to-door battles that raged through Fallujah, alive and lucky, a hyper-alert intensity that injected so much adrenaline into your system that by the time the plunger had pressed into the bottom of the syringe a sublime calmness had taken hold, a blissfulness that gave over to the all-encompassing fear of death and, by giving over, dissolved the fear until later. He was there now. Only this was different. He didn't give a shit anymore. There was nothing to go home to.

He led with his weapon and crept into a room brightly decorated with Native American artwork. Standing in the corner was a seven-foot Kachina doll with a mask of some hybrid otherworldly creature, a buffalo man bred with a bitch alien. A headdress of eagle feathers. A long wooden staff in one hand and a yellow rattle made from a gourd in the other.

He swept the room. It was empty.

He crept down the hallway and into the mirrored dance studio. His reflection stretched to infinity on all four walls. Thousands of him. When he moved, they moved, a pantomime army of identicals.

The hardwood floor was polished and shiny.

When he was halfway across the studio he regretted entering the space. He tunneled his vision toward the open door on the other side and saw the man's shadow the instant before the man sprung into the doorway with an automatic rifle.

Caleb beat him to the trigger and shot the man in the kneecap and clavicle. The man fell with his hand clenched on his weapon, spraying bullets wildly like a field sprinkler—shattering the mirrored walls and blasting holes in the Sheetrock ceiling. One of the wild bullets pounded Caleb in the stomach and he was thrown backward onto the hardwood floor, gasping, the wind knocked out of him. Both men were now on the seat of their pants—Caleb got off a quick burst and the man's head snapped back and he wilted onto his side against the doorjamb and did not move.

Caleb checked his wound. His Kevlar vest had absorbed the bullet. Felt like a horse had kicked him. Damn it hurt.

He caught his breath and pushed himself up and continued across the studio, his footsteps crunching on the shards of mirror that now carpeted the hardwood floor.

He stepped over the dead man in the doorway and came to another hallway and then turned a corner into a lavish kitchen when another man popped up from behind a wooden chopping block. The man unloaded his machine pistol and Caleb ducked behind the counter as bullets clanged through pots and pans, punctured the refrigerator and oven, shattered crockery.

There was a momentary lull and a loud hissing from a ruptured cooling hose.

Caleb rose quickly and fired a three-round burst. Deft. Precise. Two of the bullets ripped holes into the man's neck. His gun fell from his hand and he clutched his throat. He tottered and rolled off the chopping block and onto the terracotta floor.

Caleb limped over to the man and finished him off with a double-tap.

He proceeded through the kitchen and down another tiled corridor decorated with art. Pools of track lighting illuminated the works. A Cindy Sherman Hall of Horrors occupied the first twenty feet. Framed on the wall an androgynous clown and a portrait of a hairy vagina oozing a string of sausages and he took another step forward and the track lights illuminated the torso of a mannequin with both male and female genitalia. He tried not to look at the objects and images to his left and his right but it was impossible not to. He took another step forward and there was a niche with a diorama of Satan sodomizing Christ over a crucifix and then a painting of a tree with hundreds of bodies hanging from their necks and then Pieter Brueghel's *The Triumph of Death* with a skeleton holding a sword over the head of a man kneeling in prayer and beside that Dürer's *Knight, Death, and the Devil* and then he saw Death pissing into a river and he wondered if the black walnut door at the end of the hallway was in fact the portal to Hell or the deranged sloping tunnel to some serial killer's playhouse.

Then music grew out of the overhead speakers, low and gradually rising. Caleb squeezed his memory. He recognized the goopy sweet song from his childhood.

It was Barney, the giggling purple dinosaur, leading his chorus of bribed children in a frenzy of love and big hugs and kisses. It was playing on a loop. Barney.

And he couldn't help but ask himself: *Where the fuck am I?*

On the other side of the black walnut door Marlo hummed along with Barney and the children, standing behind his retooled sixteenth-century naval cannon. It was aimed at the door and loaded with a coffee can of black powder and an eight-pound lead projectile. During the retooling process he had rifled the barrel so that he could fire more than just cannonballs. This modified update had deprived the instrument of its historical value, but he was only concerned with its entertainment value, not resale. And right now, specifically, its martial value, its value as a weapon. But perhaps the most appealing aspect of the retooling was that he could now fire the cannon without lighting a fuse. All he had to do now was pull a cord to ignite the powder and the cannon would fire near-simultaneously.

The cord was in his hand.

The Barney loop was motion-activated and so he knew about where Caleb was in relation to the door. A few steps further and *poof*—smithereens. Chop goes the woodchopper.

Caleb limped onward with his weapon tucked in his shoulder. He was tempted to fire a burst through the walnut door but he didn't want to reveal his position. He hadn't seen any security cameras in the house and figured his exact whereabouts to be a mystery. It never crossed his mind that the Barney loop was an ingenious trip wire of sorts.

He was almost within arm's reach of the doorknob. A few more steps. When his prosthetic leg betrayed him and the ankle joint made a loud metallic creak—and he instinctively dropped to the floor—

Just as Marlo heard the metallic creak and figured it was time for a glorious cannonade. He pulled the cord. The projectile exploded from the barrel with a colossal boom and the walnut door disintegrated in a chaos of sharp splinters. The cannon reared up and then crashed back down and broke the ceramic tiles beneath its wheels. The world shook with seismic force as the projectile rocketed down the length of the hallway, ripping the art off the walls and then blowing through the far adobe wall before tearing apart the kitchen and then plowing through several more walls and out the house where it buried itself a hundred yards beyond and hurled skyward a massive plume of red earth.

Splinters and plaster tinkled to the floor in comet trails. Pulverized Sheetrock and adobe dust choked the hallway. A hot cloud of black powder fumes swirled in the bedroom.

Marlo crouched with his MP9 pointed into the smoky havoc. He figured Caleb had been blown to wet fragments of flesh and bone but still he waited for the cloud to dissipate and confirm his suspicions.

But Caleb had not been destroyed. He was buried beneath the pile of rubble, his ears ringing, disoriented and reeling from the percussion, but very much alive. His throat was chalky and he couldn't swallow. He was on the verge of choking. He needed to cough and clear his windpipe but he knew better than to betray his position. He could last a few more seconds.

He figured he had better get up in one quick motion. If he attempted to wriggle out the sound of the rubble falling off him would provoke a flurry of gunfire that would surely kill him at this close range.

Better do it now. He's coming for you.

He placed his palms on the tile and pushed up and gained his feet in one muscular burst. He wobbled on the splintered two-by-fours and chunks of adobe and raised his weapon to fire.

Marlo heard the falling debris in the hallway and unloaded his machine pistol toward the sound, unable to see his intended target through the curtain of smoke and dust.

Caleb returned fire, hugged against the wall. The corridor flashed like lightning inside a cloud. A bullet grazed Caleb's shoulder and spit out a piece of flesh. He flinched momentarily but did not alter his attack. He emptied his clip and slammed in another and let off a quick volley and then held his fire. He still couldn't make out anything through the haze. But over the ringing in his ears he heard a door swing open and footsteps running across gravel. He touched his shoulder and probed the wound with his fingers. The bullet had torn more shirt than skin. It was little more than a hot scrape.

He limped over the debris and into the bedroom. Smoke funneled out the open back door and he saw an unarmed Marlo bound through the cactus garden and leap over a short adobe wall and disappear. On the tile floor he saw Marlo's machine pistol. The bottom of the clip was shattered. One of his shots must have struck the weapon and disabled it.

Marlo ran across the gravel turnabout and climbed into a Dodge Charger. A real customized beast, an extra 250 horses under the hood, a full-throated scorcher with a glasspack muffler. He turned over the engine and peeled down the dirt road. He opened the console and removed another MP9 machine pistol. He racked the weapon and chambered a 9mm round. "You got lucky," he said. "The woodchopper almost nailed you." But he reminded himself that he had always been on the lucky side of things, and with a little more, he might live to see the next lunar eclipse.

Caleb emerged from the house and limped across the property and into the grove of pinyon where he had parked the cruiser. He tossed the chainsaw onto the back seat and set the AR-15 upright in the gun rack and then hauled down the dirt road through the wake of dust from Marlo's vehicle.

A half-mile ahead Marlo bucked and rocked down the rutted road with both hands on the mahogany Grant banjo steering wheel, the ferocious eight pistons sucking fuel into the cylinders and the glasspack blowing, the chassis bottoming out on the ridges and water-guttered dips, sliding around the turns, straightening the wheel as the tires found their grip again.

He sped underneath the mesa cliffs and the world opened up and he bolted across a straightaway through the parched grassland stretching in every direction. He motored toward a small bump in the dirt road over a corrugated pipe and launched into the air for several moments before landing with considerable force and bottoming out again, hurling chunks of dirt and gravel, bouncing and rocking and then regaining traction. The engine nearly redlined as he gassed the Charger ahead for the asphalt road.

Caleb motored through the swirling dust and the saddle of mesas when the land opened up again and he could see Marlo's car far ahead and below him, throwing up a rooster tail across the prairie, the wind blowing hard now and clearing the path ahead. For the sheer fuck of it he hit the sirens and lights and the desolation rang with flashing color and discord.

Marlo approached the vacant two-lane highway and downshifted into second with a loud thrust of RPMs. As the suspension lowered and compressed, the car felt like it was suddenly pushed into the ground. The tires spun on the asphalt and spit chunks of melted rubber, smoking through the turn. He spun the banjo steering wheel hard to his right and the muscular machine fishtailed. The backend whipped from side to side and then the positraction applied power to the other wheel, righting the vehicle, straight and true. He slammed on the gas and motored ahead.

Caleb wheeled off the dirt road and made a beeline across the grassland for the Charger now speeding down the asphalt. The cruiser bucked and jolted, the grassland far bumpier than it had looked through the windshield. He plowed through the barbed wire fence and made the road, dragging behind him a tangle of posts and wires. The posts tumbled and cracked about and flailed and leapt into the air off the asphalt and eventually the wire tangle tore loose.

The open road stretched to the distance, a black vein rippling in the heat.

He was closing on the Charger. He had the gas pedal pinned to the floor and it was now a race between manufacturers.

Less than fifty yards separated them. He raised the .44 magnum and thrust his hand out the window and fired down the highway. Flames shot from the muzzle as the roaring wind beat down the aftersmoke.

Marlo's rear window shattered and he ducked long after the slug buried into the passenger seat headrest. He eased on the gas and lifted his machine pistol from between his legs and fired over his shoulder. Bullets hammered the cruiser's hood, a blistering snake trail in the red, white, and blue paint.

Marlo jerked the wheel and rammed the side of the cruiser.

Caleb and his vehicle were knocked across the road and onto the gravel shoulder. The backend slid out and he thought for a moment that the car would flip. He steered into the turn and the tires caught and he was back on the asphalt before he had time to realize how close he had just come to losing it.

They continued exchanging gunfire at three-digit speed while ramming each other with their vehicles when their front bumpers hooked together and they veered off the road suddenly, interlocked and bound as one, tires blowing out from the collision with the uneven ground and excessive speed and then the cars flipped and rolled and thrashed about in a maelstrom of sky, ground, sky, shattered glass and brass shell casings and dirt and gravel and small stones clanking around like change in a dryer and their arms and bodies at the mercy of centrifugal destruction, the smell of leaking gasoline and burned rubber, engine oil, metal twisting, screeching, the vehicles dismembering and finally coming to a violent rest, overturned and mangled beyond repair.

44.

THIRTEEN AND A HALF seconds later Marlo regained consciousness. He was curled in a ball against the passenger door, bejeweled with tiny cubes of jagged glass, hundreds of them in the folds of his clothes and in his hair. He squinted and the cubes cut into the creases of skin around his eyes. His head was still in motion. He tried to find a point to focus on and stop the spinning. He searched the ground outside and found a gopher hole a few feet from where he had crashed and stared into its dark entrance. He wondered if anything was living in there when a furry head with two racing eyeballs popped out and then darted back inside.

Flames were kindling underneath the buckled hood and he could taste the malignant fumes of burning paint and motor oil. The hot discharge nearly torched his lungs. He coughed, gagged, hacked, and squeezed out of the shattered passenger window onto the soft earth. He pushed himself up, but only with his right hand. Something was severely wrong with his left. He tottered and looked for a weapon. The 9mm pistol from his console had been ejected and was now on the dashboard. He reached inside and took hold of it.

Where was the woodchopper?

Marlo crouched and stepped around his car and tried to see into the overturned cruiser, which had come to rest about thirty feet away. But the cruiser's roof was caved in and the greasy black smoke issuing from it made it impossible for him to see inside the cab. He needed to move closer.

♣

IT TOOK CALEB A full three seconds longer than Marlo to reopen his eyes. When he did, he gradually realized that he was hanging upside down from his seat belt. His nose was bleeding and dripping into his eyes and his head was whirling in the after-flash of a concussion. He saw flames spurting from the ruptured fuel line and one of the front tires was on fire and dripping gobs of molten rubber onto the wheel well. He was confused at how he had come to this place, hanging upside down in a demolished vehicle, but when he peered through the spider-webbed windshield and saw Marlo's feet approaching on the ceiling of his vision, he remembered all.

He spotted the .44 magnum a few feet away on the interior roof and grabbed the weapon. He steadied his wobbly aim on Marlo's legs and fired.

The bullet tore into Marlo's thigh. He dropped to a knee and fired a three round burst into the smoke and flames and then limped quickly behind his overturned vehicle for cover. He examined his wounds. A heavy flow of blood leaked from the bullet hole on his thigh, a direct hit through the meaty center. His left forearm was fractured and bleeding where a splinter of bone had stabbed through the skin some time during the wreck. He tried to make a fist with his left hand but it was as worthless as a paralyzed claw.

Caleb unclipped his seatbelt and crashed onto his face and rolled onto his shoulder. His head flashed again and he slid across the interior roof and kicked out the back window and pulled himself out. He crawled behind the car and craned his neck around the rear fender when—

Marlo did the same and fired from behind his.

Caleb returned fire, each man ducking, shooting, trying to find a clear shot. The flames eating away at the vehicles would soon push both of them out into the open.

Marlo stood and fired two rounds over the top of his front wheel. He tried to fire a third and the gun went *click*. He tossed the empty 9mm and limped off into the prairie.

For several moments Caleb crouched in the safety of the wreckage. He crawled to the far end of the cruiser to get a better angle. He rose up, ready to shoot a burst, and saw Marlo hobbling away. He steadied the stainless steel magnum with both hands, his left elbow resting on the chassis for support, but his vision was still shaky. It felt as though his pupils were slightly bouncing. He could feel his head swelling.

Marlo was moving out of range.

Caleb pulled the trigger and the bullet sailed wide and to the right. He took a deep breath and tried to steady his vision once more and slow his heart rate. He opened the magnum's cylinder. He had one shot left. He took another long inhale and dropped the sights onto Marlo's back and closed his hand around the trigger. But again the bullet missed the mark and kicked up a spout of dust way beyond.

He holstered the magnum and looked inside the cruiser for another weapon. The chainsaw lay on the floor, flames swirling around the blade, the burning upholstery hissing like a tar roofing kettle. He thrust his hand inside and yanked the chainsaw from the mouth of the fire.

He drop-started the saw and revved the throttle and took off across the prairie.

Marlo limped ahead. There was no place to go but the endless grassland. A profusion of blood spilled from the wound on his thigh and he was clutching it with his hand in a failed attempt to stanch the flow. He figured that the bullet had pierced his femoral artery and if he didn't tie a makeshift tourniquet right away he would soon drift into unconsciousness and sleep forever.

He could hear the chainsaw stalking him.

Panting, chest heaving, unable to acquire the necessary oxygen to propel his muscles forward, Marlo dropped to one knee and then the other.

No more four-leaf clovers, he said to himself, *no more rabbits' feet*.

He rolled onto his elbows with his legs sprawled in front of him and faced his approaching demise. An all-encompassing mood of resignation overtook him and he felt peacefully at ease. He was floating now on the sea, far-off, a tropical nowhere land with serene waves and birds of paradise. What he'd seen. What he'd done in his years in the exotic trade. The continents traveled and profited and slaughtered. The men he'd loved and the fortunes he'd made. The war always comes back around, doesn't it? And now he faced the reckoning with little discomfort. He accepted his fate with the conviction of his creed. He had lived the way he wanted to live. He had lived by no one else's prescription but his own.

The woodchopper limped into his line of sight and filled the space in front of him, a towering giant against the cloudless sky. Marlo smiled up at him and simply nodded.

With neither speech nor fanfare Caleb descended on Marlo's neck with the screaming blade and sawed off his head.

45.

E TOOK THE HEAD by the scalp and carried it dripping through the prairie dusk across the two-lane highway and up the dirt road in the darkening night and back to the compound where he nailed the head to the front door with a steel mallet and a rebar stake through its mouth.

He grabbed the AK-47 from the guard he shot earlier and limped inside. He found a mahogany humidor on the counter at the bar and lit himself a cigar with a torch lighter. He had not turned on any of the house lights and in the darkness the jet flamed blue. The cigar had a sweet aftertaste and its smoke perfumed the rooms and unspooled silken threads from its smoldering core. Many of the rooms had windows from floor to ceiling and the moonlight casting inside helped illuminate his exploration. In the darker rooms the cigar cherry floated through the night like some distant horseback traveler with a lantern. Outside the prairie and mesas were silent and there was no sound beyond the windows and adobe walls that held him inside.

He stared into the lonely country, blowing smoke in easy rolling waves against the window that swirled under and around in pinwheeling eddies, and he remembered when he and Lelah had gone camping in the mountains when he first came home from the hospital and how they sat around the glowing firelight, the warmth playing across their faces, she nestled in his arms, and how they spoke nothing for several hours for there was nothing to say that their union beneath the night sky didn't already say in a silence more eloquent and profound. They shared a sleeping bag and made love under the cool mountain and in the morning they awoke to a blood orange sunrise and drank coffee around the fire and he held her again in his arms. He said that it was good to be home and she said, "I know."

He brought the cigar to his mouth and blew the smoke against the window.

He walked over to a rustic pinewood table with a stone mortar and pestle centerpiece. He lifted the pestle out of the mortar and set it on the table. Then he picked up the mortar and lobbed it underhand through the window and the glass shattered and fell like a sheet of ice from a glacier.

He tried to count the hours since he had last slept but his faculties were shot and he figured he had been awake for no less than sixty. He wanted to lie down and rest, sleep for days, but he knew that he had to keep moving. He could sleep soon but not here.

He limped across the dance studio and the mirror shards crunched under his boots and he continued toward the sound of trickling water and found himself in a meditation room of sorts. He looked down into the pool at the marbled orange and white koi, their tails waving in and out of the pale moonbeam from the skylight.

He blew a cloud of cigar smoke and tipped the ash into the rocks and moved on.

He limped into the kitchen and stepped over another guy he'd killed and continued toward the back of the house. He limped down the rubbled hallway and over the artwork torn from the walls. He kicked a doorknob across the floor and stepped into the room with the cannon and looked around. There was an open door to a walk-in closet. He limped across the room and turned on the closet light. A safe as tall as him with a combination lock stood against the rear wall.

He moved over to the cannon and studied the firing mechanism. He was pretty sure he could make it work if he could locate the proper instruments. He found a can of black powder and a pyramid of lead projectiles next to the bed and a coil of green blasting fuse and a ramrod and figured he had everything he needed.

He wheeled the cannon across the room and aimed the barrel at the safe in the walk-in closet. He tilted back the muzzle and poured black powder down the bore. He was uncertain how much to use and poured more than he thought necessary. He then packed the lead projectile with the ramrod. He set the fuse in the touchhole and brought the cigar cherry down on the end of the fuse until it hissed with sparks and he hurried out of the room.

He ducked into the hallway and clamped down on the cigar with his front teeth and closed his eyes and covered his ears. There was a thunderous boom and the house shook and then went silent. He limped back into the room and peered into the closet. There was a deep crater in the steel door but it was still a safe. He loaded up the cannon and fired a second time. On the third cannon blast the hinges on the door gave out and the pins broke and the door was hanging at an angle.

He limped through the house and out to the garage where he found a crowbar.

He worked on the safe for a while until he pried off the steel door. It clanged onto the tiles and nearly broke his good foot.

He looked inside the safe. The velvet floor was piled with ten-thousand-dollar bundles that were bound with mustard currency straps. Hundreds of more bundles were stacked on the velvet shelves. He was staring at no less than several million dollars.

46.

ONE VEHICLE DROVE ACROSS the desert from South Tucson and the other drove north from El Paso. They arrived forty-two minutes apart at a truck stop on the outskirts of Albuquerque.

The drivers of each vehicle spoke briefly over the droning clamor and throbbing lights of idling semis that were huddled like a miniature city against the darkest hours of the night. They had little knowledge of the situation they were driving into and neither man had been able to get in touch with Marlo. After the third call in four hours they decided that it was best not to call any more and to simply continue to their destination. They spoke about weaponry and what each man was carrying on his person. They had been informed that high-powered rifles were awaiting them if needed.

The party from South Tucson tallied three men all under thirty and rode in an extended-cab Chevy Silverado. The two men from El Paso were twenty-seven and thirty-one years of age and rode in a Hyundai Sonata with factory tires and leather seats. The papers and registration on each vehicle were current. All the taillights and headlights were in perfect working order. None of the men had any outstanding warrants and each of them carried a valid driver's license.

Each party used the restrooms separately and bought an assortment of sugary snacks and tall sodas from the fountain machine and enough gum and chili lime sunflower seeds to go around.

The vehicles refueled and then drove north on the interstate, staggered a minute apart from each other.

When they switched highways in Santa Fe and headed northwest it was just past 4:15 in the morning.

47.

ALEB LIMPED BACK THROUGH the house and rummaged the garage again where he found a dusty sea bag. He shook it out and went back to the closet and loaded the sea bag with as much money as it would hold. He started counting the stacks and lost track around 280-something.

Through all of this he did not sit down. He remained standing, bent over his work. He could feel his eyes blinking more frequently and staying closed longer, burning, longing to drift away. He only needed a moment of sleep. But he knew this to be a lie. A moment would turn into hours. He was hanging on by threads of alertness. He knew that the instant he got off his feet he would crash into the dream world, without his knowing, and if he fell asleep here, he might never wake up.

He carried the loaded sea bag into the kitchen where he drank a bottle of spring water and tucked another one in his pocket. He went over to the bar and grabbed a handful of cigars from the humidor and buttoned them into a side pouch.

When Caleb stepped outside the sun was cresting in the east. At the foot of the valley he watched two vehicles turn right off the asphalt and make their way up the dirt road. He could not tell from this distance what type of vehicles they were, whether police or civilian, and he figured they were about five miles out, a good fifteen minutes from where he was standing. Perhaps twenty if they eased along the ruts and seasonal washes. From his elevated position amid the adobe walls, he was fairly certain they could not see him. He watched the vehicles disappear behind the mesas and when they reemerged within view of the compound, he would be gone.

He set the sea bag on the ground and looked at the head staked to the front door. He lit two cigars and stuck one of them in the head's gaping mouth and smoked on the other.

He threw the sea bag over his shoulder and limped into the wilderness where he became a tiny wandering shadow upon the land and the vastness swallowed him whole.

Logan and Noah Miller are the cowriters, coproducers, and codirectors of two feature films, *Touching Home* and *Sweetwater*. Their first book, *Either You're in or You're in the Way*, was a *San Francisco Chronicle* #1 bestseller. Both live in Los Angeles.